Seven Missions To Earth

By

J. R. Austin

www.Marsthebook.com

Legacy of the Red Planet Series

Table of Contents

Prologue

The Grand Cycle is but a cog in the wheel of the Grand Circuit. Just as a planet orbits its Sun, so too will a living species orbit those who naturally lead them, dancing their paths according to their attractions. A Sun, seen by those on the world below, is always a mystery at first, and so too is the proper leader of a tribe. He who brings life and prosperity to his people will become their beacon, as the Sun is to the World. That same sun orbits a still-greater object within the Universe, one controlled by the collective celestial energies that direct all stellar bodies towards what at first appears to be a mysterious hole: a void.

Eventually, after billions of Ikaran Tallas in the world of linear time, cyclical time appears to end, and yet, all ends are beginnings. This is a cycle, after all. All the matter in the Universe is compressed into that void, but at some point, the same matter is released again to start a new grand circuit. There are millions of these black voids within the galaxies that represent cycles within cycles within cycles: a Universe unending and unbounded. To this we are but a spec of sand on an infinite beach, alongside countless others. In the vastness of the Universe and all its starry expanse, there is no end and no beginning,

We can be certain of this: there are other humanoid life-forms out there. Regardless of whether we find them first or they find us, our interaction with them will be based on their level of enlightenment, not ours.

1

J. R. Austin

Chapter One:

Revelation

With pale-gray eyes and military-cut blue hair, The Tanian commander was dictating his report—but not verbally. As he sat in his chair in the command center of the ship hovering high above the Great Mountain, his thoughts were directly recorded into the device before him.

Status Report
Administrator Borosh
Ikaran Mining Project

It has been approximately twenty years (or ten of the Ikarans' tallas) since the original survey vessel made the initial landing. The locals have since dubbed this event "Candlefall." Prior to Candlefall, there was no reference point for the linear time used by the general population of Ikara, other than the days related to planetary movements or the major astrological events. Thus, linear time began to be counted in terms of Tallas After Candlefall (or A.C). For ease of reference, my administration has begun using this terminology in our own communications.

The project is fully operational and on schedule. Automated systems are completely synchronized, and all personnel have been assigned to oversee and maintain the procedures. Everyone is performing optimally and maintaining proper integration with the mechanical processes.

Our existence has been discovered by the masses, but that has done nothing to set our schedule back. We already have a core tap established, and we are structurally extracting as many resources as possible. The "Great Mountain" has provided us with measurable concealment. Ironic. Security Chief Lort assures me that we have nothing to fear from these natives.

Now that our unwitting hosts have made the effort to openly contact us, we have a lot more to do in a relatively short time. While a direct confrontation is unlikely, our response must be unified. Dealing with a civilization developing so swiftly—on a world so extremely reconditioned—needs to be carefully handled.

Fortunately, their own politics are working against them and buying us some time. I've told the Ikaran people that we would be glad to assist their planet, but only if they present us with a single World Government to deal with. I've also relayed that we have a Directive, which prevents us from interacting with any world that hasn't evolved beyond the phase of petty internal squabbling.

I then arranged secret meetings with each of their key leaders, promising each one some extra benefits if they could gain certain concessions from their peers without revealing our deal. The result has kept them fighting amongst each other. That'll buy us a few more tallas, until their Five Nations Government can come to a unified agreement regarding the Accords as we've proposed them.

Oh, and that Five Nations government of theirs is laughable: weak, ineffective, and little more than a façade. Easily handled. And of course, we still have the one we'd *first* contacted dangling on a string.

While we're making progress about dividing the leaders, we're currently facing challenges about dividing the common people. Normally, this kind of hominid species would naturally turn on each other whenever given the opportunity, but these people don't seem to care if their fellow Ikarans look different, sound different, and have different stations in society. We currently know of no way to justify a strong presence among them without first manipulating these basic fears. So instead, we're going to spend time concentrating on the Volst. Their ego is ripe for unrest. They have some "issues" that they're holding onto from previous cycles, which I hope to exploit and use to create division.

As the drilling continues, the Ikarans have no idea how many resources we're funneling away from this world. They're so occupied with what's happening above them that they fail to comprehend what's going on below them. Still, these insignificant beings are developing fairly quickly. So to avoid any missteps during the full extraction process, it's imperative that they're dealt with swiftly and completely.

Had they remained a surface-scratching agrarian culture, there would've been no need for special handling. But now that their reach has extended beyond the atmosphere, they *could* potentially become a space-faring threat to the Tanian regime (however slim that chance may be). I will keep my attention on both them and the mining project itself. But the reality is that we'll be finished here long before they can create any significant gains in space travel, much less weapons technology. In fact, they don't even have any *real* weapons of mass destruction, only some nonsense about "the grand cycle" and "one people."

As far as extraction is concerned, we estimate that the content of this world's precious heavy metals is roughly ten trillion tons. Even a safe extraction of 50% will more than cover the energy costs to maintain the Bridge *and* make this trip a wild success.

The fact that there is an even larger inward planet waiting for us is indeed a windfall. We will, of course, proceed with exploring that extraction after this world has served its final purpose.

Report ends.

Tark

"Ikara Central, this is Commander Tark Karth. We are ready for reentry."

Tark was nervous. He was the first Ikaran in space for this cycle, and genetic memory had shown that most of the first men in space had not fared well when it came to survival. Tark never outwardly revealed his fears, though not because of his ego or the need to look strong. Rather, Tark felt that showing fear was a waste of time.

"This is Ikara Central. We show you coming in at 3.4 degrees too steep for proper entry. Please adjust shallow side by 4 degrees pitch to give point 6 degrees' margin."

"Affirmative. Making adjustments now."

Tark adjusted the pitch wheel four degrees upwards, then looked over at Devane to see how the Chief Mate was doing after his first extraterrestrial encounter. As the ship gave a violent bounce upon entering the atmosphere, Devane was pale and slightly ashen.

"Devane, you look like you've seen a ghost."

"I think we—Sir, I think we cannot possibly anticipate the potential ramifications of an alien species hovering over our Great Mountain. Who in the cycle are these…these people?"

Tark did not respond. He glanced at the controls as the ship's interior heated up, and the entire vessel began to vibrate.

"We'll need to consider a strategic move before we reach the blue planet Azur. This I do not doubt, Devane."

The craft jolted again, requiring Tark's attention.

"Ikara Central, this is Commander Karth. We are activating glide mode."

Tark flipped a toggle switch, and the wings on the capsule fanned out like a dove, slowing the descent of the cumbersome craft.

"Affirmative. Remember to strap in before impact."

"Impact?" Devane cried. "Don't they mean touchdown? Impact sounds a lot more…painful."

The two men looked at each other, not knowing what to make of the implications of the slight vocabulary change. Then they quickly scrambled to make sure they were securely fastened into the vessel before it hit the water.

The craft slammed into the Ikaran Sea at an incredible speed, the heat searing across the water's surface to leave a vapor trail in its wake. Inside the vessel, it sounded like they were being dragged across a gravel pit. Then there was silence; the craft was airborne once again.

"Oh hell." Devane managed to get these words out before the

sea slapped them again.

With a loud crack, the water hit the craft, echoing another hideous rumble. With no sensors to warn the crew, they couldn't be sure if the craft was coming apart, or if everything was perfectly fine. Tark reached for the brakes of the hydrogen engine, but Devane screamed out as the commander's hand grabbed hold of the toggle.

"Wait, commander!"

The roaring sea drowned out his plea. The moment Tark activated the untested engines, they exploded. The craft blew off the breakers, sending it into a mad spin across the top of the water. Elbow-sized holes appeared in both sides of the craft, and water began to rush in.

As the landing turned into a rescue mission, Tark seemed unfazed.

"Ikara Central, this is Commander Karth. We will be scuttling the craft, due to damage on impact. Will need a water rescue team at our coordinates immediately."

"Team en route, *sir."*

Tark and Devane inflated their life vests, blew the exploding door bolts, and jumped clear of the craft as it sank to the bottom of the sea.

Once Tark and his men were rescued, they gathered at Ikara Central to brief everyone on their encounter with the "Others." The First Speaker, the Karthan delegate, the ground crew, and the Ikaran Space Program engineers were all present for the briefing.

"My fellow ISP members. Devane Urhdlu and myself were tasked with contacting a geosynchronous satellite that was discovered in position over our Great Mountain. The purpose of this briefing is to inform you of the results and findings of our expedition. I would like to start by saying this: we are not alone. What's more, I believe that we are under constant observation, and have been since Candlefall Day Zero, ten tallas ago. That would mean they've been here for a significant amount of time without our knowledge."

Tark paused for a moment, looking around the room and

locking eyes with one Jast Rathael. Jast revealed nothing from his demeanor—except he covered one eye very briefly before resuming his previous posture, which caught the attention of Tark. The gesture was so quick that no one but Tark noticed. And Tark knew that this message was being used by the initiated to indicate trust among brothers who carry a secret of the one soul, a brotherhood that started in the Catacombs of Kartha during a previous cycle. You didn't have to like your brother, but you had to keep his secrets if he asked.

Tark continued the briefing:

"The satellite we intended to contact was, in fact, a starship with humanoid beings onboard."

The room gasped as Tark continued.

"This is a troubling development, to say the least. These people (if we can call them that) look very similar to the early Ikarans depicted in paintings found in the Pole Catacombs some tallas ago. Their connection to us—and the purpose of their visit here—remains a mystery. One notable item is their airlock mechanism. It was not entirely different from our own. It's as if they too have similar genetic memories to us, and thus created items of similar design. The airlock was so similar in function and design to our own that we only had to make minor modifications to create a seal. They also seemed to have knowledge of our grand cycle."

"If they are friendly," shouted craft engineer Lemer, "then why have they kept themselves secreted away in a starship above us? We need to be suspicious of their purpose here!"

Before continuing his report, Tark glanced at Jast, who quickly looked away.

"We have nothing from the genetic memory of our GenSeers that indicates we have been in contact with these hominids before. Not in this cycle, nor any previous ones. We are the star travelers; we are the Karth Kessai; we are the ones who reach out and find others. But now...others have found us. It goes without saying that our exploration of Azur in previous cycles must be revisited in this one. We must seize the future for ourselves, not wait to find out what these beings want. I now yield the floor to anyone who wishes to speak."

Lemer jumped at the chance to be heard. As the head engineer, the idea of making a spacecraft to reach Azur tickled his heart. Azur was bigger and the atmosphere grander than Ikara, the gravity almost double. He knew that Azur was the destiny of Ikara, and in accordance to protocol, he would be the man making the craft.

"I am ready to design what we need to reach Azur. If we need weapons, I can make those as well."

The crowd cheered as Lemer continued. "I love our planet, and I love you all. You are my brethren, and I am willing to do what it takes for us to travel the stars and protect Ikara."

He was met with applause. Meanwhile, Tark quietly walked over to Jast, who was trying to escape his enquiring glances.

"Jast, I need to speak with you."

"About what?"

"You covered your eye when I was talking. You were telling me to keep quiet about what I found on that craft. You know what I'm talking about."

"Listen to me, Tark, I need for you to trust me on this. I need for you to keep this… this matter to yourself until I have time to deal with it."

"What does that mean?"

"It means I need you to trust me."

Helm

Ikara was a world steeped in tradition. Its five nations each had their own culture, purpose, and personal way of contributing.

The Volst, for example, were a nation of engineers. These brilliant people hailed from the base of The Great Mountain, but they were socially awkward. Outwardly, they seemed boorish, but they were not ignorant. After the discovery of emlash power, they created steam engines to power the homes and businesses of all Ikara. All Ikaran spacecraft contained components from Volst. If one wanted an engine made, one would be a fool not to have it engineered and produced in Volst.

Whycheral, on the other hand, was home of the GenSeers and stoics. Any Ikaran could learn to read genetic memory and become a GenSeer. But the best academies for that purpose were in Whycheral, as the best seers were often born there.

The olive-featured people of **Nathor** in the South were a spiritual people. They were peaceful in mind and spirit, which afforded them the benevolent Matron Bellelorn. She worked hard to look after her people, but sought little fame or fortune. Historically, their judges banished the Na-Ikara (those born without a soul) to the badlands. But in an act of mercy, Bellelorn took powerful steps to reverse this tradition.

Then there were **the Karthans**, living as they do on a volcanic island in the middle of the massive Ikaran Sea. They were the keepers of mystical secrets—men and women who'd laid the foundational stones of Ikaran civilization. They were guardians of the catacombs, and the eternal inheritance those catacombs held. It is often said: all Ikarans can trace their history back to the first men, and those men were Karthans.

Finally, **the Elmanith** were the high-sounding people living along the temperate coastal waterways. Their leaders were almost always well-respected, and their academies were some of the best in Ikara.

Each nation has a spokesperson, and the First Speaker of any leading family is usually the eldest heir of the previous Speaker. However, throughout the two and a half Grand Cycles, there have been a few exceptions.

One such exception was Helm Elmanith. He was born of Jast Rathael, who (through chance and the political maneuverings of Master GenSeer Marador) had become First Speaker of both Elmanith and Wycheral. As a result, Helm was able to claim Elmanith legitimacy and become Elmanith's First Speaker, even though he wasn't of Tollwyn Elmanith's loins. By the time he finally came of age and took the title of First Speaker away from his estranged father, his history—and the history of Jast—was the stuff of legends. Physical challenges, mental gymnastics, and political drama all played like scenes from a book.

Most importantly for the House of Elmanith, Helm succeeded where all his predecessors had failed: he'd maintained a spotless reputation, both personal and otherwise. That's a hard task indeed when your father is Jast Rathael, perhaps the most renowned rascal and political rogue in all Ikara.

While overshadowed by the infamous capabilities of his father, Helm still displayed a strong ability for getting to the core of a problem and figuring out a way to handle it. He also had a talent for realizing the truth and noticing details, such as the rising Ikaran winds, the increasingly unseasonal storms, and the resultant coastal flooding. He didn't yet know the cause, but it was one of the things he was keeping an eye on. By many measures, he was still a young man, but he was barely into his first talla as Speaker and the Elmanith were already starting to flourish under his direction.

Helm knew the complicated truth about his parentage. Over the tallas, he'd found out that his birthmother Gallandra had died when he was a young boy, and that Jast was his absentee father who'd divorced Ezra (the woman who'd raised him) as soon as he'd had the opportunity. Helm had thence developed an extreme dislike for Jast Rathael, but as he dove deeper into his father's records as First Speaker of Elmanith, he would discover a far more despicable truth about him.

Helm was in the upper office, trying to make sense of the forms, contracts, and documents strewn across the massive administrative desk that was part of the honor he'd received. At three and a half cubits, he was shorter than his father, and he wasn't a particularly impressive specimen of Ikaran masculinity. In fact, he was a pretty average-looking Elmanith. He had blue eyes and short brown hair. He was clean-shaven, but his skin reflected exactly how much time he'd spent working the fields of the family holdings in the south.

He dressed well, with such silks and fine clothing as a Speaker of means would have, preferring dark maroon pants tucked into the tops of his polished knee-high black boots. His shirts were usually a mix of reds, blues, and yellows, in whatever the favored pattern of the day happened to be. But they were always trimmed in gold. When outside his office, he wore a blue cape trimmed with the same rich golden color and a black-velvet tri-corner hat atop his head.

His social interactions were with far too many bureaucrats and far too few facilitators. His intrinsic family connections favored the hinterlands of Ikara, but whereas a second cousin twice-removed might be able to get you work in the mills, these same people were somewhat counterproductive in government and administration. Everyone was related somehow, and nearly all of them were ill-equipped for the tasks at hand.

Fortunately, the process of becoming the First Speaker took a few weeks to accomplish, so Helm would have time to sort it all out. It would've been far simpler if Jast had stayed in the country for the transition, but circumstances in Whycheral had made that impossible. It may have made sense at the time, but no one who'd experienced Candlefall could've anticipated how the GenSeers would interpret their failure to predict the coming of these…Others.

As word spread of the Others and images of them went into circulation, it became increasingly obvious: nothing that the current crop of GenSeers had foreseen included any possibility of aliens arriving from outside the Cycle. The complete failure to predict this possibility, and in such a public manner, was far too much for many of the GenSeers to take. Within a few weeks of Tark Karth's contact with the Others, most GenSeers had committed suicide. Their deaths were a major setback for the Ikarans, weighing heaviest on Whycheral.

With Helm now old enough—even if only by mere months— Jast resigned his position as First Speaker of Elmanith, so he could devote himself to Whycheral full-time. It had been Jast's presence alone that had been the stabilizing factor in the aftermath of this tragedy. It was staggering to think about what might've occurred if cooler heads hadn't prevailed, and he hadn't been there to offer reason in the face of irrationality.

Helm put his head in his hands, his elbows crushing the documents on the table, and his forehead pressed to his fingertips. It was daunting to have so much to absorb, so much to decide. From the first contract he'd read that morning, it appeared that Jast had been threading the needle—keeping Elmanith afloat through stacked dealings with the other four countries, all leaning on the other agreements that were in place. It was a veritable house of cards.

"Nathor has import tariffs enforced against us to the tune of a quarter billion Thals," Helm recorded in his log. "Volst has contractual construction agreements amounting to half that, but also has higher-interest speculative loans against holdings in Kartha. The operation to move the materials from Volst's docks to Kartha are the property of holding companies in Whycheral, but warehouses along the Elmanith coasts maintain them. Those warehouses owe tens of millions to the Elmanith government, and we could certainly use it. But those fees and taxes are conveniently waived as part of some greater plan. I know that the Five Nations are essential to one another, since no one seems to have enough autonomy to stand alone, but this is a *mess.*"

Being a good man, Helm was having a very difficult time rectifying the situation. Most people only have a few places to turn to in times like these, but in his case, the obvious choice was not an easy step to take.

"As much as it *really* pains me, there's only one person who can make any sense of this mess. I've got to get on the Wave and send out a call to my father."

It would be the most difficult decision Helm had made in all his young life.

Volst

Thalamas Voort strode the length of the Great Hall, his

entourage streaming behind him like a flock of midges, bickering and chirping about nothing at all. They all called after their leader, complaining about his rapid stride and unwavering momentum. His usual cape was overlaid with a far more formal Entry Cloak, which had a train that was nearly twenty cubits long. Although he enjoyed the attention it garnered, he found its length—replete with feathers and beaks of the Family's Great Mountain Eagles—to be a heavy, tedious obligation, foisted on the young by the ancient. And it slowed his gait.

In comparison to the cloak, the flamboyant nature of his hat didn't seem quite so outlandish. The single feather extending from it acted like a beacon to those who followed him. Meanwhile, the heavy tread of his boots guided the few that couldn't see the hat above the Entry Cloak.

Thalamas disliked the formal cloak, but suffered its use for one reason alone: he recognized the power of presentation. Despite the somewhat primitive appearance this monstrous morning apparel offered, the power of public opinion was still a useful tool for the young First Speaker. After all, public opinion had been the fuel behind the staunch, determined processes the Volst utilized to finally reach the crest of the Great Mountain—to much global acclaim and goodwill.

The rotunda under which they strode bore emblems that represented the Great Mountain, the heights of which were still hidden in mists and clouds. Encircling this majestic image were symbols identifying the Four Corners of the Grand Cycle, each one representing an appointed leadership: Kartha, Elmanith, Whycheral, and Nathor. They couldn't remember a time when the Ikarans looked to the Volst for leadership. In fact, it had been two and a half turns of the Grand Cycle.

Thalamas threw his eyes skyward and muttered to no one in particular, "They never followed before. They must follow now."

As he climbed the low granite stairs that led to the Rulership Dias, Thalamas Voort finally shed the formal Entry Cloak and boldly gazed upon the images displayed before him.

Viewing screens hung from the ceiling, displaying the images and recordings recently obtained from the *Observer*. The images it sent back defied explanation. The broadcast of the recordings made from that first ascent stunned the world, as evidence of the presence of the Others on the Mountain was clear and recognizable from the start. Everything screamed "Extra-Ikaran" activity: the broadcast of operational hovercraft, a visible and identifiable vehicle rolling across the barren and rugged surface, even the unidentifiable gasses and fumes rising from what might be power generators.

"The images are unmistakable," he scowled to his professional minions. He was both angry and horrified by this revelation, just like any good Volst. "It doesn't matter if these creatures are extra-planetary relatives, some forgotten clan of brethren, or a completely alien race. They are on *our* mountain! As stewards of all Ikara, it is our *right* to remain in control of the Great Mountain. We must act quickly."

"But sir," a minion pointed out, "how? The things we've seen in those first images are far beyond the capability of Volst engineers."

"Then we'll...lay claim to any and all technology discovered on the Mountain."

"But First Speaker," another spoke up, "wouldn't that be invalid? I mean, these Others can certainly claim their own technology."

"They aren't of the Cycle," Thalamas snapped. "Now just *do* it."

"But sir," a second minion dared utter, "aren't all things of the Cycle? Wouldn't these Others—"

"They are not of *Ikara*," Thalamas glared back. "The Cycle is of Ikara, and we are the *chosen* of Ikara. The Mountain is ours to look after; we are its caretakers. *We* deserve the pick of the litter. All other nations should fall behind *us* in reaching out to the Others. It is *us* who should discover their purpose and become one with these clearly sentient aliens. Whatever it takes to accomplish this is therefore justified, so just get *moving* and file that claim!"

Jast

Jast Rathael was up and on the move before dawn, preparing for the day ahead. For the second time in recent history, almost the entire crop of GenSeers had been wiped out; the first was the night of Candlefall. And Jast was trying to fix things. He had been doing damage control since the self-slaughter of the GenSeers, and was now seeking eligible applicants to canvass for any GenSeers who might have resisted the call to kill themselves. However, it'd been weeks since the suicides, and things were starting to calm down within the Whycheral borders. But Jast was still in trouble.

He'd made a flawless transfer of his holdings from Elmanith to Whycheral, capitalizing on the vacuum the GenSeer suicides had created. Their elimination hadn't freed the people of the Grand Cycle—not by a long shot—and the discovery of the next wave of GenSeers was only a matter of time. The problems he now had as former First Speaker were insignificant compared to his *real* problem. No, his dabbling in Whycheral wasn't creating the issue; he could handle that.

Instead, Jast's troubles stemmed from his son Helm. Since Jast's hurried departure from Elmanith (and all the gaps in his financial dealings that he'd left in his wake), too many unanswered questions remained, now that Helm had become First Speaker. There were illegal agreements in place, which had never been internally ratified by Elmanith. Would Helm uphold them?

Jast scowled at himself in the mirror, "It's going to be difficult to explain everything: what I knew and for how long. It'll be almost impossible to explain *why* I've done the things I've done."

He moved away from the mirror to finish dressing. Bellelorn came out of the shower, a towel wrapped around her lithe body. Her damp raven hair dropped like a thick vine down her back as she regarded her brooding husband with a hopeful smile.

"Still worried about your meeting with Helm?" she asked.

"Don't. You'll explain your reasons, and he'll listen."

"One can hope," Jast sighed. "But remember, I'm not exactly the most attentive father. It's kind of funny how ingrained I've become in Elmanith politics. I was the one that wanted out of that mess."

"Don't worry. Helm is a fair and reasonable leader. Not quite up to the capabilities of his father, but then who is?" She grinned with a wink.

As he watched her turn around to dry her naked form, he knew how very wrong she was, regardless of her convictions. Bellelorn pulled on her dress and gave her hair a toss.

"My darling, in my haste to depart Elmanith and handle the problems here in Whycheral, I forgot to expunge my office of certain incriminating evidence. I fear that is what Helm has called me to explain. The documents he could find are out of context and incongruous, but to clarify them for him, I will have to reveal something I've told no one else...not even you."

In fact, he'd kept it from everyone except Tark Karth, and even he had only been given a clue about it. Bellelorn slowly turned around, a confused look on her face.

"I know you keep secrets well, but what could be so terrible that you'd even keep it from me? You know I'll always be on your side."

"But this is like a game of strategy. One wrong move and...I don't want my loved ones to come to harm, especially you."

As Bellelorn searched him with her eyes, Jast lowered his head.

"It was right after Candlefall, when I was named as First Speaker to Whycheral. Based on GenSeer Marador's advice before he was killed, I went on a hike. Bellelorn, I met the aliens, these Tanians, and have been in sporadic communication with them ever since. Nearly five tallas. This secret has really been bothering me for some time now. You need to know before this goes any further. I need your support. I need to know you are behind me if things don't go my way."

For a long time, Jast sat on the veranda thinking, until he finally worked up the nerve to call Helm back on the Wave. His secrets were laid bare in the documents that Helm innocently held in his hands. Helm disliked Jast, and Jast feared this news might be too much for his son, but he had to face it. With the sun setting in the distance, he made the call.

"Helm? This is Jast. I wanted to get back to you, but I wanted to get the details first. Do you have time now, or should we reconnect later?"

"Now is fine," came the reply. *"Was my request clear? Did you understand why I called for your help? There are many things here that I simply cannot make much sense of."*

"Helm, this is all going to work out fine. I know you have a lot on your plate, but if you can help me with one thing, then I'll certainly do whatever I can to resolve those issues."

Helm paused. Jast's tone suggested that Helm had overlooked something; he had something in his possession that Jast feared. His father was not his usual commanding self, so what was Helm missing? He decided he would play along, figure out what it was, and maybe gain a little more leverage.

"Absolutely, glad to hear you will help. What is it you need from me? How can I help you get through these tough negotiations?"

Now it was Jast's turn to be wary. In most cases, help was the last thing Helm would offer. He was usually looking for an edge, a tool by which he could force Jast to lose ground. This situation didn't feel right. It wasn't the kind of grilling he'd come to expect, or the strongly worded threats that sometimes accompanied Helm's attitude.

"There are a few items I need to retrieve from your office."

Far across the land, Helm realized that perhaps the very questions he was dealing with were the same "items" Jast was interested in. Apparently, Helm had in his possession whatever Jast was looking for. Had he discovered an opportunity to free himself and clear up the problems of his Nation? If so, this power shift could give Helm the ability to procure Jast's help. If he could find whatever Jast wanted, Helm might be able to make a difference in the future of Ikara. Just a few moments earlier, that possibility seemed much farther from his grasp.

Keeping Jast on the line, Helm tried plumbing a bit further. He wanted to draw some critical piece of the puzzle out of the older man, something that would widen this opportunity even further.

"Yeah, I did finally start to dig through that monstrous pile of stuff you left. Is there a particular part of it I can help you find? What' are we looking for? A particular set of dates, a specific contract?"

Jast silently cursed to himself. He was now sure that Helm was already going through the stacks. He could almost hear the young man rifling the documents, seeking whatever Jast had hidden amongst the forms and contracts.

Finally, Jast chose to be a father, not a manipulator.

"Son, put down the files and go back to the chair by the window. We really need to talk, and neither of us has time for any more drama."

"You...what big secret is it this time? Do you have another son besides me?"

"No, Helm, nothing like that. It's...back at the time of Candlefall, just before it, in fact, GenSeer Marador came to me to request my help and offer me a strange piece of advice. What he asked for was for me to take the unprecedented act of becoming First Speaker of two nations, at least until you came of age, as you now have. The intention was to solve certain problems with the indiscretion that had plagued Elmanith, not just me. Anyway, from something he had foreseen, I guess, Marador recommended that after I assume my role, I take a hike to certain outer reaches. I did and what I saw there changed my life. Helm...I saw the Others. I met with the Tanians."

*"Wait...You **WHAT?!** But why didn't you tell anybody?"*

"Tell them what, Helm? That some all-powerful aliens were

watching us? That they were responsible for Candlefall and the destruction it caused? Even now, a lot of people still look upon them as helpful benefactors."

"And you don't?"

"Let's just say that I've had my suspicions. I've never had proof for anything more or I'd have stepped forward by now. What I *did* do was keep them talking, led them to believe that we were just a bunch of ignorant peasants with no defenses."

"You were buying time," Helm realized. *"Time to develop and spread the emlash technology. Time until the ISP was established!"*

"Yes, the Ikaran Space Program is the key to our destiny. I'd been dreaming of Azur for some time before Candlefall. Once I saw aliens were involved, I knew that a space program was imperative, but I also knew we had limited time. I'm still not sure what they're really doing up there or how far along their plans are, but I do know that if they were up to anything good, they would've openly announced themselves a long time before Tark stumbled upon them."

"The winds," Helm suddenly pondered, as he began to piece together disparate facts in his mind. *"The weather."*

"What's that?"

"Perhaps nothing; I'm not sure. Forget it for now. So what did these Tanians have to tell you?"

"For a while, it was difficult for me to even articulate, but they had this music and it made me feel calm, the same way Tark felt. Too calm for my tastes. That's when I got suspicious, but I kept up my charade. I'm still not sure about them, but I can tell you this: Marador told me of an impending calamity, the end of everything. And from the way he described it, I think these aliens have something to do with it. Everything I've worked for since then has involved preventing this calamity—or at least saving as many people as I can."

That's when the answer dawned on Helm. He breathed it out in response. *"By going to Azur. Father, do you know how crazy all of this sounds?"*

"And that's why no one must know. At least not yet. They're not ready. If everyone finds out what's happening, it might sabotage our attempts to save Ikara. Do you understand?"

For another half an hour, Jast explained the details of his encounter: the strange landing craft, those within it, and his periodic meetings with them over the tallas. The aliens were trying to keep him pacified, while Jast was trying to maintain his façade of planetary innocence. It was apparent that they understood that Jast was too well-known to simply disappear, so both were maintaining pretenses during their initial contact.

Helm was startled by the revelations, aghast that this planetary event had a clandestine meeting attached to it, and that the contents of that meeting involved the secret knowledge of the man standing before him. But by entrusting Helm with such a world-shattering secret, Jast finally succeeded in breaking the ice and decreasing the gap of distrust between them. Helm would now have the sovereignty his position should have granted him before: the power to create a strong Elmanith legacy, which both he and his sons would carry on. Helm would never have to worry that Jast was going to call in his markers and try to overthrow him. Now he held all the details of Jast's indiscretions and could ruin him at any moment. Helm finally had his nation's power in his hands.

Despite all this, Helm still couldn't act out against his father. What if Jast wasn't lying? Helm's intuition told him that he was telling the truth. And if he was right, there were bigger issues at stake than Jast's reputation. Helm could ruin him with a single call on the Wave, but that would also ruin Ikara's chances of surviving the coming calamity, which these Others might cause.

"Okay, you have your wish," Helm finally declared. *"Elmanith will not block your overtures towards the other members of the Five Nations Government and I will bury the details of your questionable activities. I will also eliminate any reference—implied or otherwise—to your meeting with the Others."*

"Thank you, Helm," Jast replied with an audible sigh.

21

"You did it all for the benefit of Ikara. I may have had a miserable childhood, but at least now I know there was a reason for it. A very good reason. So it looks like I have a lot of cleaning up to do around here. I'll talk to you later." Helm paused for a moment before replacing the Wave headset. Jast had almost done the same when he heard one final question.

"Wait! What happens to the one Ikaran soul if we fail?"

This inquiry caused a sense of helplessness to come over Jast's entire being. It wasn't a feeling he was accustomed to. He could've simply placed the Wave on the receiver and pretended he didn't hear the question, but something inside him told him not to.

"I don't know. I just don't know."

"You cannot fail." Helm took a deep breath. *"We cannot fail... father."*

And there it was. In that one word, Jast knew that he had a powerful ally, but he also had something more important to him personally. There was a peace between them now, the kind of serenity that involves family protecting family.

For the first time since Helm's birth, they were reunited as father and son.

Chapter Two:

The Accords

Borosh was in the command cabin of the ship, looking over hovering displays of reports carved in light. Meanwhile, a female attentively stood nearby.

"Understand, Amishari, these Accords are a mere plaything for us. The Ikarans take it as a great burden, but it's just another distraction for us to make use of."

In her dark jumpsuit, Amishari looked less like a military officer, and more like a high-placed functionary. Her manner was curt, efficient, and very tight-lipped. She looked much like any one of the Tanians, with pale hair tinged with a bluish-white that hung to the middle of her back. But her eyes were different from most Tanians; they were a severe shade of blue.

Borosh went over the reports hovering before him as he conversed silently with his subordinate. Indeed, Tanian communication within their kind hadn't required sound for millennia.

"These Ikarans are ignorant as to our true intentions here, and that works in our favor. In fact, I don't think I've seen a species more trusting. It isn't difficult for a technologically superior race to become like gods to an indigenous people; all you need is a common language and sufficient time. We have the advantage here. We have more than a half million tallas' experience in space exploration and planetary acquisition. We're powerful, skilled traders and diplomats, raiders, and conquerors. These Ikarans have had their source of power, their emlash, for what, a decade or two? They can't compete. They are little more than herd animals."

"More like children, I would say, sir," Amishari replied in her clipped psychic tones, gently touching the pendant she was wearing. A simple keepsake from days past, it was a modest blue stone at the center of a pair of entwined triangles, hanging from a golden chain looped around her neck. "And children need discipline and guidance. We do need to keep in mind that their advancement is quite aggressive."

"And that makes them easy targets. If they want technology, we'll give it to them. Just enough to lure them in and absorb their culture before we're through with this rock. We'll give the natives colored glass beads and lead them to believe they are diamonds - anything to avoid violence and keep any losses within acceptable limits. Remember, even just *one* of our lives is better than *all* of theirs."

"And overtly exterminating a species is always more challenging and costly than coaxing them into a trap," Amishari blandly added.

"Exactly," Borosh replied. "We've done it before, and it works every time. Of course, you should know that better than me."

For a moment, her impassive face blanched ever so slightly with a faint grimace, which earned a smile from Borosh before he turned back to his displays.

Such a brief slip might've been easier to hide if their communication had been verbal. But with their manner of psychic communication, meaning and emotion were conveyed in an instant—far too brief to think about hiding something if you're undisciplined. The Tanians had spent millennia developing their nonverbal language, one wherein a microburst of emotion revealed a significant portion of a person's demeanor and attitude. For the uninitiated, it was very difficult to hide any emotion or thought pattern, but among the higher classes, deception still remained a possibility. So Amishari had a way to cloak her true emotions from the prying minds of these takers. This slip was a rarity.

It was more than that, though: they'd taken the subsonic waves that every mortal being can feel before they hear them, and discovered how to engage the mental state through harmonics. Even over long distances, they could convey intricate messages to those that could comprehend them, and simple emotional conditions to those who could not. Emotions such as: 'We're friendly; trust us.'

Amongst themselves, theirs was an emotionless language, taking all that had emotional meaning and twisting it to meet their needs. There was little happiness or sorrow among the Tanians, only existence. Singing, however, afforded them command and control of the conversation by engendering in their targets a modicum of susceptibility, and opening negotiations in a more advantageous state than would otherwise be possible. Music soothes the savage beast and speaks of peace and plenty, but it has another beneficial side effect. By using their singing voices before interacting with an alien species and observing their reactions, the singers could develop an understanding of how the target peoples think. They could then use that very understanding of the language and perfectly emulate an emotion they could never truly feel. This skill gave the Tanians a distinct advantage when negotiating with innocents such as the Ikarans.

In addition, the Tanians were very generous with their resources, lavish with their praise, and deep in their seeming appreciation of Ikaran privacy. It was the interstellar equivalent of fattening up the cattle before the slaughter.

"Administrator Borosh," Amishari said after a moment or two, "I feel it my duty to remind you that we have never engaged a species like the Ikarans before. As a unified body, the ethical code of the Ikarans is undeniably strong. For millennia, they've observed the course of this Grand Cycle of theirs, following its permutations and alterations with diligence and dedication to that greater reality. So long as the messages are consistent and aimed at the whole of Ikara, there will be no point of leverage, so the Ikarans will inevitably turn on one another."

"Correct! This creates a challenge in keeping their eyes off us. We must introduce division, but we cannot do it overtly. We can possibly achieve this under the guise of praising some aspect of outward diversity. Since we can't create a race war, what about creating a financial crisis that'll cause classist segregation? Which is why these initial Accords are defined in such simple terms, Amishari. The First Speakers of every one of their nations will readily accept them. By creating a central government then dividing these people, we create a need for us to use force to maintain peace. Once the power is in our hands, we can create a crisis and empower ourselves by being the ones to solve it."

"How so, Administrator? They are trusting, true, but they have such a united front: a concern for what is good for their world and their people as a whole."

"Yes, that is troubling, but if we make the right moves, that trust that will be their undoing." Borosh grinned. "It means we can approach them individually and make such offers as benefits the individual, while not seeming on the surface to threaten the whole of their world. Undermine the individual by emphasizing them as being parts of different groups, Amishari, and you undermine the whole of their precious societal structure. They know very little of guile or deceit; as you yourself just said, they are like innocent children, unaware of what predators exist outside their own little world. Of course, it is this innocence that makes negotiations within their own kind far simpler. That's how they have been able to connect their entire world in transportation and communication networks in only a few decades. The main things now separating them, other than outward appearances and a few historical biases, are mostly artificial cultural and language differences."

"By offering to level the playing field," Amishari realized, "these cultural differences might then be expanded into outright jealousies."

"*Now* you're getting it." Borosh swiped a hand across one of the displays, changing it to a political map of the world beneath them. "When we needed to further our mine holdings, instead of going to Whycheral, I went to these Volst because they see themselves as being underdogs in the previous cycles. And now they view themselves as the Chosen. They happily support us. On the other hand, if there is a point in the Accords dealing with issues of physical operations, then it's the Karthans, since they imagine themselves as spearheading the way into space. Fat chance of that."

"So you've been playing one off against the other without them realizing it."

"Like I said," Borosh nodded, "innocents. It hasn't even occurred to them that they have no way of enforcing our end of things. Amishari, as of yet, this operation has not turned a profit. It will in time, but for that to happen, we need to get these locals under control. These Accords serve only to placate them while we operate free of interference. All they have to do is sit back and enjoy their new prosperity, while we pump their planet dry. They have more in common with herd animals than real people. Animals being led to the slaughter."

"By the time they discover otherwise," Amishari stated, "it will be far too late."

Here she stepped over to one of the displays, and with a projected thought, she called up something new: displays of text, accented with elaborately drawn borders and symbols from the five different nations.

"I'm just trying to get a better understanding of the operation," she continued, "so that I may be of more efficient use as your assistant. On the surface of it, the terms of these Accords weigh far in favor of the Ikarans, but that is by design so that they will come to rely on the advances that we will be supplying them."

"Basic economic law," Borosh grinned. "Give them too much too soon, and unless they know how to handle it, their economic and political structure will start to overheat. Runaway economic growth begets inflation, which begets graft and corruption, which creates a secondary marketplace. This will magnify the already existing dissent of the Five Families directly in opposition to their Five Nations government. The result? A need for increased governmental presence." Borosh was clearly pleased with himself as he communicated his master plan of division. "This Great Wheel of theirs will break under the pressure. And what do we ask for all that we give them? The mountain heights above Volst and the badlands beyond; lands undeveloped by the Ikarans, lands they have no interest in."

"Except for the mineral content to be found there," Amishari pointed out.

"Minerals which the Ikarans see no use for, even after we told them of our interest in them. It was an offer these primitives couldn't *wait* to take up. Even the wariest of them could see no harm in allowing their 'Tanian Brethren' access to such useless land."

"Brethren?"

"The term fits into their mythology of the Great Cycle. I've convinced them that we merely follow a different Wheel. By doing so, I sacrificed my ability to destroy their faith. I cannot simultaneously tell them we follow the cycle, then destroy their belief in it. I made this change in protocol because I felt it was a better tactic for this extraction."

"So we give them miraculous technology," she enumerated, "such as replication processes that take mere moments instead of hours, and in return, the Mountain is considered our property entirely. It sounds…most efficient, Administrator. I would even say brilliant."

"All we have to do is remain secretive about our *real* capabilities," Borosh said, "and as it turns out, that is *very* easy. If they petition, I deny. If they present a unified front, I will pit one nation against another. If they demand a tour of the facilities, I provide them with a very carefully planned tour of utter insignificance. We simply have to conceal our true intent from them, but with their eyes on their new toys and their new sense of group diversity, they won't give their resources (or us) a second thought."

Borosh broke from their silent communication to emit a short chuckle and shake his head before continuing, once again telepathically.

"Amishari, in all of Tanian history, while not every mission has ended with a successful extraction, there has never been a mission that has been unprofitable. Ikara is not about to be the first. "Well…except for Nimbusi…" Borosh paused for a moment before continuing. "But that was simply bad planning. The violence and unnecessary bloodiness…I prefer a cleaner elimination. A slow boil, turning into a roaring flame that eventually snuffs out the baby-eyed mutants. Rather entertaining, I must say." Borosh let out another small chuckle.

"As you say, Administrator," she deferred, bowing ever so slightly.

"I shall *love* the moment when they realize that their deaths shall be at the hands of their benefactors. The few who will be left over will then have no choice but to become one with the Tanian Empire. Oh so glorious. Glorious!"

He spared a moment for a wide, toothy grin, then resumed a more professional attitude as he turned to face his expressionless subordinate.

"Now, if you are finished with your report, I wish to make some small adjustments to these Accord agreements. The locals have a big signing ceremony planned in a few days."

"Yes, Administrator," she nodded.

"Oh," Borosh added just as she was about to turn away, "you should attend that signing. Having an assistant by my side will make me look more important in their eyes."

"Yes, Administrator."

With a curt nod, she left. Any thoughts she might have on the whole matter remained secure behind the disciplined veil of her mind. In the coming decade of her assignment to this planet, she'd see the pattern just as Borosh had outlined it, and witness the inevitable gilded cage that the Ikarans were making for themselves.

The Ikarans had a passion for the stars, which they'd recorded throughout their history. So the Tanians offered interstellar trade and trans-dimensional travel, as well as commerce opportunities over time: promises they never intended to keep, but which acted as a perfect lure built upon the actual developments the Tanians *did* share. In the coming tallas of the Accords, improved interconnection between population centers revolutionized trade and transport, while simple progressions in technology improved many aspects of daily life. Tanian recommendations allowed Ikarans to avoid many of the challenges of rapid tech advancement, and a great many diseases were defeated through the simple procedures shared by their Tanian allies.

One subject that'd caught the passing eye of Amishari, however, was that of the Nathorn Healing Singers. In her spare time, she searched for all documented information the Tanians had on the subject, displaying it before her as she later sat down to her desk. *Songs that heal? That sounds more like a psychic focus, or harmonic carrier wave, than superstitious custom. In fact, almost like...*And that was when she brought up another, far more detailed file, which described known influences of Tanian harmonics over the minds of other species. She looked from one to the other, pondering. *Could it be?*

Of course, the GenSeers might have been able to foresee the dangers of having too great a reliance on unearned advances, but they had all committed suicide when the presence of the Others was revealed. Even if they had not, with such wonders now being given by their Tanian Brethren, a growing number of Ikarans were starting to view 'Seeing' as something of a superstition anyway.

However, there were a few foresighted Ikarans determined to make proper use of such Tanian gifts. A hundred tallas before the emlash, the Volst-built Karthan-operated gliders, which were lighter than aircraft, had been expensive curiosities. But now, with power supplies and motors, they became more practical. But more importantly, the use of such powered aircraft were becoming a testbed for what would be needed for the real objective: interplanetary spaceflight. The goal to reach Azur.

Behind this goal, carefully maneuvering events out of sight of their Tanian Brethren, was the secretive hand of Jast Rathael.

Jast

From Jast's vantage point, the conversation with Helm had gone very well, and the considerations he suggested were accepted with the appropriate amount of respect. In other words, Helm arranged the Elmanith contingency exactly as Jast had expected. Helm was nothing if not predictable. He did just the opposite of what Jast recommended when it was useful, but otherwise, the two agreed on much.

Jast, of course, didn't personally attend the Tanian talks. He had sent a Whycheral acolyte—not yet a GenSeer—to observe and report, along with Halgor. Fortunately, the ascent onto the height that he'd made as a youth was still not a subject he would have to explain, not with Helm now in agreement about the matter. After his talk with Helm, he'd taken the precaution of sending a message through diplomatic channels. Within a few weeks, he'd received confirmation that his name had intentionally vanished from the various versions of the First Contact dialogue. It was one thing to have the Karthans wondering about his complicity, but for the whole of Ikara to have questions was a completely different situation, one he could not reconcile.

Before the official signing ceremony, Jast had sent for and received the final draft of the Accords from the Tanians. Now, as the rest stood atop the Mountain signing and looking pleased with themselves, Jast sat back in his study, carefully examining the agreements.

He read them grimly, nodding to himself after every point. Of course, there would be windfalls for all Ikarans, but there were some points in particular that he was looking for.

"And there they are," he smiled to himself, "just the minor points I need to free my people. Now all I have to do is stay the course, and keep an eye out for the one thing I do not yet have…an ally on the *inside* of the Tanian Complex."

Thalamas Voort

Thalamas Voort had accomplished something no other member of the Volst dynasty ever had. Through his direct relationship with their new allies (the Tanians), a Karthan had come to them begging. Oh, it would never be seen that way in the public eye, for too many of the Ikarans held to the ancient prophecies and the Grand Cycle. Ikara would forever see Kartha as the adventurer and Volst as the engineer. But the irony of a victory, which was engineered by his People and resulted from being adventurous, set his heart in a good mood for the first time since the discovery of the Tanian outpost.

The months of talks now concluded with the finalized Tanian Accords, which were about to be signed right here, high upon the shoulder of the Great Mountain on the Volst *Observer*.

Administrator Borosh, chief of his delegation, was dressed in his more formal gray uniform and high boots, with a blue cape that matched the design popular with Ikaran elite—a fact that was not coincidental. He was attended by a female assistant and some other Tanian functionaries, most of whom did not speak, including his Security Chief, Lort. As usual, Lort was dressed in his pristine uniform, and though he stayed mostly in the background, there wasn't a thing that his dark gray eyes missed as they shifted rapidly back and forth. There was lots of pomp in the dress of many in the delegations from the various nations, and as much grumbling as smiles. The favored tone for the entire agreement was simple: everyone was mutually dissatisfied with something.

It was, however, somewhat dampening Thal's spirit to see so many of the Tanians walking about in the *Observer*. He and Borosh had agreed a forty-percent staffing threshold, but at one point, Thalamas was certain that they were working well past that. With the primary talks now concluded, Thal decided it was time to talk to the Administrator. Privately.

The plasteel and girder construction of the *Observer* left a fairly open inner construction, whose sturdy yet transparent walls allowed Thalamas a clear view out across Ikara's mountain vista. There, he could see the monstrous building the Tanians called the Matter Transport System (MTS), now overshadowing the other constructs. Its former small frame was completely engulfed by the full-scale version. It was the Tanian Bridge to the stars, a wide enough bridge to easily pass thousands through at a time.

Everyone couldn't see the same picture, though. The earlier images, those that had already slipped onto the broadcast waves, were now stock footage, looped and provided daily by the Tanians for the benefit of the Ikarans at large. The purpose was simple: keep the remainder of Ikara away from the truth, with promises of inclusion keeping the Volst starry-eyed.

But Thalamas Voort was no fool, and while his people expected him to serve Ikara as well as their Family and Nation, the gloves were soon going to be coming off. From the rhetoric spouted by First Speaker Jast Rathael of Whycheral, there would be more challenges after the Accords were signed. That concerned Thalamas greatly, for the Accords averted most of the Five Nations government's problems. But direct negotiation by the families could, over the longer term, implicate Volst in the trade agreements and demonstrate a certain amount of complicity.

Thalamas shook off the negative thoughts, and instead rehearsed what he would say to Borosh. Volst would soon be the heroes of Ikara. His people needed rewards for their loyalty—not insignificant trinkets, but real value from the Tanians. Thalamas Voort would make certain this would happen, and when he did, his would become an epic name in Volst, just as Tark had in Kartha.

"First Speaker Voort," Borosh greeted him. "How nice to meet you outside of the Accords discussions. This is my assistant, Amishari."

"My Lady," Thalamas said to her with a broad sweep of his hat and slight bow before re-donning it in the same continuous motion, his sense of self-importance clear in his smile. "It gladdens the heart to see a lady who can be both efficient *and* beautiful."

J. R. Austin

They were standing at the far end of the *Observer* as the rest mingled with various Tanians. The Ikaran Representatives congratulated themselves on the signing, each delegation taking their copy of the freshly minted document. Thalamas had waited until the majority of the handshaking with Borosh had been done, then chose his moment to catch the alien alone, away from other Ikaran ears.

Now," Borosh continued, "how can I help you? If there's a problem with the Accords, then perhaps you should have brought it up during the discussions."

"Oh no, nothing like that," Thalamas assured him. "It's just that a thought occurred to me."

"And what would that be?" Borosh smiled.

Here, Thalamas looked out across the wide plateau atop the Great Mountain, then to the unparalleled view across Ikara behind them.

"Well, I don't know," Borosh said with a slight shake of his head. "By the Accords, we must offer our technology equally to all five nations."

"It's just that, it seems to me that we—that is, Volst—have a closer relationship with the Tanians than the rest of Ikara. After all, it is our *Observer* upon which we stand, and it was our engines that took the first Ikaran up to meet you."

"I suspect what you mean to say," Borosh completed for him, "is that Volst's importance has been vastly underappreciated by your fellow Ikarans."

"Exactly so!" Thalamas beamed. "It is our generators that supply all the energy needs for Ikara and our engineers that head up the design teams that create the wonders to ease every day of Ikaran life. All we wish is to serve Ikara, but it appears to me that we could do a better job of that with, say, better and safer designs for our generators."

"Well, I don't know," Borosh said with a slight shake of his head. "By the Accords, we must offer our technology equally to all

34

five nations."

"And so you shall," Thalamas pressed, "but it would benefit the people overall if you made it a practice of giving it to Volst first. We *will* be the ones to help the rest of Ikara make sense of it, after all."

"I do see your point," Borosh agreed with a slow thoughtful nod, "and I think I may be allowed to do that, but my superiors may need a concession. Just a small one, mind you."

"And what would that be?" Thalamas eagerly asked.

Borosh looked up with what appeared to be a genuine look of concern. "Well, I do not wish any Ikarans to get underfoot or accidentally injured in the process of our operations here, so you could simply encourage fewer visits and minimize curiosity regarding what we do up here and in the badlands. This is purely to ensure the safety of your people, of course."

"Oh, I quite understand," Thalamas assured him. "Coming from a long line of engineers myself, I know how the likes of diplomats and functionaries can get in the way of dangerous machinery if they aren't careful. Volst will ensure that any curious Ikarans stay out of your way."

"Good," Borosh said with a sigh of relief, "then we have an agreement?"

"With just one small favor to ask..."

Thalamas' gaze drifted in the direction of the MTS building, a wistful sigh escaping his lips.

"When you are ready to let us walk the stars, I would deem it a great favor if Volst went first. Karthans aren't the only ones with the urge to explore."

Borosh let out a wide grin, while beside him, Amishari maintained her leveled, disciplined features.

"Speaker Thalamas, it would be my pleasure."

The Tanians left, leaving the representatives from the Five Nations to themselves—on the Volst *Observer* atop the Mountain—to discuss the Accords and their own particulars. *Let them have their privacy*, Borosh thought to himself. *This is where they start plotting and scheming against one another.* He had planted the first seed with that fool Voort; now he had to let it grow.

The Meeting

"It is easier to build a nation than it is to build a bridge."

So began Helm Rathael, and despite the difficulties ahead, he was right. Helm said these words during the shrill talks that erupted in the shadow of the Tanian Accords, and in the presence of the leaders of the Five Families. He was dressed in the silken finery that was be expected of a Speaker, complete with his flowing gold-trimmed blue cape and favored velvet tri-corner hat, though the latter was currently removed and sitting on the table beside him. All were present except for his father, Jast. Halgor, his father's *de facto* representative, was seated opposite him, though not particularly paying him attention. Helm imagined that Jast had trained him to intentionally ignore him and be as nonplussed as possible during any interaction.

But he was pleased to see that everyone else were more attentive. Although they had already signed the Accords, there was still some disagreement amongst the group of leaders. After receiving pressure from advocates of the Accords, such as Thalamas Voort, they had all agreed to sign, but the dissatisfaction and unease others still felt shined through during the post-ceremony discussions. Helm, while not entirely distrusting, was one of those who still felt uncertain, and he wished to make that known. He had practiced this speech on the way from Eleman, and was glad to finally present it without a Tanian presence. He badly wanted to be able to trust them, but since he knew that they had contacted Jast first, he feared that his ambitious father may have corrupted their ability to negotiate. Then there were the indefinable suspicions his father had posed, too.

"My dear Lady Bellelorn, distinguished Speakers, and gentle Halgor, I want to make a suggestion, a call for alliance, if you will. By sheer force of will, we have been brought here and made signatories to an Accord that has provided us with great benefit, in exchange for land and mineral rights on property we all would agree seem to have no value whatsoever.

"But the agenda of the Tanians is yet to become clear," Helm continued. "We are at the brink of a momentous change, one that may lie beyond the limits of the Grand Cycle. A great power stands before us and it is true that with power comes strong personalities to seek it, but we must remember that this is not always for the betterment of the people or the Cycle.

"I ask you then, in our present situation, to consider what purpose we have for holding this new thought, this singular government, together? So compelling is the Tanian case, so easy this road to advancement, that I fear that these Others will draw us from the direction that the Grand Cycle has set for us. Any temptation that would do so surely is itself a danger, for should we swerve too greatly from the path, how then would we ever know when we find it again?"

Helm gently nodded in the direction of his compatriots and equals, but as a precaution, he did not do so toward Halgor, whom he considered to be only a placeholder for his father—a stand-in, not a leader. As he concluded, he looked at the Volst First Speaker to his right. His first thought was to surrender the floor to Simoth, the young dark-eyed Karthan delegate whose role naturally should have been the historical forerunner. However, Helm realized that the location of this meeting took precedence over tradition.

Thalamas Voort looked like he was sitting on a pile of gold that nobody knew about. Add in his goatee and mustache, and he cast a nearly devilish demeanor as he looked about at his peers. It left the others wondering why. Perhaps the Tanian Accords represented success to his people, or maybe it was just the view that such a rarefied elevation presented. For whatever reason, Thalamas sounded more than a little excited about the future.

"My dear associates," he began, "Speaker Helm is onto something. I have noted on several occasions during the talks that one of us offered what seemed to be Tanian thoughts for consideration.

It may be that we are all sympathetic to their purposes, that we are simply that kind and understanding, but I am concerned that the only liberties offered to any Ikarans were those made towards our Eastern neighbor, Whycheral. Could it be that we need to isolate ourselves from the Tanians directly in order to actually make headway in a future round of talks?"

Helm choked a bit at that reference, catching Thalamas' eye, but shook it off and remained silent.

"My dear Lady Bellelorn," Thalamas continued, "what would you say about this situation? Should we create some form of planetary bond, some structure, with which to engage the Tanians? That they invited us all here undoubtedly has some intention. They had the opportunity to make contact with my nation, or with Whycheral, but instead they followed our customs and let a Karthan lead the way. As possibly the most removed from this debate, what would Nathor wish us to consider?"

Caught a bit off-guard because she expected to be left for last in the discussion (as would be protocol under the Grand Cycle), Bellelorn looked up from behind her brilliantly raven bangs and extravagant eye makeup and took *them* by surprise with a slow-panning gaze. The purpose of such was to give the Matron an air of mystery and command, and the effect, counterpointing a brilliant amber and crimson gown, succeeded on both counts. She looked like someone set apart, elevated above the rest, and hence ever-respected by them all.

She sighed, and instead of remaining seated as the previous speakers had, she stood and shifted her position, visibly turning away from Halgor (as if he wasn't an accepted member of their group). Halgor felt the slight, lowering his head in sadness towards the floor.

"In the intervening tallas since Candlefall, our individual nations have made tremendous strides towards a unity that, according to the Grand Cycle, has precedence and is quite acceptable. The Jowhar of the Whycheral, the cutting off the head as it were, certainly devastated the whole of that Nation and put its Family to grief, but Jast Rathael has brought Whycheral from the edge of despair and only now is rebuilding a Whycheral Council worthy of all Ikara. I am, however, opposed to drifting away from or intentionally circumventing the Grand Cycle. We have been, and will always be, Five Nations guided by the Five Families' principles. It is unfortunate that not all of the Speakers could be present, but we have accomplished much in these Accords and for that I am glad, but therein lies a reminder – we have already signed these Accords, we have already made the agreement, and any discussion in the contrary is redundant now. Concerning our intent for the future, however, perhaps we need to have the Speaker of Whycheral present, though again, there is much that has happened that falls clearly on the Grand Cycle and as such, did not require such protocol."

With two and a half cycles of history and nearly a quarter million tallas of experience as a race of beings, Ikarans were far more than a gathering of individuals. Indeed, the guidelines and instructions concerning their culture, community, and communications were hard-wired for a coherent civilization. It was true that the music—the interference that drove individual Ikarans to heights of greatness and others to madness—was from an alien source. But adaptation was a tendency embraced by Ikarans, and it served to unify them, rather than isolate them.

The rapid nature of their cultural advance, from tribal to regional to national, was just such an adaptation. The development of the Five Nations government seemed to encompass a plethora of interests. The similarities between individual desires and familial needs meant that there were far more complementary characteristics than cultural differences. Family traits that had long identified members by eye color—a genetic change that came about after the burning men—now shifted back, in a sense. Now, as before, one's work ethic and knowledge would represent those best suited to the tasks at hand. While a decision had already been made in terms of the Accords, those at this meeting had the task of deciding if what lay before them was another such adaptation, or if it was outside the Grand Cycle entirely.

Bellelorn retook her seat, and there was much open discussion, some of it louder than others. Despite the very clear outward division between each nation, inwardly, each was essentially in step with the others, and all aligned behind Elmanith. Though they never truly embraced a singular government, in the end, all agreed to step in line behind Helm. It was the voice of Thalamas Voort, though, that made the fateful declaration.

"My friends," he began once the general discussion had died down, "I think we are all in agreement. For what crosses us, whether the Tanians mean us good or ill, we must face it as a united world, a singular people. The Grand Cycle demands it. As we've already agreed quite publicly during the Accords ceremony, so we must privately agree amongst ourselves. We further agree that there is only one amongst us able to hold the responsibilities of such a leadership position firmly and fairly in hand. Elmanith. Helm, my friend," he said, turning to face him, "I am afraid that this historic responsibility falls to yourself. This very day, upon the top of this very mountain, the government of the Five Nations is born, and you are its first Speaker. Guide us well."

Helm would guide them, taking the reins with more gusto than even he expected, politely nodding his head to the cheers and well-wishes. He understood more fully than Thalamas Voort what had truly been accomplished that day; for now, the very dream that his father had been working towards could come to be. Boasting a long coastline and an operational fleet that was the envy of even Kartha, Elmanith had accomplished the impossible. Within five short clicks of the Grand Cycle, there was no longer a shortfall among any of the Five Nations. These final talks were the turning point. With a unified Ikara, they could now turn to the goal that ever-haunted their collective dreams.

They could reach for Azur.

Jast

Jast sat back in his desk chair, looking over the report. Halgor stood attentively before him. The tall servant's old blue rag partially stuck out of the top pocket of his vest, and his ever-present bronze ring with the symbol of a key was still on his finger, even after all this time. Occasionally, Jast would reach down to give his pet laravel a scratch, but his full attention was on the report.

"Hmmm. The terms of the Tanian Accords seem rather one-sided. Ikarans reap quite a few benefits, including being supplied with several technological breakthroughs. The problem is that these breakthroughs are along the course of our own current researches. They certainly save us some time with trial and error, but the fact is there is nothing that we wouldn't come up with on our own in a talla or two anyway. What else…? It looks like different regions will receive different benefits, depending on need. All nations received pledges of support from the Tanians for a variety of projects. Rails and control fixtures for the rail projects, new and next-generation plastics for food storage and transport, advances in geothermal power generation, internal combustion engines for conveys and flitters. On the surface of it, despite its limitations, it would seem to be a bounty unrivaled in the history of Ikara's Grand Cycle. Maybe that's why this thing sailed through the committee in less than five days, not that Volst in particular seem anything less than ecstatic about that."

Jast turned another page, Halgor patiently waiting while his master studied the agreement.

"Administrator Borosh certainly wants to keep us away from the Whycheral Highlands and the Na-Ikara Desert, though. They're both designated as off-limits to *any* business. Interesting, but not nearly so as the journey itself, I gather."

He looked up at Halgor, setting the papers aside on his desk while the large man offered his own report.

"I did as you said, Jast," he quietly rumbled, his one drifting eye occasionally losing focus with his master. "While the GenSeer

41

acolyte was involved with the meetings, I wandered around taking pictures." Halgor took out an envelope and handed it to Jast. Jast pulled out a stack of pictures and looked through them while Halgor continued. "I collected images along the way as well as up at the *Observer.* If an area was off-limits, I'd just wander in, snap a few, then wander out. A couple of times, one of the Tanians saw me and challenged me but I just played dumb and they let it go at that."

"Exactly why I picked you, Halgor. As large as you are, few people would figure you for being as intelligent and perceptive as you are. Well done."

Halgor replied with a smile and remained silent, while Jast continued to look through the pictures. When he was finished, Jast set them down atop the desk, leaned back, and sighed.

"I may finally have enough evidence to begin building a case against the Tanians, as to what they are hiding, Halgor, and I can tell you now that it's nothing good. That old GenSeer was right; Candlefall announced the coming final Cataclysm for Ikara. It's just a matter of proving it, assuming it's not already too late."

Chapter Three:
Missions to Azur

Thalamas Voort

"Thal-A-Mas! Thal-A-Mas!"

It was a day of celebration, and the crowds cheered as the parade swept by below. First Speaker Voort looked out from the second-story balcony of his home, before him the great square of the Volst capital, and across from him the Government Hall. The space between was crowded with a throng thousands strong. As the parade went by, banners bearing his name and image flew about, and children chanted his name. Thalamas waved beatifically at those below.

Beside him stood an advisor, a bookish man with a clipboard and a constant nervousness about him; it was as if he expected to displease someone at any moment, and thereby bring his entire world crashing down upon him. Thalamas waved a bit more before offering a comment to the advisor, maintaining the smile upon his face for all to see while doing so.

"They love me, Malath."

"There is…is nowhere in all of Volst where you are not known and loved, sir," the bookish one replied. "You arranged for the advances being given by the Tanians to c-come to us first, and that has given us un-paralleled p-prosperity."

"And the recognition that Volst has so long sought," Thalamas added. "No longer will we take insults. Not from the pompous Karthans, those arrogant Elmanith, the wily Whycheral, or even nascent Nathorn. How can the world *not* see Volst as the Chosen now? The primary generators for all the energy needs of Ikara are on Volst land, operated by Volst engineers, and now are using the new, safer, Tanian designs. It is Volst that heads up the design teams to take advantage of all this new technology. Technology that saves the lives of *all* Ikarans. And even better, Volst has been promised access to the MTS, where all others have been refused. Volst, not Kartha, will be the first to see another world. It is a perfect arrangement from which Volst prospers. All we have to do is keep silent, Malath."

"Uh, yes sir. About that sir, the Tanian excavations seem to be p-progressing satisfactorily, at least according to Administrator Borosh and what little imagery we can get back from the *Observer*. The Tanians still have not given us any specifics about their operations and their sites are completely off the communication grid. Not so much as a single Wave transmission that we can detect."

"They have a right to their privacy." Thalamas shrugged as he resumed his waving to the crowds.

"But s-sir, of what images they do send back," the nervous man fumbled through the papers on his clipboard to find the right one, "there is evidence of some deterioration of the soil base around the site of their operation."

"I know of that and I brought it up with the Administrator. He assures me that it is a temporary condition that will end once they have completed their processes."

"Well, th-that may be sir, but then there is the matter of some disappearances."

"Another reporter get lost climbing the mountain?" Thalamas sighed.

"A-actually, sir, there is a growing list of disappearances, and not just from mountain climbers. Curious journalists, yes, but also some citizens who have been voicing their concerns over the Tanians and the Mountain. Just vanished in the middle of the night."

Thalamas paused for a moment. His concern for his people was genuine, but so was his ego. And often, these two qualities would clash in the most interesting of interactions. Then he remembered the parade below and re-plastered on his smile for the public's consumption. He kept one hand loosely waving as he grew thoughtful.

"That could be of some concern. I may have to talk to Borosh about it, see what he knows. When was the last disappearance?"

"Just last night, s-sir. In fact, it was Thegal Rost, the very analyst who had been examining the pictures of the soil erosion and who had been due to make a report of it for your examination today. He's vanished without a trace, along with any sign of his analysis."

"I'll admit, that sounds rather...convenient."

"Agreed, sir."

"Perhaps we need to keep a bit more of a careful eye on our other-world friends. Just in case."

"Agreed, sir," Malath quickly nodded, shuffling once again for other papers attached to his clipboard, "and with that in mind, I have already been examining the Accord papers more carefully myself. It seems as the Accords protect the Tanians against any form of direct challenge from the Five Nations Government, but neither does it deny any Nation or Family the right to protect itself. I'm not exactly sure what to make of it, sir."

"Neither am I," Thalamas pondered. "I am very pleased with the direction Volst is taking, but we should deal with the Tanians just like any other Nation. Carefully. At the very least, we can use these suspicions to press the Tanians for a few extra benefits in exchange for keeping our mouths shut. We've entered into a golden era, Malath. With the Five Nations government now in charge, we can keep any proposed actions against the Tanians tied up in committees for a full talla while the Tanians keep giving us the benefits that we've long deserved. In fact, by the time the various committees finish dissecting and analyzing any given proposal for action, we can see to it that the end result that gets voted on bears little resemblance to the original, and Volst will be left with clean hands. Then the more we learn about what the Tanians might be up to on that mountain, the more we can hold over their heads with the implied threat of exposure."

He pondered a bit more before his attention was drawn back to the cheering crowds below, and he once again resumed his cheerful hand-waving. Soon after that, his doubts were forgotten, lost amidst the obvious evidence of his success, literally parading before him.

A few minutes later, the ground rumbled. It was nothing that anyone paid attention to at first; tremors were quite common. But as the seconds ticked by, the rumbling grew stronger, until even Thalamas paused in his waving to grip onto the railing and glare around in annoyance.

"A tremor has to happen *now* in the middle of my parade? And why isn't it stopping already?"

The rumbling continued for a few more seconds, just enough to topple some decorative masonry from a higher level of the government building onto a suddenly alert crowd. Then at last, it began to diminish. Just enough time to earn a scowl from the Volst First Speaker.

"That was a bit more than the usual tremor."

"Yes, sir," Malath nervously replied. "We've always had more quakes than the rest of Ikara, but they do seem to have been increasing of late. That was a particularly strong one, though no one seems to have been hurt."

"Hmm, curious." A moment to ponder, but then Thalamas saw the parade below coming to a hesitant pause, and immediately shrugged it off in favor of a broad smile and fresh waving of his hand. "No matter. Even force quakes aren't going to mar this day."

Again seeing their leader greeting them with smiles and an open hand, they resumed their cheers, and the parade picked up its previous pace. With the pomp and glory laid out before him, Thalamas very quickly forgot about the quake.

The Volst geothermal emlash power stations had all been fitted with the Tanian-supplied improvements, and they now littered the flank of the Great Mountain to supply more than adequate power for a global grid, with nary a single fault or interruption to its flow. Even better, it was Elmanith that had paid for their construction and not Volst, and with just one request. Elmanith insisted that a protected embassy (of sorts) be constructed to replace the *Observer* station. It would have to be free of Volst influence and built to Elmanith specifications. It was to be a seismic and chemical composition research facility, and it would be administered by the ISP. Thus was built the Volst Oversight Platform.

The one charged with its construction was Thollum Woll, the chief engineer for the Great Mountain Project, which oversaw all Volst projects about the Great Mountain. He was an aggressively patriotic Volst, who chafed at the idea of working with any other Nation—particularly the Elmanith, who nearly all Volst considered the weakest and most petty of the Five. He balked at their instruction and chortled at their missteps along the way, but he did work with them. At least Thollum got to name the thoroughfare leading to the facility. He named it Woll Street.

The Tanians stayed aloof from such local matters, letting Volst negotiate with the other Nations, rather than doing anything directly. Borosh knew that Thalamas Voort would cover for any Tanian mistakes, as long as he kept him supplied with new toys. And in turn, for anything he missed, there was always the final solution of the Tanian Security Chief. The latter was a last resort, however, for Lort's solution would be rather brutal.

Only a week after the Oversight Platform opened, it happened: The ground beneath a portion of the Platform gave way, resulting in the loss of Ikaran lives. Borosh himself attended the memorial service, Amishari by his side, while Lort and his security team remained in the background to keep a careful watch on things. The ceremony was held atop the old *Observer* and attended by a group of Ikarans dressed in a wide variety of bright colors, who had the chief Administrator marveling to his assistant.

"I'll admit," he shrugged, "they make for a colorfully dressed set of natives."

"It's called a culture," Amishari replied with a trace of sarcasm in her thoughts. "Many worlds have them."

"Well, it looks good enough but has no place in a truly civilized society. That's one of the little things they'll have to abandon if we take any of them with us across the Bridge."

"Speaking of which," Amishari told him, "Thalamas Voort has been after me to ask you when the Bridge will be opened to Ikaran travel. He wishes for Volst to be the first to make use of it."

"Yes, the man thinks himself some sort of actual leader, instead of the feather-covered, bead-wearing primitive that he is. I'll talk to him."

"It seems as you have your chance right now, Administrator; here he comes."

Thalamas Voort approached them with a purposeful stride and a look of determination about his face. Borosh held out his hand in the fashion of the local greeting, but he was barely into his first words before the Volst cut him off.

"Thalamas, how do you-"

"The collapse occurred because of one of *your* mine shafts," Thalamas said, getting right to the point.

"And you're supposed to keep such things away," Borosh quietly countered.

"The data you supplied said there was nothing there to stay away *from,*" Thalamas scowled. "In fact, it was easily hundreds of miles away from the next nearest mining tunnel. It was supposed to be safe."

"Mining has its dangers, as you well know," Borosh shrugged. "It's a tragedy, but this is why we can't have too many people on the mountain. What would you have me do?"

Thalamas stepped up very close, his voice dropping to an angry whisper.

"Right now, I'm about to give a speech that will be witnessed by several hundred people and transmitted by Wave to the entire planet. Exactly what I say might depend on what *you* say to me right now. The other nations view Volst as being slow and stupid, but our engineering skills prove otherwise. We are methodical in our ways, often to a fault, but once we have finished analyzing a problem, there is *very* little that we miss. Little details, the likes of which many people at this assembly would find very interesting."

"Okay, I see your point," Borosh admitted with a shrug. "Your people are very diligent workers, so how's about this: you do some mining for basic metals anyway, but I will allow you to mine into some currently restricted sections of the mountain. However, the bulk of the resources you retrieve, you will give to us. The work will be dangerous, which is why we could use some workers as methodical as those of Volst, but in exchange your people will be well paid, both in manners useable here on Ikara, and in Tanian credits…for use *off* world."

Thalamas' eyes went from angry to bright as he immediately perceived the implication.

"You mean-"

"No doubt your Five Nations will want to launch an inquest into this disaster. As part of this I will invite an investigative team to make the first trip to Tania. That team will be comprised entirely of Volst personnel, since this happened as part of a Volst construction project. In fact, you will insist that it be all Volst and I will reluctantly agree. The real mission of this team, however, will be to bring back whatever you need to know to be assured of the safe passage of the rest of Ikara. Thalamas, when the time is right, Volst will be the first through the Bridge."

"Volst," Thalamas beamed, "the first to the stars. But how will we choose? Which ones of Volst's people will go?"

"Why choose," Borosh shrugged. "We have the capacity to transport everyone."

"Everyone?"

"*All* of Volst's citizenry, my friend. Every man, woman, and child. When the time is right, of course."

"Oh, of course," Thalamas smiled, now putting out his hand. "Administrator, you have a deal. I speak in a few minutes. All will be taken care of in that speech."

They shook hands, and a very happy Thalamas Voort walked off to rejoin the memorial, leaving Borosh and Amishari to converse more discreetly.

"He's nearly like a Tanian," Borosh remarked.

"Yes," Amishari blandly replied, "I *had* noticed. Physically and ideologically, you could be brothers." Amishari was referring, of course, to both men's love of power and glory, though Borosh differed in his far more murderous ways and lack of naiveté. Borosh, of course, missed her real point completely.

"They simply understand the importance of production schedules and industry secrets. By the time this day is up, they will be running a mine for us and be well paid for their troubles."

"In Tanian credits."

"Collectable once they reach Tania, of course," Borosh shrugged, eyeing his assistant.

Amishari said nothing but stared blandly, directing her gaze at Thalamas Voort as he spoke.

"This incident was a tragedy for which Tania takes its share of responsibility, but it is not without its lessons. Even now, an investigative team is being organized by the Five Nations government, one in which Volst will have a strong presence. We *will* find the reason behind this collapse and take measures to assure that this sort of tragedy never happens again. For now though, let us hold a moment of silence for those dear departed souls."

He took off his large, eagle-feathered hat, hung his head, and said not a word more, which prompted everyone else there to do likewise. It was a moment of silence for the dead Ikarans who had been on the Platform. By the time they looked up, Thalamas had stepped aside to leave the podium for the Tanian Borosh. More than a few displeased looks from the audience greeted his presence, as feelings fell somewhere between frustration and distrust. When the Tanian spoke, however, it was in pleasing tones, and a general feeling of goodwill seemed to radiate from him.

Actually, it was, in fact, radiating from him in the more literal sense.

"We Tanians grieve at the loss of *any* life so believe me when I say that, as an empathic species, we feel this loss as strongly as do you Ikarans. We will, of course, cooperate with any investigation into probable causes, and I hereby call for better safety standards for *all* projects in and about the Mountain. That said, as tragic as this all is, I am reluctant to remind you that this would never have happened if it were not for the insistence of increased access to our activities at the top of the mountain. We will, of course, be happy to comply with any future demands for access, but as our work progresses, the chance of missteps and similar tragedies will only increase. Please, for your own safety, stay away from Tanian operations. It is simply too dangerous for untrained personnel."

"Administrator," Thalamas called out as he stepped back towards the podium, "surely you can understand our concerns. Perhaps if you just allowed a small contingent from Volst? We are, after all, better trained than the average Ikaran to know what types of dangers to look for."

For a moment, Borosh paused as though he was considering this request. A glance showed a small sea of faces regarding him with fixed gazes, including several members of the Five Nations government, as if by pressure of gaze alone, they could force him into agreeing. Borosh saw this, sighed, and put out his hands to either side in a gesture of surrender.

"Very well. Volst may be your representative contingent, but no others and not too many of them. We seek only your safety until our project here is completed."

He ended with a slight bow of his head, for which he got collective applause, before leaving the podium.

In the end, all but a few Volst specialists left the Bridge complex, while the *Observer* was completely shuttered. For safety reasons, the job of keeping an eye on the Tanians would now be left entirely in Volst hands, who would willingly or unknowingly turn many a blind eye on what they might see.

Borosh
"Come in. You're one of the men from the Volst Oversight

team."

With only a curt nod for a reply, the tall man in the heavy coat, colorful shirt, and leggings went into Administrator Borosh's office. The office seemed a strange place to him. The design was clinical. Its function centered around what looked like a simple plasteel desk with rounded ends, which had chairs that molded around the back of the one sitting in them (almost as if the administrator secretly wished he were a judge). The room had displays that hovered in the air just above the desk in front of Borosh, seemingly bearing none of the physical input that one might expect. Everything was white, clean, and devoid of any real sense of having been lived in.

It made the man from Volst feel a little uncomfortable.

Borosh motioned to the open seat opposite his desk, but the Volst simply shook his head. He preferred to remain standing. The Administrator picked up a pad made of metal and plastic, which had glowing figures written across its top surface. To Borosh's merest touch, it was accompanied by lines of text visibly floating an inch above its surface, and a three-dimensional picture floating above this text. It was a picture of the Volst and the others on his team. Borosh selected the one corresponding to the one standing before him, watching as the display swiftly changed to a different block of text, accompanied now by just one picture hovering above it. He smiled up at the tall man.

"I just wanted to talk for a bit. I've been so busy with my many duties that I have not had the time to properly get to know much about Ikaran culture. I figured this is the perfect excuse. So, let's just talk about anything you want. Tell me about Ikara, the way the different factions are laid out and why. Tell me about Volst. Anything at all. I've already interviewed two of your companions, so I do have a couple of basic questions, but start anyplace you like."

The Volst was hesitant at first, but the man's eyes held a trusting look. Then he couldn't help but feel a bit more relaxed in his presence.

"You...just want to know about Volst?"

To Borosh's confirming nod, the Volst cautiously continued.

"Well…there are five nations, each descended from one of the original five leaders who in turn are descendants of the burning men. Volst is a nation of engineers—but I think you already know about that…"

The Volst's narrative meandered quite a bit at first, wandering from the types of clothing each nation preferred to the man's opinions about the behaviors of the other nations. Throughout it all, Borosh patiently listened, occasionally offering a guiding question or two, which steered the discourse more to his liking. Borosh was searching, but even he was not quite certain for what. Something, anything he could use to better pacify these Ikarans. After an hour, he saw it: a suggestive glimmer hidden behind the mention of prophecies.

"Well, yes, we have many prophecies," the Volst shrugged, long since taking the offered seat and feeling more relaxed and comfortable. "The old GenSeers say it's all stored in our genetics. We have prophecies going all the way back to the First Cycle. Nothing before that, of course; the GenSeers say our path was broken at that point, so we really don't know about anything before we-"

"Tell me about some of these prophecies," Borosh said, curious. "Any one at all."

"Well, all of them are about what the Grand Cycle has spelled out for us. How one day the Cycle will lead us back into the unity of the Agora before we leave to reclaim the stars. Then there's the one about-"

"Wait. Agora, you say? What is this Agora?"

"The Agora?" the man shrugged. "I don't know too much about it myself, but it's some sort of shared mind that's supposed to bring peace and unity. I can't see how *that's* going to happen myself but that's what the prophecy says."

"Interesting," Borosh mused. "From the sounds of it, this Agora may be very much like what my own people have with our mind-to-mind communication. We may have a lot more in common than either of us first thought, my friend."

"Really? It's just an old legend, you know."

"But one perhaps based on old facts. And if it is, then it suggests that one day you may communicate in the same manner as ourselves. You may very well become just as we are."

"Well," the Volst hesitantly admitted, "that sounds like it might be good...I guess. To become like you."

"*Just* like us," Borosh replied, the grin spreading across his face with the stealthy pace of a slithering snake. He would be talking to his own technicians about the possibility of Agora, he decided. "Just like us indeed..."

Mission One

Simoth Karth was still rather young compared to most of the grey-haired ones in key positions of government, but he was bright and clever (almost too clever, by some accounts). He was an average-looking Karthan with average brown hair trimmed in an average way. Even his clothes were average: his shirt a deep green and his jerkin the color of the tossing sea. He paced angrily about his office, not at all pleased with what lay atop his desk: a folder filled with papers, the designation on the folder simply reading "Mission One." It was the summary of the first mission to Azur. A mission that was already underway.

He paused for a moment before his window, looking out at the early morning sky. There was a light in the distance, the flame of a bright candle seeking up towards the firmaments. He saw it and bit his lip with frustration, before spinning around to confront that one folder across the room on his desk.

"The *day* our first mission launches and *that's* when Jast gets the mission briefing to me? What's he pulling *now?*"

He threw a last glance toward the rising flame beyond the window until it disappeared into the glare of the morning sun, then turned back towards his desk.

"Too late now to do anything about it," he angrily sighed, "might as well see what we've gotten ourselves into."

He walked over to his desk and took his seat. With a last sigh, he glared down at the one folder and carefully opened it up to read the first page.

It was a preamble, a summary of things to date. But Simoth knew it for what it really was: a sales pitch designed for the people who controlled the purse strings.

"In the aftermath of what some have called the Tanian Awakening, the people of Ikara have made monumental advances in transportation, communication, and navigation. During this short period, those advances fundamentally changed the relationship between both the individual Ikarans and their developing Nationalistic cultures. As a result of its virtually global appearance, the astronomical event known as the Candlefall has become synonymous with these changes and it has been renamed 'The Ikaran Illumination' to downplay the role that the Others played in its origin. It is therefore important to note that the concept of a mission to Azur has been a cultural one dating back through the two and a half Grand Cycles that we have been able to research through genetic memory. We have been to Azur before, and knew we would go there again.

"Ikarans born in recent generations have been introduced to an open universe to explore. Though it was a cautious and qualified offer with smooth words, the Tanians have promised us the stars. Ikara, however, cannot wait and we are determined to reach the stars with or without the Tanians. Now, through the combined efforts of the Five Nations, virtually all Ikara has participated in the study and research for this project.

"*It has only been a half a talla since the government of the Five Nations was officially ratified and the Ikaran Space Program birthed in full, and yet in that short time we have set our sights on Azur; a planet that our best calculations estimate that our current technology can reach within six months. This mission will be the culmination of our highest ideal, our greatest achievement, and a benchmark of our accomplishments."*

Simoth flipped the pages aside, looking for something of greater substance. He muttered:

"I supposed I can see their point, but the ISP has taken absolutely no input from the aliens and not made use of their greater knowledge on the basic sciences. There's still huge gaps in our understanding of planetary dynamics and the Universe at large. I just know we're going into this too fast for our own good. Our ambition is outstripping our diligence.

"Long before contact with the Tanians, we were developing mechanisms for making a first mission a tangible possibility, with support from every family in every region

"Support," Simoth snorted to himself, "and money pouring in from every Family around, which only means that everyone wanted one of their own on this first crew. Political expediency over competent choice. That is the danger I've been trying to point out to Jast, but he's just so determined to get these missions started. Almost as if he's in a race against something." He continued to read.

"The parameters of this first mission limit us to a crew of five...

"And that's what's doomed this mission even before launch," he sighed. "Each of the Five Families wants to have one of their own in the crew, and once everyone else realized they'd have no-one from their own faction on board, their donations started drying up. It's underfunded and...Wait, what's this?"

He looked at a couple of charts on a page, then shook his head and sighed.

"Falsified results. I got a report on the *real* data before Jast changed it around. Okay, so I'll admit he's done a brilliant job of keeping this moving forward, even though it's so publicly popular yet privately despised, but from what I can make out from the other papers I've received, he's as near as *selling* places on the First Mission! And here's the crew roster. I know these names and none of them really knows what they're getting into. Vadas Elim? Third in line for

Speaker of Elmanith if something happens to wipe out Helm and his entire family; more politician than scientist. And Nord Ratham? His only claim to fame is that he wants it so much he's the only one willing to speak out against what everyone knows is best for Nathor, just so people will notice him. Then we have Nahl Vahst, who is the one person I'm sure Thalamas Voort wouldn't mind if he were to suddenly declare allegiance to Elmanith, except that he happens to be his wife's cousin and the son of a rather prominent owner of one of their energy production companies. Maldren of Whycheral? The last time *he* had a reliable vision, I think my parents were trying to conceive me. They're *all* chosen by favoritism and nepotism. None of them have been through the rigorous training they'll need for fear that they might not measure up. Why, half these…now what's this?"

He turned a page and read some more, a puzzled frown crossing his face.

"This doesn't make sense. There's references of working with the Tanians in some of this, and quoting sections of the Accords, but…these are the parts of the project that have been the slowest to develop, with the greatest cost overruns. It references the equal partnership clause of the Accords and the Tanian advisor, but…," he flipped a few more pages, frowning ever the more, "…dividing work evenly amongst the nations, with political considerations taking precedence over whoever everyone *knows* is actually right for the job, waiting on approval from the advisor, agreement that certain elements must involve technology supplied by the Tanians instead of our own…All this was in the Accords? But then on the next page, it seems to indicate that we did it all on our own *without* their help. And then these figures on the next page don't add up. It's like there was more than enough money for the project, but…some of it's being funneled elsewhere. I don't understand. What is Jast up to?"

He looked up, as if expecting an answer. His gaze wasn't simply focused on a random patch of empty wall. Seated in a chair in the shadows sat another. The beauty of Bellelorn, the Matron of Nathor, hidden from direct sight of any window view. She replied in a quiet voice, as if afraid that even here, safely within Simoth's Karthan offices, she might be overheard.

"I'm not entirely sure," she replied after a moment, "but it seems he has been hinting. I've been very excited about the ISP and the First Mission. Indeed, in my time as Matron, while I've done my best to feed the poor, protect against homelessness, and look after the betterment of the Nathorn people as a whole, it has become rather banal at times. This mission put some excitement, not only back into my own life, but the lives of the people in general. As you know, I committed to supplying storable sustenance packs for the mission crew, but now I've just received word by Wave that not all those packs made it onto the launch vehicle. We have little in the way of technology or designs with which to support the mission, and a few are even starting to say that Nathor has not truly been supportive of it. Including that Nord Ratham you mentioned, by the way."

"From what I'm reading in this report and in others," Simoth told her, "it's almost as if Jast himself has been sabotaging this mission from the start by changing the crew members around. We've lost some of our talent in the process, and there are also rumors he's gleaned some wealth off the top of the mission budget."

"No," Bellelorn said with a light shake of her head. "Jast has been the one pushing for a long time to get Ikara to Azur. He would not sabotage his own dream. Not to mention he doesn't need the money."

"Then what, Matron, is going on? I know you at least suspect something, or why come here in person instead of just telling me on the Wave?"

For a long moment, her only answer was silence. Then she got to her feet and softly walked across the room, until she was looking at Simoth from the opposite side of his desk. There, she bent down until she nearly had her mouth to his ear, and spoke in the barest of whispers.

"He whispers into my ear at night when we are about to be

passionate. The Tanians are watching this first Mission...and us *very* closely."

Due to the Tanian observations, most of the flight had been under stealth protocols. It wasn't until a few months after launch that news came out about the First Mission. Contact was resumed with the mission crew by Wave, and those last few days' reports had taken a dire turn. There were issues with equipment and fuel, as well as the solid fuel breakers. There were food shortages, faulty equipment, and a fuel shortage too. Every day since communication had been reestablished seemed to bring a new, ever-more-calamitous report from the Mission crew.

"We're starting to ration our food supplies now. Nahl wanted to celebrate our achievement with a feast a couple of days ago and we discovered some of the food had either not been stored properly or was completely missing from the packaging. We're also having some issues with the Wave, as you can tell."

Not even half a day later, another report came.

"Our sensors didn't detect it until nearly too late. Azur's moon is larger than the engineers told us, big enough to throw off our calculations. Vadas is updating the calculations now, but we're having to guess at the gravity of the thing; it seems to be pretty big in comparison to our own moons."

By the next morning, they could hear the stress in the voice reporting.

"It's definite, that moon altered our course a bit, but we think we have it corrected. All we have to do is make sure our food and oxygen—What was that? It sounded like-"

Those listening heard what sounded like a loud 'ping,' then a sudden hiss just before the transmission cut off. It was nearly a full day of anxious waiting before the next transmission would come to nervous ears. It was the *final* transmission from the crew of Mission One that they would receive.

"We're calling it a micro-meteor. Only about the size of-"

cough, *"sorry. As I was saying, only about the size of a grain of volcanic sand, but enough to penetrate the hull. We finally sealed up the hole, but not before we lost precious oxygen, not to mention the equipment that little chunk of space rock damaged. In fact,"* cough, wheeze, *"we have some dead crew members due to cockpit contamination and lack of oxygen; I am sorry to report Nord and Nahl have expired. We're still on course for Azur, but thanks to that little rock, the emlash sensor and controllers have been compromised. We have nothing with which to control our descent. We recommend next time someone design some sturdier housing for the equipment, not to mention about the hull. Still, we-"*

Cough, sputter, gasp. Then there was a pause before the voice resumed, this time with something new in the timbre: the sound of wonder.

*"I...I can see it. So round and blue, the clouds and all that water. It's...It's beautiful! Control, we aren't going to make planetfall; we're already heating up from contact with the atmosphere. But press on...Ikara must return to Azur. Don't let our failure stop you; we knew the risks and gladly took them. Azur is waiting for us. On behalf of the crew and their sacrifice, I will try to maintain a running commentary of observations for as long as I can in hope that the data will benefit the Mission. During the last few intervals before this broadcast we've crossed at least three radiation barriers while applying breaking thrusters. These barriers emitted radiation very different than what we experience on Ikara and have damaged our equipment, possibly beyond repair; you need to shield against **that** as well. Due to navigation equipment failures, our angle of descent is too steep and fast, and at this point we're going to heat up much faster than previously anticipated. Air heating up now. Craft plunging almost directly down; the pull is enormous. We advise future descent involves a more controlled and gradual angle of entry. We're gaining too much speed in relation to the gravity. Protect the equipment from these radiation belts and micro-meteors. I am sending data now before the ion field possibly blocks our transmission. The heat...not*

sure how much-"

The transmission cut off with a snap of static, and then... nothing. It was apparent to the ground crew that the great Ikaran heroes on Mission One had perished before the transmission had made it home, incinerated in the Azurian atmosphere.

It was most unnerving for Jast to watch a message sent by dead men. The tape showed the craft traveling at speeds far higher than needed to even leave the Ikaran atmosphere, and far too fast to enter Azur's safely. From the look on Jast's face, it seemed like it was all on his shoulders.

"Damn, damn!" he exclaimed as they helplessly watched the data on the tape roll in. "We should have known this was going to happen! There! Right there! See those radiation levels and the speed indicator?"

Everyone in the control room gathered to see the tape in Jast's hands as he continued.

"That's our mistake. We were approaching the entry point with too much velocity and the breakers did not engage properly. And... and here! The navigation system failed. Look at those radiation bands! We don't have those here, not like *that!* We can't shield ourselves against that level of radiation. We must create a new emlash board that will work through it. The entry protocols were correct, but once the emlash system was fried, they had no chance! They could have made it. They could have, but we failed them. We didn't do our jobs!"

As the ground crew examined the incoming data, Jast stormed out of the room. After that, events proceeded more rapidly than the Mission's pace.

————————

It was a particularly rainy afternoon in the Elmanith capital of Eleman. Jast was finalizing the debriefing files of Mission One and preparing to address the Five Nations government about its outcome. Rain wasn't uncommon along the Elmanith coast, but the intensity of the downpour was unusual. The upper reaches of the nation had suffered increased flooding, and the losses were mounting among the fishing crews, who couldn't risk the increased ferocity of the coastal storm patterns. Then there was the wind. Storm winds were taking on an increasingly reddish hue, with an accompanying increase in electrical activity. Due to all his efforts to keep a lid on the Tanian activities on the Great Mountain (and their suspected impact on global weather), Jast seemed to be wearing down as the deaths kept increasing.

Immediately after the loss of the First Mission, the Five Nations government held a meeting, whose sole purpose seemed to be finger-pointing. It looked like the new government might break apart then and there, until the delegate from Kartha found a more convenient scapegoat. He was a smart kid named Simoth, who Jast knew had been sent by the Family to keep an eye on the ISP. He was also in line to take over for Kael Karth when the Speaker was ready to retire. Before that would happen, however, Jast knew that Simoth had a lot to learn about what was really going on.

Simoth stood up and patted a stack of folders before him as he began speaking.

"The disastrous end to Mission One was a tragedy for all Ikara, but particularly for the families of the crew. Vadas Elim, third in line for Speaker of Elmanith. Nord Ratham, noted political figure of Nathor. Nahl Vahst, a prominent son of Volst. GenSeer Maldren of Whycheral. And finally, mission leader Talren of Kartha. A moment of silence, please, for this lost crew."

After a heavy pause, Simoth continued, his hand once again patting his stack of folders.

"As we mourn those lost, one cannot help but wonder if it could have been prevented. I have here enough evidence to make an accusation, even if not conviction. It's circumstantial at best, but still enough to cast a shadow over one of the main proponents of the ISP. Jast Rathael has-"

"Excuse me." It was Jast who unexpectedly spoke out in loud, clear tones that immediately drew attention away from Simoth. "But

I would like to offer my resignation, effective immediately."

Those assembled raised their voices in confusion. Questions were launched at one another and in Jast's general direction. They would have little time to wonder, however, as he did something even more unexpected when he stood up to speak:

"I fully accept all responsibility for the failure of the First Mission. There may have been problems stemming from a number of sources, but as chief administrator, the whole of it ultimately falls into my lap. However, in this resignation, I hereby wish to nominate a replacement for my position. I nominate the young delegate from Kartha, Simoth Karth. He is young but brilliant and capable, and so it is with no reservation whatsoever that I nominate Simoth Karth as the new chief administrator for the ISP."

Jast sat down and let the controversy rage around him, not the least of which was a surprised look from Simoth himself. No one was going to question Jast's appointment. Who could be more qualified to give the nomination, and who else would be more accepting than Simoth Karth himself? After much talking, two things came out of that morning session: the formation of the Five Nation Council on Interplanetary Travel to oversee all future missions, and the appointment of Simoth Karth as its head. Before they adjourned, they scheduled the first meeting of the newly formed Council on Interplanetary Travel to be held right after lunch.

Jast had found time enough to size up Simoth, even before the morning meeting. Bellelorn hadn't visited the young official without her husband's knowledge—but rather, with his planning. He hated to use her in such a manner, but it was the only way. And she had agreed to assist. Jast found his administrative position had now become too public to do what he needed to do. So he had to find a young replacement who could weather the next several tallas, but one who was also cunning and intelligent. He'd delayed sending the First Mission briefing file to Simoth on purpose, then sat back to see if he was smart enough to connect a few dots. After the call, Bellelorn (the First Speaker of Nathor) verified that he was all of the above. And Bellelorn's report on her meeting with him confirmed the rest.

The Karthan seemed determined to return Kartha to its rightful place as leader of the most ambitious, unifying exploration ever devised by Ikarans. Jast didn't have anything against that, but some things needed to come in their own time.

With Volst giving up their Observation platform to the Tanians, Elmanith had used their own broad, safe coast as a launch facility for the first experimental, unmanned tests for Mission One. The coast was easier to get supplies and building materials to anyway, and the Karthans had agreed to its use. With no precedent for unoccupied space exploration, no thought was given to precautions or best locations. If Elmanith could get it done, they were happy as long as there was a Karthan involved.

Now that the First Mission had met with such disaster, however, Kartha seemed determined to put forth itself as the most qualified nation to lead future Karth Kessai missions.

That afternoon, the first meeting of the Council on Interplanetary Travel was about to convene. Simoth Karth looked out through the gallery window to the rain-soaked streets beyond, thinking to himself how wet it seemed, even for Elmanith. He turned away and stalked into the ISP main conference hall, a flurry of conferees scattering at his approach like a flock of coastal seabirds before a capital ship.

Other members of the new ISP council hadn't yet arrived. Without a thought for propriety, Simoth took the central position and shifted the nameplate of Jast Rathael to his right, as befitting a noble ascending to precedence in a vassal state. By the time the last of the five representatives and their retainers had assembled, the necessary materials to support his position had been disseminated, and even the displaced Elmanith leader Jast was attentively listening to the youth from the Island.

"Let it be said now, as it has been through the Cycles, that Kartha knows its duty. Adventurers forever and leaders among the

Families, we represent all Ikara in this endeavor to gain dominion among the planets and eventually among the stars, we now know that we stand on the threshold of our destiny.

"Some would say that my youth precludes me from making the decisions for my nation. On that, I would agree fully, but if the question is instead, do I have the wisdom to speak for my People among all the Ikarans, the answer is very different. For the spirit of adventure that lights my heart and drives my passions is the fire of youthfulness, and that is the very *heart* of adventure.

"Before our morning session, our esteemed administrator Jast Rathael opened the meeting with his own resignation and my nomination as head of this Council. After looking over a summary outline of future mission planning, our first order of business, then, is to confirm the crew for Mission Two. This mission is to not only orbit and investigate possible landfall on Azur, but to test the possibility of a landing and subsequent re-launch from the planetary surface. In keeping with history, tradition, and the Grand Cycle, such a necessary mission must be led by Karth Kessai, those called to be Adventurers among the Stars. I am here to nominate just such a leader, not only in the name of Kartha, nation of adventurers, but in the name of all the Ikaran People. Thus, in the quiet rains of Elmanith, in the very heart of Eleman, I offer for nomination the name of the preeminent Scholar of Kartha, the self-proclaimed Walker among the Others, Devane Urdlu."

Beginning one's own ovation might be considered pompous, but that's exactly what almost immediately happened as Simoth clapped his hands. He had calculated that the choice of a lesser advocate from the Karthan position would bring confusion, but he never expected abject disbelief. It was uncomfortable to be the only person clapping in the large conference room. But eventually, full dozens of seconds after it had begun, the hushed roar of a very surprised collection of space scientists and advocates arose. At first, only a few here and a smattering there joined in the accolade, but then there were more as the implications finally sank in.

J. R. Austin

A Karthan would lead Mission Two, and the hold upon Ikaran destiny that many saw within Jast Rathael's hands had shifted during that engagement.

Helm

Helm was beside himself.

It wasn't the weather. It was true that the weather patterns had shifted dramatically over the past couple of tallas, with the windstorms and torrential downpours preventing transports and conveys from travelling. That he could handle.

It wasn't the quakes either. True, they seemed to be ever on the increase, but that just meant that the Volst engineers got the pleasure of designing ever-more-stable structures.

It wasn't even the stress of his position. The food-supply accounting processes were spotty again, but taking on the administration of all Ikaran commodities and distribution had sounded like a good compromise. And his penchant for detail meant he would eventually get it all balanced out.

No, he was beside himself because he had once again failed to take a stand against his father. In the past two to three tallas since the creation of the Five Nations government, the operations of the individual nations had become an onerous task, no longer the clean slate and bright beginning that everyone had dreamed of. A people who'd grown accustomed to comfortable self-management did not sit well with a unified leadership belching forth orderly regulations and operational guidelines. Helm's role as First Speaker was no longer to guide and direct the Elmanith, but to express their will and represent them to the other Nations. They were unprepared and unwilling to accept and follow orders in that fashion.

So it came to be that the Five Nations Council finally had a meeting to seek a solution for their problem of a lack of central leadership, and of the overwhelming reality of administering an entire world. It was the results of that meeting that had Helm reeling.

"I expected my role to be more of a figurehead," he said as he leaned back tiredly in his desk chair, his tri-corner hat tossed to one side. "A mouthpiece. I never wanted to be a true leader; I don't have the energy or will for that type thing. The idea of true leadership is for the naïve...the uninitiated if you ask me."

He glanced at the fresh mound of papers on his desk and shook his head. So much work, so many people demanding wisdom and answers (things he felt he didn't possess).

"That day on the Mountain, we had presented a united front to these Tanians. The Five Nations quickly ratified the Accords, and the world was made right with that one action."

He sighed as he thought over what had happened since, shuffling slowly through a few of the documents before leaning back in his chair once again.

"But it seems that the challenges were more than anyone had expected. Our haste in meeting with these aliens may have actually done more to *harm* each of our individual nations. I've heard the doubts about how sincere the leaders of the Five Nations really are, whether they truly have everyone's interests in mind or just their own. People are not stupid, we have never needed a central government of such magnitude before and the more power it has, the less accountability it operates under. Then there are the Tanians themselves; negotiations with them went rather quickly...perhaps too quickly. I cannot help but wonder what they could be hiding to be so generous. They are not Ikaran, they do not have a soul our seers can detect. They have no deeper purpose that would cause them to be benevolent. They could be nothing more than empty shells supporting a life form. Something that goes to the dirt eventually like a piece of trash, no eternal quantum state of existence. If this is the case, they are very dangerous and any agreement they make is meaningless."

Helm shook his head once again before looking up at the man who sat opposite him: the man who was the council's solution to its problems *and* the source of his current headache.

"And then there's the fact that you did not attend in person. My own father, First Speaker of Whycheral, the only one who had not shown up to represent his people. Why is that, father?"

Jast looked back, his expression schooled and noncommittal.

"I had my reasons," he finally replied. "You have to remember how busy I am."

"Some say that you care more for what happens within the borders of Whycheral than for any treaty with these Outsiders."

"The Accords are a farce," Jast stated quite bluntly, "designed to pacify us for a time. The only good thing to come out of it was the unified Five Nations government. I'd hoped that would keep things moving along for a bit longer, but it seems jealousy and in-fighting are becoming more prevalent behind the scenes."

"It's done some good initially," Helm admitted. "Volst builds power resources into a leveraged asset, Whycheral continues to be in charge of travel and storage resources, Nathor is actively exporting tools for healthful personal improvement, Elmanith focuses on creature comforts, and Kartha expands its dominance of adventure and exploration. But outside of that, every nation seeks its own favors from the Tanians and the quarreling has made its way into the governmental chambers. Each of the Five Nations are now striving for control like a pack of hungry laravels."

"The problem is," Jast explained, "that the Five Nations government was built in the manner of a council, with no single strong official to be appointed as its leader. That was done to assure equality, but ultimately it has become its undoing. That is why they needed a central figure, a Chancellor to relieve them of the difficult burden of the drudgery of administering to Ikara as a whole, so they can do so with their own individual nations."

"A position for which you so eagerly volunteered, father, despite your antipathy towards the Tanians."

"I *am* the most qualified," Jast shrugged. "I have stepped up before when there was a need, all the way back to Candlefall when the GenSeers were killed. And I've helped the Five Nations to get the Space Program quite literally off the ground."

"All very true, but I'm still skeptical. You failed to attend the single most important meeting of the Grand Cycle; the one meeting that formed the body to which you are now Chancellor. How much of this has to do with what we suspect of our Tanian friends?"

"Perhaps quite a bit," was all Jast would say. "I'm now in a position to glean more of the Tanian objective and I do get along with that Tanian, Borosh."

"You despise him and all Tanians," Helm reminded him.

"That doesn't mean I can't put on a presentable face and play nice. Besides, most of our dealings are by Wave, minimizing any personal interaction that might give them an advantage."

"Father, this is all just too crazy. Almost as crazy as when you suggested one of my kids will pilot a spacecraft to Azur."

"Someday, one of them will. Dantu, possibly, though more likely Micah."

"Dantu was just four at the time, Micah only three, father."

"I didn't say it would happen this talla. Helm, enough of this bickering, I'm here for a purpose. If I'm to administer the Five Nations properly, I'll need a Speaker Regent and I want that person to be you."

"Me? Father, I'm no leader. For one thing, I'm not underhand enough."

"You don't have to be a leader, just an administrator. I'm both Chancellor as well as First Speaker to Whycheral. This might sometimes put me into conflict, so I'll need someone I can trust to catch me."

"You mean, until they catch you at something and toss you out as Chancellor? I give it two tallas."

"That long?" Jast smiled. "With all the political maneuvering and factions vying for Tanian favoritism, I'd give it a lot shorter time than that before the whole Five Nations government simply folds in upon itself. Helm, it is not one truly unified government, but a five-headed beast ready to bite itself."

"And you want me to help you ride this beast," Helm sighed.

J. R. Austin

"Great."

The Plan

In the following months that led up to the Mission Two launch, the governance of the Nations of Ikara continued to stabilize under the leadership of Chancellor Jast. However, political intrigue continued to abound as nations jockeyed for favor with the Tanians. Such maneuvering made it difficult for Simoth to keep the ISP functioning beneath the radar of political intrigue.

It took some time for Simoth to go through the secretive files of Jast's administration of the ISP, files that indicated that Mission Two was already on the drawing board by the time the First Mission launched—and apparently funded by some of the money missing from Mission One. Not for the first time, Simoth wondered what Jast was doing.

Simoth had other problems though. The current state of affairs with the Five Nations government drew his ire and taxed his patience, but he was determined to keep the ISP and the next mission going. So he contacted his cousin Tark Karth, the one person he could really trust, the one person who'd been involved in behind-the-scenes activity enough to offer some advice.

The response was an invitation from Tark to meet with him in the Catacombs.

"You and Devane risked everything to meet those aliens," Simoth said as they strolled the dark tunnels, their only lighting being an occasional lash-lamp mounted onto the wall, "and while that's good, I think it's hampering our efforts."

Simoth was dressed in rather nondescript navy-blue pants and a brown jerkin, a hood drawn over his head until they were deep into the Catacombs. Walking alongside him, Tark was also dressed as commonly as he could, but his gait and bearing would always give him away. Tark was not a man to hide in the shadows. Not at all.

"A daring thing to say in an age when even questioning their motivations is suspect. The Tanians are very popular with certain

70

peoples."

"So I've noticed. In fact, I suspect that's why that you suggested we meet down here. Tark, the Second Mission was to be my crowning achievement, even after Jast bungled the first one. And now…Kartha is supposed to be the one to lead such adventures, but Volst wants to take that away from us, claiming their closeness to the Tanians means they are *chosen*. Then there's the Tanians themselves. In the Accord talks, I watched that Tanian Borosh win one condition after another just from his smooth talk and the fact that everyone seems to look at him as some sort of savior. I didn't see Helm, or anyone else for that matter, lift a finger to object either. With their conditions, along with our increasing dependency on their technology—all of which seems carefully screened—they've created a reliance with no *real* technological advancement that we can use for the betterment of our people. Then there's the breakdown of the Five Nations government. I'll be bold enough to say that the Tanians, by requiring a one world government, have stratified us by even the most superficial differences, a problem that has all but eliminated our chances for effective extra-planetary travel."

"You say much that most ears do not want to hear," Tark remarked as they walked.

"And I'll say a lot more. I think that Jast Rathael's working *for* those aliens. I think he sabotaged the First Mission on purpose. The dream of every Ikaran has been to return to the stars, but between Jast and the Tanians, that dream is being taken away! They should call the Tanian Accords the Tanian Pacification Protocols because that's *just* what it's done."

"It looks like I selected well. He's perfect."

Simoth spun around to see the source of the familiar voice. There, stepping out from the shadows of an adjoining tunnel, was Jast Rathael himself. His beard was long and flecked through with traces of gray. He no longer dressed as he had in his youth, with knee-high leather boots and a blue and gold tunic. Instead, he simply wore voluminous green robes with a blue and gold trim. A sign, perhaps, that he no longer needed to present himself as an imposing figure, that merely his name alone was now enough. At his side was his pet laravel, Voldoth, and behind him the ever-present Halgor. Simoth was surprised at first. He cast a suspicious eye on Tark, then back on Jast.

"Is this some sort of setup?" Simoth snapped. "Tark, what's this about? Is the infamous Jast Rathael here to ambush me in revenge for taking him out of the limelight?"

"No, nothing like that," Jast said with a reassuring smile. "In fact, I'd like to thank you for doing that for me. I'd drawn too much attention to myself to be effective in what needed to be done. Now as Chancellor, I would be unable to show any overt favoritism for the ISP."

"Chancellor?" Simoth said with a confused look.

"You should be hearing the official announcement soon," Jast told him. "Now come."

Jast started walking down another branch of the tunnels, motioning the others to follow. Simoth walked alongside him, Tark now falling back with Halgor and the laravel, content to let Jast explain everything.

"As you have said, every Ikaran dreams of reaching for the stars, and yet here we discover that these Others have been atop our Mountain doing who knows what. Even I don't know exactly what—at least nothing I can prove—but you may have noticed the change in the weather. Or the increased quakes."

"You believe the Tanians responsible?" Simoth asked. "But what has that to do with the ISP?"

"A lot." They walked a few more steps, Jast gathering his thoughts before he spoke again. "Before he died in Candlefall, the Master GenSeer Marador warned me of a coming Cataclysm. Candlefall was the first step towards that Cataclysm and the reason why I've been such a proponent of reaching for Azur. You may have noticed, however, that the Tanians don't seem to want us to leave. Maybe they fear what we could become or maybe they fear we'll discover what they're really up to. If you look at things in a certain light, everything they've done has been to pacify us, to keep us planet-bound and at each other's throats. Ever wonder why?"

"So we don't start asking the wrong questions?" Simoth ventured.

"Very good," Jast nodded. "Our desire to venture out into space is the one thing that has always united us, long before the Five Nations government. That's something the Tanians don't yet realize. They're using elements of the program to try and pull us apart and while that seems to be working to a certain extent, with the way I have things set up, the Five Nations government could completely fall apart and the ISP will continue, though away from the watchful eyes of our alien benefactors."

"That all sounds noble enough," Simoth admitted, "but for one glaring fact. It was *you* who sabotaged the success of the First Mission and that alone has ripped apart the Five Nations rule and threatened the ISP. What do you have to say about *that?*"

At first, Jast said nothing, instead directing them quietly down another branching tunnel and deeper into the Catacombs. When Jast spoke again, it was with words that Simoth would find both surprising and shocking.

"The First Mission *had* to fail. The Tanians were watching it too closely and I suspect that had we successfully made planet fall while they were looking, the consequences would have involved far more direct interventions on their part. Right now, it's a game of seeing who can fool who, but I have no doubt that had they the need, they could bring a *lot* more to bear than we've yet seen. Enough to flatten every city on Ikara."

"So, wait," Simoth paused in his step. "You *sacrificed* those five lives on the First Mission?! In the control room you broke down. You swore like it was your own family members who'd died."

"It was acting, and damn good acting, if I do say so myself. I did it for a higher purpose: to save millions more lives. The Tanians have now seen us try and fail. They won't be looking too closely at any other attempts from now on, which is good because any further attempts that may gain the public eye will have them waving the Accords in front of our noses to get us to stop. Their promise of space travel at their side? Either an outright lie or not what it seems. They promise something that, at best, will end up with them assimilating us until there are no more Ikarans."

"But…you sent those five people up there *knowing* they would die! The radiation belts? Did you know about that? What about the equipment issues and the fuel?"

"I had to make damn sure they didn't make it, so I reduced the fuel loads and even removed a large portion of the food supply. In hindsight, that was an unnecessary cruelty. Oh, and even if the emlash navigation systems had not failed, they would have burned up anyway. We sent five of the most useless people we could find," Jast reminded him, "or didn't you notice how the selection process was geared more for political benefit than any other consideration? The truth is, we *did* find a number of very good candidates; we just didn't put them aboard Mission One. Ratham had conspired with Elim to kill both myself and the Matron; he was drunk in a bar half a season ago talking about it. He bragged he would maneuver himself into the position of Speaker of the Quorum then to Vice Regent to put him close enough to slit my throat. That's incredibly abnormal activity for an Ikaran. A few days before we picked him to fly the mission, I heard that he sealed the speaker position. You would think he was one of the soulless ones by the way he spoke and maneuvered. It was like he thought he could move against the prophesies of Marador. I say their deaths were a great house cleaning. The Tanians have no idea how powerful the Cycle is, and we're using this to our advantage."

Another turn in the tunnel, and it started to widen as they walked. Simoth sought the words to express what he thought, only to find that he didn't know what he thought of any of it at all. Jast used the opportunity to continue his explanation.

"We all know that it was Karth who led us to the stars so long ago, and so it will be Karthans that will lead us once again, but it won't be from where the Tanians will ever see. The one point in our favor is that they truly know nothing about our cultural history. Volst built a launch platform atop the mountain, so they figured all they had to do was get the Volst to surrender it to slow us down. Tark here actually assisted in that matter. They saw Volst as the leaders of exploration, and Volst helped things along by thinking themselves as chosen – a fiction the Tanians helped to nurture, by the way. The truth is, it was always my intention that a Karthan should lead the way... for the *real* missions."

Several emotions flicked across Simoth's face, a multitude of questions that found their first voice as he recalled some of what he'd read in the ISP documents, recently acquired from Jast's old office.

"I read in your papers how the first two missions were already planned before the Accords were even signed, but I also saw indications of several more planned. This first mission was the distraction, but the rest..."

"The First Mission had to be rather public. It was the only way we were going to raise enough funds, but that very publicity doomed it to failure."

"I found some of the missing funds already earmarked to Mission Two," Simoth stated. "That's what it was all for then? Mission Two is the real mission to Azur?"

"You're only partly right. We *did* gain some valuable insight into space travel from the First Mission and yes, some of the funds acquired went to the second mission, but from the beginning, this was all planned as a *seven*-step process. Before the Tanian Accords were even ratified, once it was determined that an Ikaran landing on Azur might be possible, the missions were specifically focused on breaching the theoretical boundaries of previous Grand Cycles. Seven missions in all, with the seventh step being colonization."

"*What?!* There's no way we can hope to do that in our lifetimes! You're talking moving, what, dozens of people to Azur? We don't have the launch capability of doing that, even *with* the funds you've hidden away."

"And that would be our biggest advantage of all, for our alien friends have no knowledge of our oldest of legends, nor the secret that Kael Karth has been keeping all the long tallas of his life...a secret which I will now pass onto you."

They stopped where their tunnel turned into a wide cavern, where Simoth was soon to discover that it wasn't a chance course that Jast had been leading him along. Behind him, Tark suppressed a smirk, and even Halgor grinned wide as Jast stretched out an arm to indicate the large cavern before them.

"Behold what those secreted funds and backroom deals have bought Ikara."

The cavern was enormous, both in the seemingly endless span reaching into the darkness and in the height above. It wasn't the stretch of its size that immediately caught Simoth's attention though, but that which lay within it. Lit up by emlash-powered work lights, scaffolding was scattered around with crews of workers and technicians from all nations. There was a busy hive of activity around the one glaring central fixture.

The gleaming metal hull was still tarnished in places—eons-old engines being worked on by the crews, a sleek design only now waking up from its long slumber. It was the very center-point of *all* Ikaran legends. It was a vessel of space, but one whose size dwarfed even the Tanian vessel hanging in orbit above the Great Mountain. It was a colony ship, made for the generations.

Simoth stepped fully into the cavern to get a better look. And with every step, it seemed the great vessel only grew larger. He had no words, no argument. Somewhere behind him, Jast spoke, but his attention was fully on what lay before him.

"*The Slumberer* can hold hundreds, at the least. Some very capable engineers told me that it would take several tallas to revive it and a lot of technology that does not yet exist. The things we develop for the Missions? That which we can glean from the Tanians? All of it, the *real* purpose, has been to get this vessel of our ancestors fully functional. Missions Two through Six are designed to pave the way for the final launch. You may question my methods, but the final plan has always been to save what I could of Ikara from the coming Cataclysm. You will be the face of the ISP and the Missions, but know that *this* is our true purpose. Just try and remember to maintain your open dislike for me outside of these catacombs and not to draw too much attention to the Missions from the Tanians."

Simoth nodded vaguely, shocked. Everything made sense now, but he wasn't sure if that helped or just made things worse.

"How long has it been here?"

"Practically forever. It was sealed down here in perfection, made of metals that are from outside Ikara; highly nonreactive yet strong. We are still exploring its incredible potential. The pilgrims that have been going down into these Catacombs for the alleged reason of some ancient observance? Workers and technicians for the *Slumberer*. Simoth, *this* is the big plan."

Mission Two

Under Simoth Karth's leadership, Mission Two's objective became more aggressive and ambitious in nature. Based on the results of the Mission One research, it was determined that an equatorial landing might be best. The rotational velocity of Azur very nearly matched that of Ikara, meaning the crew's landing wouldn't be completely dissimilar to landing at home. Telemetry for tracking progress would be problematic, so to best capitalize on the mission's duration, a secondary function of Mission Two would be the placement of a recording satellite.

It was known as the Azur Orbital Laser Altimeter (AOLA). Its primary function was to graph the planet and report altitudes of all potential landing zones for future missions. It also harnessed a transmitter and an advanced laser microphone system. The communication system could facilitate data and verbal transmissions with future missions between Ikara and Azur, as well as facilitate communication between mission groups on the surface of Azur. Soon, the Ikarans would have a complete map of Azur and be able to communicate with anyone with the proper equipment on the surface.

The Mission Commander was Devane Urdlu, and it was with baited breath that Simoth and the rest of the ground crew at Ikara Central listened to his reports as they came over the Wave.

"On course and approach looks good. As we learned from the Mission One data, we have aligned to a shallower angle of entry and also, we used a couple of orbits to slough off some extra velocity. The new emlash sensors have confirmed what Mission One learned the hard way: the gravity of Azur is just about double that of back home. This planet is a monster, but we'll master it. Commander Urdlu, Karth Kessai, reporting."

There was some cheering in the control room at the report, but Simoth silenced them all with a wave, grabbed the microphone, and gave a quick nod to the Wave operator. A flick of a switch, and he was transmitting back to the faraway crew.

"Acknowledged, Mission Two. Confirm the deployment of AOLA before entry."

There was a long pause before they received a response. One of the things they'd quickly learned from both Missions was that the Wave was not the instantaneous communication it had always seemed to be back on Ikara. Given a great enough distance, even the Wave could seem like a frustratingly slow method of communication. Simoth was midway through his lunch when he was alerted to the latest incoming transmission. His plate was still rattling on the table by the time he was halfway down the hall.

"Satellite deployed. We're buckled in and on our way down now. Heats up quite a bit on entry but we should make it fine. Still, you may want to install something to keep the extra heat out for the next mission. We're heading for a landing on a chain of islands along the southeastern coast of the largest landmass. By the Cycle, I wish you could see this view."

The craft rode down from the heavens on a pillar of flame

burning brightly in the dawn sky. The ISP had underestimated the intense heat the craft would experience, so some of that heat made its way to the crew and their gear. The parachutes deployed to slow the craft, and shortly after, Devane signaled the engagement of the thrusters. A large roar popped through the ship as the landing engines activated, and the entry chute was jettisoned.

"Blue flame alive... I repeat, blue flame alive. Adjusting trajectory to the landing zone."

The control room was cloaked in silence, none knowing what to expect. This was the most critical segment of the mission: the surface contact. You could hear a pin drop waiting for the next transmission. The ISP members waited...and waited, until it seemed like all was lost.

"Mission Two," Simoth finally called out into the transmitter, "what's going on? Commander Urdlu, are you there?"

Alas, there was not a word, not a single breath from the landing crew. What had been the greatest step for Ikarans now seemed another tragedy. The loss of Devane would be a major blow to the program. If the ISP had to send nonhuman organisms to Azur to test equipment (instead of actual Karth Kessai), the delays would be significant, costly, and most likely impossible to overcome. The loss of the second ship, along with the crew, might even signal the end of the ISP. No one would want to fly to Azur if it guaranteed certain death.

The speaker made a static, cracking sound.

"Ikara central, this is Commander Urdlu. We have made surface contact. I repeat, we have made surface contact, and we are whole. We had a close water landing. We missed the beachhead by several dozen cubits."

Devane wanted to scream into the wave, but he remained as cool as a Karth Kessai could be. The ground team erupted in laughter, and were soon passing hard drinks around. For this historic event, Simoth had made an exception to his militaristic ways by allowing alcohol into the ground station.

"Commander," Simoth replied as someone stuffed a full shot glass into one hand, "you had us worried."

"No reason to worry sir, it was just the delay between entry and touchdown. I was concentrating on making proper contact. After all, there is no reason to communicate until we have actually achieved an objective. Also, I was holding my breath. The air in here is rather foul, and I almost passed out when I opened my helmet. Tomas has ventilated the situation."

Simoth replied with a chuckle and quick swig of his drink. It was a significant moment for the Ikarans of the third cycle. Not only had they made first contact with Azur for this iteration, but the craft, having landed with only minor reentry damage, would quite possibly be able to make it back with its discoveries.

"Beautiful place down here, but the gravity makes us feel like we each have an extra hundred units' weight on our backs. It's slow moving even with the hydraulic powered suits. We'll be sticking pretty close to the ship during the Deployment part of our mission, until we're sure exactly what's out there. Okay, got to rest. Next transmission as soon as I catch my breath..."

Sometime later, on faraway Azur, Devane reported to Simoth and the ISP once more.

"Crew fanning out now," he said, whilst his crew pulled the activation string on their deployable raft and began to load it up with gear and food from the landing craft. They used a quarter of their Koru light time before they could begin construction on a defendable zone.

"Let's dig a perimeter ditch along this line," Devane ordered as he pointed from the beach to a cliff overhang, then pointed to the center of the construct and continued. "We can cut a square into the landscape. Let's go three cubits deep and put the shelter there."

The Ikaran transportable shelter system was literally from another world. Covered in a thin, foldable, cloth-like metal that could stop fast-moving projectiles of any reasonable mass, the shelter was outfitted with a one-way mirror system (which allowed those inside to see out, but kept anyone on the outside from seeing in). The covering was also paired with a unit that cloaked it from intruders and passersbys. With the push of a button, the shelter cover could mimic the surrounding area and allow the Karth Kessai to observe any and all activities without being detected. Chief Mate Zoltan placed the shelter system under the cliff hang, so the Ikarans couldn't be approached from the top or the back without warning.

"Let's dig the trench nine cubits wide," added Zoltan, it being his job to oversee strategic deployments for this scientific expedition. "This will trap any fast-moving vehicles that could get close. We have no idea what to expect but based on GenSeer readings, there may be alien life down here and they could possibly be very advanced. I'll cloak and anchor the craft just in case we've been spotted by any potential aliens."

"Good thinking," Commander Urdlu called out over their short-range wave system, before a call came from one of their other crewmen.

"Chief Mate Zoltan. Engineer Dall requesting permission to remove atmospheric suits. Outside pressure and content look good according to the monitor. We should not have any problem breathing, nor with the mechanics of mobility."

"Negative, Engineer," Zoltan responded. "We will proceed for one more day with these suits as per protocol."

Zoltan wasn't happy with the unprofessional nature of the request, and wanted to shut it down as quickly as possible. Karth Kessai were scientists and fighting men; Zoltan didn't want to start breeding an environment of weakness and tolerance. In the course of history, it's not the complainers who have made the advances for the universe, but those who were disciplined and willing to only take risks when there was something to gain.

Of course, Dall wasn't complaining or resisting. He simply wanted to experiment with the new atmosphere. It was the kid in him wanting to come out and play, but judging by the Commander's scowl, it was obvious that his curiosities were not considered amusing.

Early the next morning, Devane toyed with Dall's suggestion, and began to remove part of his atmospheric suit, grunting to himself as quietly as possible.

"Ugghh..grunt…hmmfffp…"

I can barely breathe, he thought. *It's very difficult to move and breathe in these suits, but without them, we're useless for now.*

He tried to hide his true feelings, but the look on his face made it obvious that he did not think highly of the idea. However, since the Commander didn't actually order everyone to wear a suit nor rescind Chief Mate Zoltan's previous statement, Dall wasn't going to give Devane the chance to cancel his plans for a day of full atmosphere. He not only removed his large green helmet with the black lenses; he unlatched the entire suit, and let the world of Azur hit him.

"Wow…whoaaah," Dall cried out as he tried to steady himself under the immense gravity.

"Engineer Dall," Commander Urdlu barked, "since you volunteered, you will remain without an atmospheric suit for the entire day! Let us know how you feel in the morning. I want you to stay close to the vessel today, create a stable launch platform for our return launch, and repair the reentry damage on the ship. Oh, and get our launch calculations in order. According to the time on Andar Azur, we need to launch towards Koru's rising to take advantage of the planet's orbital push."

"I guess I really asked for that one, Commander," Dall sighed.

"That you did. Here, put on this red shirt, you are under review." Devane reached into his command bag and tossed an ISP red shirt with insignia to Dall. He then turned his back and left with the remaining five members.

"Ikara Central this is Commander Devane Urdlu. We have begun collecting specimens and data on more than a thousand life

forms...Yes, a thousand! And we've not even begun to touch the bulk of what there is over here. We've got reems of data transmitting to the recording satellite and we're packing the Mission Two craft full of specimens. Just the bugs alone will have our guys busy analyzing for ages, and then there's the fish. Recommend a water tank for the next Mission, because there's this eight-limbed creature you're just not going to believe unless you see it for yourself. Chrono-freezing just won't do this guy justice. All in all, I believe even if we were to stop processing organisms at this very moment, this mission would still be a success. We've made one massive leap forward for all of Ikara."

As the return-mission launch date approached, it seemed that Devane's assessment would hold true. Other transmissions revealed more incredible observations from Commander Devane Urdlu—more reasons for celebrating back at Ikara Central.

"This is Commander Urdlu recording day two of Mission Two. We have encountered what appear to be long ago abandoned cave dwellings on the Equatorial side of the island. This side seems to have at one time been more hospitipal for humans than the magnetic pole side. Inside of these dwellings, we have found basic stone tools for cooking and hunting. It is not surpising to find human habitations, but are these people still alive somewhere? We have yet to encounter other humanoid types. The ship has been repaired and I have the plant and animal specimens chronoed and ready for the ride back home. We are all increadibly sore from moving in this extra gravity. In addition, engineer Dall appears to have taken sick; he was the first one to remove his atompshere suit. The rest of the crew is remaining in gear, as am I."

"This is Commander Urdlu recording day three of Mission Two. Dall's condition appears to have worsened overnight. Nathorn Medic Tomas has said that the healing songs are not working and is using conventional methods to determine the cause of illness. Dall has voiced some skepticism regarding the singing, repeating rumors that it's part of the Tanian pacification protocols. If that's indeed

the case, it would explain why it is not working on Azur, but until we know the nature of the illness we really can only speculate. As Commander, I have remained in suit for the duration, except one brief moment when I experiemented with atmosphere transference. I fear the rest of the team may have been exposed to whatever is harming the engineer."

"Commander," Simoth called over the wave, alarm clearly creeping into his voice, "how quickly can you return the crew to base?"

"Without our engineer, we're about two full days from launch. Luckily, the hardest part of the return setup was completed by Dall on day one. Most of what's left is lower tech work."

"You have one opportunity to launch early tomorrow at zero-seven-five-one Andar Azur. Is it possible to make that launch time? If you are more than a fraction or two off launch time it will require more work in space to get you on track. That launch time will give you maximum push from Azur's orbit."

"We will do our best to make that goal."

The transmission that came from the Commander the following morning was not as hopeful.

"We were preparing for launch...was skeptical...Chief Mate Zoltan and Tomas have studied Dall's blood samples and believe it's biological in nature. They think it's alien bacteria, Simoth, but no such on Ikara has ever made anyone sick before. No-one even considered that common Azuran life forms could make someone sick!"

"In hindsight, this is an obvious risk," Simoth admitted. "That common microbes that support carbon life on one planet might be deadly to similar life forms just one planet away, we'd not considered this. Our planet is more hospitable to human life than Azur and this may be our one great weakness as a race: our inability to fight off basic microbials on Azur and other planets."

"I say we bolt like hell from this place," Devane added, "and come back to see if we can find a humanoid test specimen to examine

and see what we can pull from their DNA. We may also be able to find latent Ikarans who have come to Azur from previous cycles. If we can awaken their genetic memory, we can learn more about this place in one sitting than we would with twenty tallas of observation."

"I concur Commander, but we do not know if people still live there. Something may have happened and the signs we see now are very possibly from long lost civilizations."

"Time is zero-six-three-one Andar Azur," Devane announced as he ended the transmission. "We are a go. I will get the team together."

Devane clicked off the transmission and went to gather his crew. Then he noticed that Dall (the only crew member wearing a red shirt that day) was missing. Certainly, his attire would make him easier to find.

"Where in the hell is Dall?" asked Devane, clearly annoyed.

"He's on the Equator side of the island commander," Second Engineer Arn chimed in. "I have been trying to get him to come with us but he invoked the Karth Kessai right of 'Interpid Quietus.'"

"I have no power to make him violate his rights," Devane sighed. "If he would rather die here a free man than under the rule of the invaders who seek to end our way of life, then that's his choice, but I wish to speak with him first. Come!"

Once Commander Urdlu stood facing a resolute-looking First Engineer Dall, he wasted no time in getting right to the point.

"Dall, we have no idea what kind of savagery awaits you if we leave you. These aliens down here, we have no clue what they're into. Do they eat people? Who have they cross-bred with?"

"I understand the risks, sir. I may not die immediately, or possibly not at all, but it is my right and there is no protocol or reason within the Grand Cycle to not grant a Karth Kessai his wish regarding death. I am a star voyager now, and with that comes certain universal rights that even the Commander cannot overcome."

"Then it is between you and God now," Devane replied solemnly. "I will honor it, of course."

"It is for the best, Commander."

"You understand, First Engineer Dall, that we are not coming back this way. We have no missions planned for this part of Azur again. If we leave you, you are going to be here forever."

"I understand completely Commander. Please tell my wife I did not intend to stay but I cannot risk spreading this to the crew. Let her know I did not stay for selfish reasons." Dall bowed his head towards the commander in silence, looking down at an image of his wife on his lumen device. He said no more.

"I pray by the Cycle that something good comes of this, Dall. We will remember your bravery. As Commander of Mission Two and the Sovereign representative of Ikara on Azur, I release you of your duties and grant you the title of Arch Viscount of Azur. Until we cross the stars together again, my Karth Kessai Brother."

Dall was normally not an emotional man, but he shed a tear as he looked downward. Devane laid his battle blade and hydrogen gun at the feet of Dall, and returned to the launch site.

"Fellow Karths," Commander Urdlu announced once back on the ship, "we will be leaving Engineer Dall behind as per his request. He does not wish to burden us nor risk our lives with his illness. He has invoked 'Interpid Quietus', and so we will remember him as a hero among the Karth Kessai. Prepare to launch!"

"Just cleared atmosphere of Azur."

That was the beginning of the last transmission Simoth would receive from Mission Two.

"The sickness has already taken hold. Arn is coughing in his suit and looking lethargic. The others are staying quiet. The illness appears to be spreading. We've loaded all we can into the satellite and are also transmitting what data that we have from here. Also, the satellite is not performing as designed and we have forwarded the error codes. If Arn is any indication on how this is going to go, I don't think we'll make it. Setting course to splash down in the water 14 clicks hemisline side three clicks Koru rising side of

Kartha. Maybe you can recover the logs and what we've gathered. I am inducing the crew into a hibernation state for the trip back. This will slow the disease's progress and give us a chance of survival."

Commander Urdlu was not sounding well himself, and he made no more transmissions after that.

The vessel splashed down where Devane said it would, and a hazmat crew quickly converged on the craft. The first on the scene was Tone, a young girl from Nathor with a degree in science from Elmanith. Using a wave frequency, she blew the emergency bolts on the craft and jumped into it. She was in full gear, so couldn't smell the decomposition that had taken place in the oxygen-rich containment. Therefore, what she finally saw was all the more shocking.

"They're dead! They should already be out of hibernation. They're all dead. By the Stars beyond the great black, no-one is alive!"

She took a moment to regain her composure before following up via the Wave transmitter built into her suit.

"Someone get the logs, I'm checking everyone to be sure."

One by one, she checked the pulse of each crew member. Arn was pale, and she could see bacteria on the inside of his helmet. There was no saving him. Tone proceeded along, checking each crew member one-by-one as she tried to keep a level voice during her report:

"It appears Dr. Tomas has only recently expired, possibly hours before landing. He shows signs of recent movement, it is possible he awoke from hibernation and the stress to his system was too much. The Chief Mate and GenSeer both expired days ago. Both bodies indicate they have passed rigor mortis, but with no insect larva to examine, I cannot give an exact time. The GenSeer had actually taken his helmet off before passing; he's just sitting here in his seat with a blank stare on his face...I suspect he died shortly after waking up from hibernation as well."

Tone finally arrived at the Commander. His gear was still clean, and his skin was pale and ashen. But it appeared that her first impression was incorrect, as the commander's chest was moving when she placed her hand on it.

"We have a breather! The Commander's alive!" She reached for Devane's wrist, then called out, "I have a pulse, I have a pulse! Someone help! Please, help!"

Her screams into the Wave did not go unheard. Almost immediately, a team of waiting hazmat specialists descended onto the vessel.

"Are there any signs of broken bones or any other issues with moving the Commander?" one of the hazmat team members asked while shifting into position.

"No, he is clear to be transferred," Tone said as she stepped back to let the team work.

Without hesitating, the well-trained team pulled Devane out of the craft and put him on a stretcher.

Simoth and the other ground crew waited in the medical facility to see what had happened to their hero.

"It has to be something special to make landfall on Azur. Something fantastic. To do so and die is a tragedy I cannot imagine," Simoth said in a somber voice.

"I am Dr. Szarkor." A familiar, middle-aged Nathorn man with an ISP medical uniform approached Simoth. "Commander Devane Urdlu is in a critical condition. I am afraid we have no way of helping him. We have not developed the medicines nor the procedures to assist patients whose immune systems have been biologically compromised in this particular manner. Due to the fact that Ikarans have not stepped foot on Azur since the second cycle, it is unlikely his body will be able to fight off this infection. As long as the Commander is alive we will try to keep him comfortable, but we will not allow him visitors."

"No visitors!" Simoth raged. "We have to debrief this man. We spent a small fortune making this mission work!"

"I am sorry Simoth, but these rules are for your safety. If he regains consciousness, we will reconsider."

Realizing there was nothing to gain by fighting to see a comatose man, Simoth became expressionless. He looked at his fellow teammates. With his hands by his sides, he opened his palms, turned his back on the doctor, and walked out.

Once the Mission Two vessel had been cleaned and deemed plague-free, its logs were recovered and very thoroughly analyzed, along with everything that remained onboard the small vessel. It wasn't long before a team of Nathorns and Elmaniths went through the data and confirmed the existence of the tiny Azurian bacteria. They were different from Ikaran ones, for these bacteria had a proven record of being quite deadly, at least to Ikaran, humanoid life forms. Several options were raised about how to protect future missions from these biological hazards, including genetically altering some Ikarans for survival on Azur and in space travel.

With these Azurian microbe samples to work with, Simoth quickly assigned a team of scientists to develop a way for future crew members to have immunity from them.

Most observers deemed Mission Two a complete failure, and its landing site was marked off-limits for any future missions. For others, the findings within the vessel were a wellspring of information about the flora, fauna, and weather conditions on the surface. In fact, all of this data would make the later missions much safer, and it would aid the Ikaran scientists in the preparations for the very secretive seventh mission.

Simoth was the focus of public dissatisfaction throughout the Mission Two debriefing and analysis, and he found the ISP receiving to be a lot of pressure—from the likes of organized crime, corporate graft, and other manipulation, as well as from the still-hidden Tanian agenda. Given what Simoth now knew of what lay at the bottom of the Catacombs and what Jast had hinted at, he understood that a successful mission to Azur had become a necessity. Without it, planetary morale would plummet; the people came to see that the Tanians could travel dozens (or even hundreds) of lightyears to get

J. R. Austin

to Ikara, but they couldn't even colonize their neighboring planet. Simoth suspected that the Tanian commander was counting on this kind of depression and dissatisfaction.

Amishari and Administrator Borosh were discussing the failed Ikaran space missions.

"I do not understand why we need to put resources towards stopping the Ikarans from space travel. If we openly try to stop them Borosh, we will tip them off that our intentions are not good. We do not wish to hasten their advancements. Besides, their fatality rate should be more than persuasive. They may lose interest eventually without our intervention. People do have a tendency to want to stay alive," Amishari said as she touched the pendant hanging from her neck. She and Administrator Borosh were discussing the failed Ikaran space missions.

"I will consider this. I do not like the idea of these simple beings advancing further. There are things we do not clearly understand about their 'grand cycle'. Things that trouble me. I fear if we let them continue in their progress, they will be more difficult to extinguish."

Amishari threw Borosh an emotionless look before responding.

"I doubt these simpletons have any destiny beyond being a source of labor on Azur. Except maybe the Karths, who might be eligible to serve as our veiled pawns in the fight against the indigenous people. Beyond that, I would not trouble myself with such things."

"Perhaps, but we certainly cannot allow all of them to go to Azur, it's too much to manage," Borosh replied as he considered Amishari's view.

"Agreed."

Mission Three

The Ikarans knew that they needed to launch the third mission very quickly. With two failures in a row, the pressure for more advances drove the ISP to be politically swayed, so instead of due diligence, Simoth was forced to use what he could as a favorable lure for a third mission. Despite his best efforts, however, there were those who took advantage of the situation. Several administrators beneath Simoth (and a few on the Council he headed) shifted from passive corruption to more vigorous activities. Demand for swift results drove the suppliers' prices up, caused shortcuts to be taken, and made minor officials easier to bribe. Even Simoth found himself greasing a few palms in an effort to speed things along.

In the second week of early spring, the Tanians demanded a second Commission to be held. The demand was voiced through their closest ally, the Volst, and in retrospect, it was perhaps the first sign that the Accords were in jeopardy—or were a sham.

Invitations were sent by courier to each of the Five Nations' First Speakers, requesting their attendance in the most polite terms. As had been the case in the Accords Commission, the meeting place was to be the Volst *Observer*, the place all had agreed as the most remote, neutral, accommodating place for such a meeting. Most believed this decision was a concession by the Tanians to the many requests levied on them, since the Accords had first been accepted. The problem, then, was to determine when the commission would be held. Elmanith suggested later spring, Nathor preferred early summer, Whycheral was ambivalent, and Kartha demanded they delay until late fall.

Tanians, however, are not patient.

Tanian Flitters landed at each of the Five Nation's headquarters. Tanian troops in atmospheric suits emerged, calling themselves 'escorts,' and marched straight into each of the Halls of the First Speakers.

"We are here to escort you both to a Security Committee Conference," one of the escorts said. "Please get dressed and follow us."

"Jast," Bellelorn whispered with a look of both fright and hope.

"Don't worry," he whispered back. "We'll just do as they say."

Although Jast knew better, he did not argue, and, following his lead, neither did Bellelorn.

So without incident, the escorts returned to their craft with every attendant First Speaker in custody.

Details of the Security Conference were never made public, but Helm had made an official announcement that Jast had written.

"Upon advisement from the Tanians, the intent of the Ikaran Space Program is being shifted to a focus on the environment in the polar regions. Plans are to abandon Azur for now and instead use our flight missions to more completely explore certain aspects of our own environment."

It may have been called a security meeting, but with that announcement, the real intent was obvious. It had begun with a full-scale kidnapping of Ikaran leaders and ended with a clear Tanian boot print pressed firmly to Ikara's exposed political neck. When Simoth was able to meet with Jast in the Catacombs again, they both more plainly knew the Tanian intent.

"It's quite clear that the Tanians do not want us to go to Azur," Simoth said with no preamble. "Whatever they're doing here on Ikara, I'm guessing they have planned for Azur as well."

"They don't plan on making the same mistake there as here on Ikara," Jast agreed. "They won't be as politically careful on Azur."

"Your announcement has everyone at each other's throats," Simoth told him. "I don't know if you've heard but at the last meeting of the Five Nations government, there was a lot of finger-pointing. Officials from Volst expressed their concern over Karthan excavation and the extensively open plundering of the Ikaran heritage that is known to be held within these very same Catacombs. They don't know about what you're doing down here but apparently, they've heard the rumbling and are taking it for tomb robbing."

"I planted that story myself," Jast admitted. "Not my best one, but likely enough to keep the Tanians from investigating the *real* cause."

"Kartha has apparently responded with allegations that the Volst are building vast subterranean tunnels with Tanian assistance right beneath the Great Mountain! Some climatologists had a good look at the Volst construction budget and put the pieces together. Others are saying such tunneling could endanger the Mountain *itself.* What do you say about *that?*"

"Beneath the Mountain you say? Hmm...What if it's not really the Tanians assisting the Volst but the other way around? We may have discovered the aliens' real purpose for being here...They're mining, and in a really big way. That may also explain another report I've received from one of my other concerns. It seems as energy production has been dipping a little; that could be due to a loss of heat from the Tanian mining."

"Well, whatever the reason, all this has turned the ISP into a political game of catch. All these delays and budget problems are coming close to aborting the mission entirely."

"I've been keeping track," Jast told the younger man, "and you're doing a very good job of pushing ahead with the Third Mission. I agree with your choice of Tark as Chief Mate for this mission, and I see that the vessel is being built for a larger crew and corresponding supplies, greater fuel capacity for the launch and recovery phases, and you even got Nathor at work supplying solutions for those tiny disease bugs from Mission Two."

"I suspect you had a greater hand in that than I did," Simoth sighed, calming down. "I'll admit, I used a few of your own tricks to get what we've needed, while still funneling a few more personnel over to this project down here."

"For which I am grateful," Jast said with a slight nod. "My position as Chancellor does not give me free enough reign to do everything I need to do."

"Some of our funding came as a result of that kidnapping of the Speakers the Tanians performed. What went on with that, anyway?"

Simoth felt concern mixed with anger, as even he was not sure if any of it was directed at Jast, the aliens, or both. Jast responded in a lower tone, as if afraid that they might still be overheard here.

"They quite sternly *suggested* we abandon our space program or they'll start taking back every technological goody they've ever given us. Of course, we need that stuff to continue with our project down here, so we agreed and that was that. Well…for now, at least. We are working on replicating their technology"

"Except that we didn't agree…not really, did we Jast?"

Jast simply shrugged, admitting nothing, which was as good as a definitive answer to Simoth.

"We've chosen a landing site at a cleared area in the middle of the fourth-largest continent, a hundred clicks from the summit of the main defining mountain range," Simoth continued with a tired sigh. "The milder climate, dryer atmosphere, and heightened elevation above the Azurian sea level should mean optimum sample collection, safety from bacterial infection, and longer-duration soils testing. Nathorn also promises to have some sort of preventative serum ready for the crew to protect them against future infections."

"Good. We'll need a proper understanding of the life cycle of Azurian plants as well as the soils samples to gain some further insight into the history and planetary origins of Azur. Any evidence yet of sentient life forms?"

"Not yet," Simoth admitted, "but we'll know more once the Mission nears Azur."

"When will it launch?"

"Early in the morning. We're hoping to hide it in the glare of Koru as it rises. This is not the optimal time of talla to launch. That window has passed as the planets are moving out of retrograde, so we will need more fuel than the last mission required. I have the techs working on that now. We've also employed radar cloaking technology for this launch and with a little luck, we will not be spotted by the Tanians. Between the light of Koru blocking physical observation and the cloaking tech, we should be fine."

"Let us hope. You're doing excellent, Simoth."

"As a lightning rod? I quite agree. Still, I suppose it's necessary to give the Slumberer the chance to awaken to save the Ikaran people. Anyway, I've got a mission launch to attend to. I guess I just came here to vent after seeing the Tanians so much more open about their intent."

"Look at it this way," Jast said in parting, "it will make it a lot easier to ask people to keep some things secret from now on."

Of that, Simoth had very little doubt.

While the glare of Koru kept the eyes on the ground from observing the Ikaran craft, the cloaking technology hadn't yet been perfected. Sensors that could pick up cosmic driftwood from an entire planetary orbit away wouldn't be stopped by a little extra Koru light or the new Ikaran technology, particularly once the craft left the Ikaran atmosphere. The first to see it was Assistant Amishari, as soon as it appeared on the display in her office.

For a brief moment, she looked at it as the scanners tracked the primitive launch, then entered in a command code.

"Hmmm, these Ikarans are a tad on the defiant side. They are clearly risking everything to get to Azur. I think they underestimate the capabilities of the Tanian regime."

She clicked the send button. The next message to appear on her display were the words "Target Ignored," before it disappeared from her lumen screen. No one in the Tanian base would be seeing anything of this launch or its mission. Since the target had been specifically ignored by the assistant, communications transmitted to and from the vessel would also be undetectable.

Amishari returned to her work, the expression on her face as bland and unchanging as before…save perhaps for a very brief hint of a knowing smirk.

The first transmission from Mission Three came while the vessel was still in orbit around Azur.

"Ikara Central, this is Chief Mate Tark. We have recovered the satellite recordings and are now in the process of installing a more sophisticated altimeter system that uses one of those new focused-

light devices. That should help us discover a few new things about this world."

The next report came not more than an hour later, and from the tone in his voice, all could tell that Tark was bursting with barely restrained excitement.

"We have our telescopes aimed downward to get a better view of the surface as we orbit. Quite the view up here. In fact, why don't you see for yourselves."

The transmission switched from voice-only to the new image-transmission that Simoth had ordered to be installed, and the monitors in Ikara Central flickered to life. The technology had worked in the lab, but no one knew if it would work on an interplanetary scale. They had worked, however, so that's why nary a soul in the Control Center could speak, or even breathe, as the image appeared.

The static cleared, revealing a fuzzy image at first, but then, with another flicker, it snapped into crystal clarity. They were looking at another world.

"Azur," Simoth was first to whisper.

A large blue ball curved off into distant reaches, vast puffy clouds engaging in their slow drift across the upper reaches of the atmosphere. A grandeur that no one there could've imagined spread across the single monitor before them.

Caught up in the excitement, it was a few moments before Simoth remembered to quickly motion to one of the techs, and a few seconds later, the transmission was echoed across several more monitors scattered about the Control complex. A hundred faces now paused in their work as the panoramic view continued.

"I hope you're getting this," came Tark's eager voice, *"because the show has just begun. Switching to Telescope Two..."*

The view changed to one zooming down through the atmosphere, bringing the mountains closer, then resolving into great forests, lakes, and a spread of plains so vast that it made Simoth's mind boggle.

"That one plain there looks bigger than the entire Na-Ikaran

Desert," Simoth gasped to himself.

The telescope zoomed in a bit further, zeroing in on some movement. At first, it looked like a large brown mat crawling its way across the surface of the plain, but as the view cleared, it revealed itself to be a vast herd of four-legged creatures.

"They look like the range-bova that hunters of the past once used for food," Simoth pondered, "but…there's got to be thousands in that herd. *Tens* of thousands!"

They watched as the view drifted around the curve of the world, bringing them one new sight after another, with occasional comments by an eager Tark.

"Got a desert coming into view. Looks similar to the Whycheral badlands…only, like a lot of things on this world, a bit bigger."

Simoth could only nod in silent agreement as the promised sight came into view, but he would soon discover that they had yet to see the best that this mission had to offer.

"Getting some activity on Telescope Three now," Tark reported. *"We're just starting to pass over the largest continent and…well, see for yourself."*

It was close to the Equator. There were small clearings in the jungles that the telescope was barely able to focus on, but they were just big enough to reveal one occurrence that those clearings contained. As they drifted over to the night-side of the world, many of these clearings suddenly lit up with small fires. Nothing expanded in the way of a natural forest fire, but they were contained throughout the time they watched it. As the craft flew across over to the day-side, those fires extinguished themselves.

"Campfires," Simoth realized with a gasp. "There's life everywhere! *Intelligent* life everywhere!"

"We got some more of the same in a desert we're viewing through Telescope One," Tark said. *"I swear, is that Simoth I hear screaming and jumping up and down right now?"* He laughed. He was not far off in his assumption. *"Okay, we've got a landing to make so switching off the image feed for now. The next time you hear*

from me we'll be down on the ground. Here's hoping those injections the Nathorn medics gave us work against those little death-bugs they got around here."

Simoth grabbed the microphone for a quick response to the transmission, the joy he felt evident in his tone.

"Imagery received, and spectacularly so. Eagerly awaiting your next contact."

"Ikara Central, Chief Mate Tark here. We've landed magnetic side towards Koru rising from the original intended landing zone. I place it at 43 degrees three clicks. The plains we saw took on a different look upon descent and we also wanted to be a little further from the cluster of those campfires we saw from orbit. There is no doubt in my mind we have been spotted, but as a scientist I did not want to miss my chance to make contact with advanced alien life if we have the opportunity. Oh...and those big herds we saw? You should feel the ground rumble under your feet when they pass. Switching feed."

The view that appeared this time was from ground level. It was a bit shaky, as if the equipment that produced it was being held by hand, but the image was panoramic nonetheless. It was taken from the top of a hill, overlooking a vast grassy plain punctuated by distant clusters of trees. Somewhere in the distance, there was something that looked like a lake. Large herd animals strolled absently across the field, the cries of birds in flight drawing attention to the sky above. Also in the view were several of the Mission crew, one of whom was pointing off towards the lake. The view then slightly shifted, zooming closer in the direction that the crewmember indicated. What they saw there had everyone at Ikara Central staring in shock.

Clustered near the lake were the tops of what could only be some sort of straw and leather huts.

"That confirms it," Simoth slowly stated, his voice a bare breath of whisper. "Azur has intelligent life. Tribal, but definitely there.

Those empty dwellings from Mission Two were probably inhabited as well, but now...now we know there are still people on Azur."

The lens held there for a moment or two, then Tark himself stepped into view. His trim muscular figure was dressed in the typical green Karth Kessai voyager suit, his face flushed with excitement and new purpose.

"The gravity takes some getting used to, but maybe the Nathorns can do something about that the way they did with the microbes. Listen now as I say this. Azur is here, waiting for us, beckoning to us. As much as I love Ikara, *space* is our home, and Azur, the next in many stops as we travel the Grand Cycle. We belong here. Those huts you see? They may even be our cousins – if not before, then soon to be. Whatever it takes to get here and establish a presence, we *must* overcome. I am Karth Kessai...for the first time in my life I feel that I am a *true* Karth Kessai, descended from a long line kept too long from the path of exploration. Take a long look at the view around me, for this is ours to claim, not anything the Tanians would give us."

Every transmission after that was watched with great anticipation, but the point had already been proven, more so when the crew of Mission Three failed to sicken as had those of the previous mission.

"Ikara Central, this is Chief Mate Tark. We are in good health and wish to proceed towards the primitive village we showed you on the heads-up lumen display. I think we can make contact and possibly find a subject to take back to Ikara with us. We have an historic opportunity here to learn more about these aliens."

"Chief Mate Tark, I would advise you to move cautiously with that idea. We have you protected against common microbes from Azur but we have no idea what kind of microbes humans here carry. However, for the sake of science and exploration, I will not forbid your request." Back on Ikara, Simoth had a proud look on his face as he spoke.

The next morning, as the fog lifted from the valley, Commander

J. R. Austin

Tiedyn Rowel and Chief Mate Tark began the trek to the village.

"Chief Mate, what do you expect we will find when we get to the objective?"

"Relax Rowel," Tark stated in an authoritative but somewhat genial tone, "no need to be formal now. No-one is watching or listening. We don't need to act important."

Commander Rowel had won his spot on the flight crew through nepotism, but despite that, he'd done fairly well in training. He had, however, yet to earn the complete respect of his men. For this reason, the more experienced Chief Mate Tark Karth was the one actually running the mission.

"This rising fog will give us good cover," Tark continued. "Let's hope we don't have to fight anyone. That would make our scientific observations more difficult on future contacts and even with our preparation, the gravity here has us in a sluggish state. Anyway," Tark said, flashing a grin at Rowel, who then nodded in return, "I prefer to keep my study subjects alive."

The green flight suits made them extremely visible to onlookers, so each man used wet soil to break up the solid pattern of the suits. Their blades were out, but guns holstered. To make a more camouflaged pattern, Tark had made stripes across his boots and gloves with some of the soil, and so Rowel followed his example. The two men slowly proceeded towards their intended objective.

Back at camp, First Engineer Bar was talking to the Second Engineer.

"Do ya think we should have followed em, Fish? I mean, it makes me nervous that the only two guys that can fly this thing are running around out there in those misty clouds. Is it just me, or are we really in danger of becoming citizens of this place a little earlier than we'd anticipated?"

"I...I have no freaking clue, but let's check the systems so when it's time to bolt like the emlash, we can get out of here."

Karp moved a little closer to the vessel to give it a thorough inspection. He heard a hiss and a crack, and simultaneously realized that the surrounding foliage (which was doing an excellent job hiding the ship) could also work as concealment for an attacker. Out of the corner of his eye, he saw it: not a person, but an object thrown by someone or something. It missed his head by a hair, and the spear burst to pieces when it hit the ship's number-one return engine. It had not, however, left the vessel entirely unmarred.

"Oh man! Oh man! We've got a problem now!" screamed Karp as the fuel began to leak out of the engine in a cool, gaseous cloud.

"Get it sealed. Make it quick!" Bar barked when he realized he could feel the air getting cooler around them. "Give me your gun; give me your damn gun!"

Karp handed his weapon over to the First Engineer and went straight to work on the more important issue at hand: ignoring whatever had decided to attack them as he opened the latch on his toolkit. He was trained by the ISP to have faith in his fellow crew members, and that training was now proving its worth. His job was to ensure they still had a way home, and leave it to another to look after his safety.

Bar stepped between Karp and the aggressors with a fission gun in each hand. The primitive men looked at him with wide eyes, then the tallest one called out.

"Da Budaro!"

Faster than the well-trained Ikaran could fire, the dark alien man threw a spear, which hit Bar directly in the center of his chest, the obsidian rock shattering into his heart and lungs. Bar looked as if he was unfazed by the attack and unloaded into the alien hominids. The sky lit up as far as the eye could see, and a thunderous report terrified every living thing within that same range.

"What in the Cycle was that? Did someone open fire?"

Tark had seen the entire dawn sky light up like the Candlefall, followed by the thunderous clap of the hypersonic boom and ignition, leaving little doubt in anyone's mind that a fission gun had just been fired.

The ship," Rowel said, his calm tone impressing Tark. "Cleary, there's a problem. We need to get back to the ship."

"Leave the gear," Tark snapped. "Let's move!"

Both men ran towards Koru rising. When they made it back to the ship, they found Girard (the Nathorn medic) administering first aid to Bar.

"The engine is stable, Commander," Karp reported. "We lost a fraction of our fuel, but we still have enough to get us free of the atmosphere by my calculations. I've not had a chance to check on Bar."

"What the hell happened here?"

Tark looked around at the bits of flesh and blood left by the attackers. Then Rowel exclaimed, with eyes as big as a newborn baby's:

"Wow, these guys were blown literally to bits."

Neither man had yet realized that their First Engineer was mortally wounded.

"What's going on with Bar?" inquired Tark.

"I can't stabilize him here," Girard reported, lowering his head. "He's not going to make it. The songs don't work on Azur and his injuries are too severe for conventional medicine."

"We need to secure the ship," Tark exclaimed. "We are aborting the mission and returning to Ikara!"

As Karp was going over his numbers, he then reported, "by my calculations, Chief Mate, we have just missed our launch window."

"If we stay and fight, we will have to kill all these primitives," Tark responded in a no-nonsense tone, "and if one of them so much as nicks one of our vital instruments with those stone tips, we're moving here permanently. I don't like either of these scenarios so we are getting the hell out of here."

From the look on Tark's face, he might get them back to Ikara by force of will alone, which wasn't something that Karp would argue with.

"Roger that, Chief Mate. I'll recalculate our trajectory and fuel once we are in orbit."

The Nathorn medic picked up one piece of the hominid flesh from the ground, placed it in a chrono-capsule, and sealed it. "I am taking this small sample for genetic study, Commander."

"Affirmative," Rowel replied. "Take it to the lab when we return and tell the techs to hold it until I make contact. Chrono-freeze the First Engineer before he actually expires and place him in the mammal containment. We might be able to revive him back on Ikara."

"Why does it seem the engineers are the ones always getting hurt on Azur?" asked Karp nervously.

"Well, I suppose if we all waited around long enough in this place, we could all become victims of horror," Tark sharply responded. "Ya know, you get a little plaque in the ISP Headquarters when you die down here, Karp. Are you going for that, or would you like to get home?"

The ship blasted into the heavens, and to the men of Azur who'd survived the witnessing of their arrival, it was as if the gods were departing. The mystical craft left a streak across the sky, as its ominous scream penetrated the souls of the men watching it.

When they finally made it back into orbit and were on their way home, the report that had Simoth on the edge of his seat was that of the crew's continued health. When they later landed near Kartha, they selected a few to recover them under cover of night, who had the privilege of watching the Mission Commander step out of the craft with Tark by his side.

Alive and well.

The crew were immediately examined by the Nathorn medical team. The First Engineer was moved from the ship's chrono-chamber to a re-emergent facility designed for animals brought from Azur. Most of the other crew suffered from anxiety and physical stresses, but doctors determined that the greater gravity of Azur was the primary contributing factor. The serum that the Nathorn had devised had successfully warded off the sickness that had doomed the previous mission, and with that, the success of Mission Three was complete.

By the time the Mission Three crew had returned, Mission Four was already in its final stages of preparation.

Mission Four

Due to infighting, corruption, and greed, the Five Nations government was nearing collapse by the time Mission Three had returned, but the ISP was almost completely loyal to the Jast-driven consortium. This dedication was indirectly due to the family operation of Elmanith, tacitly allowing the Jast Consortium free rein to push through the fourth mission, which would now include retrieval of actual artifacts from Azur. The mission was launched in record time, once again with the rising light of Koru from the coast to minimize Tanian observations of the event.

Unannounced on the Wave, the objective of Mission Four was to initiate contact with the sentients discovered in Mission Three and observe their culture. It would take some work to overcome the last contact, which had resulted in the deaths of at least two of the sentients encountered there.

Unlike previous missions, it was determined that, with their greater passion for living things, Nathor should take point on the mission. So to be equitable and utilize the larger craft to allow more personnel, all Five Nations were also represented.

Still, there was one thing that worried Jast, something he feared to even mention outside the safety of the Catacombs—at least until the day when Bellelorn came up to him with a small slip of paper.

"A message came in for you over the Wave," she told him.

"Who from?" he asked as he took the paper.

"That's just it, I don't know. The voice sounded oddly neutral, like it wasn't real."

"Artificial?"

Jast opened the slip of paper, read what was written on it, and cast a gaze up at Bellelorn. She knew what it said, and met his eyes with a look that suspected far more than her words would say.

"Jast, did you want to take a pilgrimage today? I think you wanted me to remind you."

Her eyes briefly drifted down towards the paper, to which Jast gave a very slight nod before stuffing it into a pocket.

"Yes, I am about due. Maybe I'll bump into someone."

Bellelorn gave a knowing nod, and that was all that was said. Jast would not utter a word more until he was back down in the Catacombs, waiting for Simoth to show up.

When Simoth arrived, his smile told of the recent success of Misison Three. "I got the message from Bellelorn in the usual way," he said as he approached. "I'm quite busy with preparations for the next mission, so I gather this has to be important."

In a way," Jast began. "Regarding those preparations, how do you plan on keeping the launch from the Tanians?"

"Same way as before, under cover of the glare of the morning Koru rise and our cloaking devices. It worked once."

"That's what has been worrying me; the fact that it *did* work. Simoth, it's occurred to me that if our emlash sensors can determine so much about Azur from its orbit, then how much better must the Tanian sensors be? A little Koru-glare and emlash camouflage shouldn't be able to stop them."

"And yet it did," Simoth puzzled. "So what are you trying to say?"

Jast took out the slip of paper and passed it over to Simoth.

"When I got home today, Bellelorn told me there was a message just in from the Wave. It was an oddly inflexionless voice that drew her suspicions enough to write it all down instead of saying anything aloud. The message is actually not addressed to anyone specific and it contained only that which is written on the paper."

Simoth unfolded the paper and read aloud what Bellelorn had written down.

"I can cover your tracks again, but try to be more careful in the future."

"It's referring, of course, to the Mission Three launch," Jast explained. "Simoth, the Tanian sensors *did* pick up the launch, but someone covered it up for us."

"The Tanians?"

"One of them; someone sympathetic to Ikara. We appear to have a friend on the inside."

"Well, that's great," Simoth said uncertainly. "Isn't it?"

"It's someone in a significant but risky position, a person who will want to maintain his cover at all costs, so we have to be careful."

"Agreed. I'll see what can be developed to foul their sensors. A different metal for the outer hull, or a type of paint or something. I'll get some people going on it immediately."

"Good," Jast nodded. "In the meantime, I've got some other business to tend to."

Jast started to turn away, but had taken only a few steps when he paused for a last word over his shoulder: "Oh, and burn that paper before you leave these Catacombs."

Landing in a jungle area had initially been planned for Mission Four, but in the end, that was not to be. Starting with the launch, the mission was a fiasco. It had a myriad of difficulties, mostly due to corners cut by the various Families, who were trying to reduce margins and still meet the Five Nation treaty requirements. In the end, adhering solely to the minimum specs on any type of project is a near-guaranteed way to ensure its failure. One can plan a mission for many tallas, and on launch day, any number of unforeseen complications can arise. Therefore, adhering solely to the minimum stated specs can never account for such unexpected surprises, and for Mission Four, they were not dealt with appropriately.

For instance, on launch, one of the hydrogen thrusters was misbalanced, which meant the mission almost ended before it had even begun.

"Ikara Central, this is Commander Tiedyn Rowel. We have a thruster engine rattling on us. If it keeps up, it will sever its connection to the main body and cause an explosion."

For Mission Three with Tark Karth, Tiedyn Rowel had been the Commander in name only; he or his family had literally paid for his spot in the ISP. Regarding fear and skill, he was just like any Karth Kessai after training, but now he'd been Commander of two missions, making him the most experienced star pilot on Ikara. And experience does not wait on protocol.

"I have disengaged and aborted both thrusters at only seventy percent of use. Engaging main engine."

"Commander," called the ground controller through the speaker grid, "that engine is not suitable for leaving the atmosphere. Its fuel mix is for interplanetary travel only."

Simoth stood quietly in the background, secretly hoping that Rowel had the fortitude to press on. He certainly wasn't going to step in and stop him.

"That's a negative, Ikara Central. The engine is firing and is able to work in this low oxygen environment; we need only clear a few thousand clicks to be in the proper orbit zone. Once there, I will orbit with the planet's rotation and use that to make up for lost fuel."

The ground crew knew that this plan simply wouldn't work. They'd already taken into consideration the power needed to break free of Ikara's gravity. And by not using the stage-one thruster until burnout, the remaining fuel wouldn't be enough to get them free of Azur and back to Ikara. Rowel also knew that once the craft hit Azur, there would be no turning back. The Commander looked around at his experienced crew and nodded, each one looking him in the eye and nodding back. They knew this vessel would never return to Ikara.

How in the name of homemade sin am I going to explain this to my wife, Rowel thought to himself.

"Commander, you need to abort the mission and return to base."

"The crew understands the dangers and has voted unanimously

to continue on at any cost. We are requesting permission to continue on. For the sake of all of humanity and the future of Ikara, we cannot be permitted to fail. We have to make peace with the people in the landing zone. The zone is otherwise safe for us and we do not have time to try yet a third location for landing. We must make contact there so we can create an operational facility. Tell my family I am sorry."

There was a brief pause as one of the ground crew looked over at Simoth.

"It's your call, Director."

There was a very long pause before Simoth made it official.

"We will press on." Even as Simoth said the words, he couldn't believe it. He'd just laid his reputation on the line by sending those men on a one-way mission. In his mind, he consoled himself with this fact: at least they were willing.

"You have a green light, Commander. Push ahead and Godspeed." The ground controller's voice echoed through the cockpit of the craft, as a sense of finality came over the crew,

"I think you just screwed those guys, Director," Lemer said, stepping over to Simoth to voice his disapproval. As the chief designer of the craft, he clearly was not happy with the decision.

"I understand you are attached to the craft, Lemer, but we have to make sacrifices for the future. These men are experienced and willing to make that sacrifice. We can build another craft and we will."

"Director, these craft are designed to make multiple trips. We keep losing them and the budgets keep getting smaller!"

"Bear with us, Lemer, just bear with us. We have a plan."

"I can bear with you until the end of time but we have shortcomings, we have losses, and we have people dying on another planet. Now we need a new budget and new craft and we will be starting at zero with no new information from Azur."

"We can still communicate through our Orbital over Azur and get scientific data. We will make this work, Lemer. Listen to me and believe. Your mind is the most powerful tool you have. If you think we will fail, we will and we'll need to replace you with someone who believes as I do, that we will succeed. Do you understand?"

"I do," exhaled Lemer, almost begrudgingly. Ultimately, though, he knew the Director was right, and even if he wasn't, it was best to shut up and keep his job.

First Engineer Karp was the first to notice an issue with their atmospheric suits.

"Commander, sir! My suit is not holding air properly. I just did a compression test and it failed."

The hissing noise was hard to miss, but Karp was from Volst, where stating the obvious was a national pastime for his people.

"Dear Father of the Cycle, what in the hell are we supposed to do with hissing suits?" Rowel was clearly beside himself with the misappropriation of priorities by the ISP. Chief Mate Theon Bar had an idea, though, and was soon patting Karp's shoulder with waterproof-backed tape and giving him a grin.

"There! That should do it Fish!"

Karp was not amused, but it worked. Their problems had only just begun, though. When the craft was ready to enter Azur's atmosphere, Lamvok discovered that someone had mixed the old calculation methods with the newer, more scientific system they'd learned from the Tanians (which worked in decimals and powers of ten). As a result, the crew's miscalculation had caused them to miss their preferred entry point. Lamvok noticed the discrepancy right after the craft had passed through the heat phase of entry, but before he could say anything, there was a sharp report followed by a loud hiss.

"We have a leak," Lamvok said in the calmest manner one could, in accordance with his training. Chief Mate Theon then reached over and calmly covered the hole with his favorite tape, repeating the motion of patting his hands on the tape, then moving them across to make sure it'd sealed. He then nodded to Lamvok, who continued his report to Rowel.

"Commander, we have come in at the right and proper angle but wrong coordinates. We are going to stray significantly from our designated touch-down zone. Also, that tape might not hold, not that it matters at this point."

The craft was rattling hard now, sounding like a cart of bottles tumbling down a hill. The Commander braced himself and glanced over at the tape that Bar had placed over the hole.

"Can that really hold?" the Commander calmly asked.

Boom hassssspt!

"I guess not," he blandly elaborated. "All hands, suits on and remember your training: focus on what we can fix, ignore what we can't. Now give me some numbers."

"Just grazing the thin upper atmosphere now," Lamvok reported, "it should be easier to equalize the pressure of the cockpit now."

"That's something, at least," the Commander agreed. "Theon, let's get as much air under our front nose as possible. We'll glide all the way in if we have to."

"Working on it, sir," the Chief Mate responded as he fought the controls while adjusting cockpit pressure to normalize the leaking cabin. "We're still going to miss our intended target, though."

"By about half a continent," Commander Rowel said with a nod as he looked at the instruments. "Still, if we can walk away from it, then it's a terrific landing in my book. Everyone strapped in? Good, because this is going to be a bit bumpy."

Lamvok looked over at the Commander, knowing he was a man of great wealth who'd left it all behind for this mission and his people. In a moment of weakness, he asked Rowel in a whisper, "Commander, do you ever get scared?"

The Commander replied instantly. "Scared? Lamvok did you just ask me if I get scared? Hell no, I don't get scared you can't do anything with a space craft full of scared people!!"

Ultimately, the craft fell short, plunging down into a mountainous region at an elevation well above the tree-line. Some local natives might've seen the burning star plunging down from the heavens, but no one would know what that meant for possible survivors. All the natives knew was that they'd seen something crash down into an area with limited options for sustenance and survival.

To their credit, the resilient crew (who'd come to understand each other better than any previous group) decided to continue the mission, despite the odds. The improved telemetry allowed for reporting from the site for more than a month—twice as long as the provisions should've lasted—and with no indication that it was operating on anything other than remote land.

Except, perhaps, for one.

Before the telemetry stopped, there was a last message. The curious part was that it wasn't in a voice that the recording data could identify. That message, which was recorded four days after the last identifiable one, was simple but eerie.

"This is Terra. This is my home."

Jast listened to that message with interest as he readied himself for another meeting before the ISP committee. Simoth would have to chastise him before the Committee for his involvement in the problems with the supplies, and he'd perhaps offer political punishment. Jast understood why: to keep the greater plan safe. In truth, while Jast hadn't initiated or approved the cost-cutting, he'd made use of it and funneled some of the difference down into the Catacombs. What held his interest now, though, was that one message; for while others viewed it as a sign of the failure of the mission, Jast couldn't help but smile at the success it implied.

"Ikarans," he said to Bellelorn as he hugged her close, "can live on Azur."

J. R. Austin

Chapter Four:

Mission Tark

Borosh looked out towards the Great Mountain as Lort sat at his desk and worked on a diagram of the Bridge. "Lort, I have big plans. Plans beyond this puny planet and beyond even the company. I've discovered that this planet is nothing compared to what power the Ikarans have hidden away. They hold within their realm of influence and control a secret of true power and if I can harness it—when I harness it—I'll have the secret to Universal dominance!"

"What!?" Lort, confused, looked up at the Administrator. He couldn't be serious, could he? "What do you mean?" He was taken aback by the sheer discipline Borosh had managed while hiding these darker thoughts from the rest of the team for so long—unless he was joking, of course.

"We are going to find it," Borosh said with a sincere passion that Lort couldn't deny. "Somewhere between here and Azur, we are going to find that cradle of supremacy." His demonic grin widened. "With it, we will control the absolute destiny of the physical universe!"

The Administrator paused for a moment, looking down his nose at Lort. "You, Lort. You will be by my side when I make my final step into eternal greatness. I will be invincible! Indestructible! And every living thing will bow to me or suffer immensely. My apotheosis is coming, I can feel it."

"You...you're scheduled to retire at some point Sir. How will this 'universal domination' happen then?"

"The details are already taken care of, I just need to find someone who can be responsible for the shard that will carry me to my destiny. I've decided that that person will be you, Lort."

As head of security, Lort knew only too well that it was beyond his realm of knowledge or expertise, but he could sense that he needed to appease Administrator Borosh.

"Very well Sir," he said. "Tell me what I must do and I will take care of the dirty side of business." Borosh turned his back to Lort and looked out over the Bridge again. "In due time, Lort...in due time."

Mission Five was to be the most ambitious project yet, so ambitious that it was several Ikaran tallas in the making. In fact, it was ambitious enough that its costs finally began to gain the notice of the Five Nations government, even with Chancellor Jast Rathael there to cover it up.

The initial briefing for Mission Five had gone rather well, though. Simoth stood before the ISP Council and read the summary, with Chancellor Jast Rathael there as the official government representative.

"Mission Five has a two-fold purpose. The first is to see to the rescue of the Mission Four crew. Based on the last mysterious transmission, we believe them to still be alive and surviving. However, from the evidence we have been provided, we know that Azur has an indigenous population of sentients or proto-sentients. As such, our second goal is to find, observe, and make contact with this local population in a first-contact protocol. We hope to open a dialogue with them."

"That's quite a large crew you have listed," Jast pointed out, looking up from the briefing papers. "Some eighty people. That sounds a bit excessive."

"But necessary," Simoth responded. "We don't know what manner of specialists we may have need for when dealing with the aliens, plus the Mission crew will be building a listening station on Azur, with the idea of an eventual manned colony. Such a station will require construction workers and a variety of specialists."

"I suppose I can see their point," Jast admitted. "Please continue."

Simoth spared a brief glance to the Chancellor before shuffling the next set of papers laid out before him.

"There are certain medical concerns that have arisen. Though it seems at the moment anecdotal in nature, it does appear that with the help of our friends from Nathor, we seem to have overcome the problem of infectious pests, but there is still the matter of the greater gravity. It takes ninety days to get to Azur with our current usable technology, during which time there is nearly no gravity, followed by double our current gravity once they arrive on Azur. From the medical data we obtained after examining the crew of Mission Three, we have determined that this combination of extreme stresses can be too much for all but the most stalwart of Ikarans. Our doctors and GenSeers suggest that this may be a result of having spent too much time Ikara-bound, that we may have lost some of our space travel genetics. Our solution for this will be two-fold. First, while the GenSeers, together with our medical researchers, seek a way to revive the greater adaptability the Grand Cycle suggests we have had in the past, the Mission Five craft is being designed with new artificial gravity technology that we gleaned from the Tanians. With this, the mission will start out from Ikara at our normal gravity, but through the course of the ninety-day trip, the gravity level will gradually increase in force until it has equaled that of Azur by the time they reach that world. This should give the crew's bodies time to adjust and allow them greater mobility on Azur than the crews of Mission Two and Three had."

"That has been a concern of mine," Jast acknowledged. "I am glad to hear that it was addressed."

"Thank you, Chancellor. Next is the budget. Each of you have before you a copy of the initial budget estimates – subject to governmental approval, of course."

The meeting discussed the budgetary particulars, with Chancellor Rathael there to ask detailed questions on behalf of the Five Nations. It was all a fiction, of course, that Jast and Simoth had discussed in another walk down in the Catacombs (as they'd previously decided on the brief argument they would make over the crew layout). Simoth would put forth the perceived needs, and Jast would object to why a given item was budgeted so high. Then one or the other would give grounds.

"Chancellor Jast," Simoth said at one point, "the problem with the past Missions has been the slapped-together way in which they were assembled. For Mission Five, the lowest-bidder process has been entirely eliminated. However, if you're worried about the cost to the Five Nations Government, know that Mission Five will be paid *entirely* by the Karth Kessai Foundation."

"Well then," Jast said with a slight grin, "budget approved."

Of course, no mention was made of the fact that the Karth Kessai Foundation was built upon the resources of the Karth Family and the Elmanith Conglomerate, which itself was backed by Jast Rathael's Legacy Fund. Ultimately, the budget was exactly what Jast had desired it to be.

Eventually, they arrived at the question of who would be the Mission Commander. Simoth made the nomination.

"I nominate Tark Karth as Mission Commander for Mission Five."

"He's your cousin, right?" Jast immediately objected. "Showing a bit of nepotism?"

"Tark is the single most qualified person in the entire ISP," Simoth responded, his voice rising.

"And friends with the Tanians," Jast pointed out. "I'm not sure if he'd be the right one to actually *lead* a Mission to Azur when the Tanians themselves have made it quite clear they want us to remain planet-bound. By traveling, we are forcing their hand. I don't think they have the fortitude yet to stop us by force; it would show their hand and I think they are unsure of their dominance."

"Tark is first and foremost Ikaran," Simoth pointed out. "A true Karth Kessai, our best pilot and field leader, and very knowledgeable in every aspect of Mission systems. If there is one better qualified, then I would like to hear it!"

With Tiedyn Rowel lost with the rest of the Mission Four crew, and Tark being considered a hero after Mission Three, there was really no one else qualified. So Jast had no opposing nomination (another of his plans). In the end, Jast shrugged and nodded his acceptance of Simoth's argument.

"Then if there are no further objections," Simoth stated, his dark eyes taking in all attendees in a glare that panned the room. "Tark Karth is hereby named as Commander of Mission Five."

After the meeting was adjourned, Jast could honestly report, with witnesses present, that he had argued for the better interests of the Five Nations government. And yet, through careful planning, he and Simoth had succeeded in what they'd set out to achieve.

Naturally, over the coming tallas, there were cost overruns, all of which Jast tried his best to sneak through. That wasn't difficult when everyone else on the Five Nations Council was trying to sneak through appropriations for *their* own particular pet projects. The Council was rife with corruption and political scheming, but rather than use his position as Chancellor to try and eliminate it, Jast was using it as a smokescreen to shield his own activity with the ISP. Finally, however, there came a day when even the blind, self-serving eyes of the Five Nations Council started to notice that Jast's reign did nothing to quell the problems plaguing them.

The first objection came from the Volst Speaker, Thalamas Voort.

"We all know the problems this government has been having," he began, his bearing as vigorous as ever, "what with all the constant arguments and corruption, but it is the job of the *Chancellor* to rein everyone in, the job of a *strong* leader. I do not believe that Jast Rathael is that leader. Indeed, I believe the opposite to be true. He has proven himself a weak and ineffectual leader who has allowed far too many special interest appropriations to be budgeted through this esteemed body. I move that Jast Rathael be removed as Chancellor, and further that the position be eliminated altogether. We were doing fine enough with just our equal voices to guide this government."

J. R. Austin

"Your motion is recognized," Jast acknowledged after a pause. "Is there a second?"

All eyes searched the others, wondering who would be the one to start the vote, but what they failed to notice was the nearly imperceptible nod that Jast gave to one particular Speaker before she spoke up.

"Nathor seconds the motion," Bellelorn said, with a visible trace of trepidation.

"Then we take it to a vote," Jast stated. "All in favor of removing me from office and eliminating the position of Chancellor, respond."

The vote carried. While Jast did his best to hide his true emotions, he wore the beginnings of a knowing, satisfied smile.

Tark looked at the wondrous ship of their ancestors in the Catacombs. It was looking a lot shinier now, its hull polished, the engines refurbished. He admired it for a bit, a sigh escaping his lips as the other stepped up behind him.

"I'll never get to pilot that beauty, will I?"

"I'm afraid that honor will go to my grandson Micah. Besides, you have a very important job of your own to tend to."

Jast stepped up beside the other, taking a moment to admire the impressive vessel before continuing.

"I'm no longer Chancellor, nor for that matter is anyone else."

"You did say that you saw that coming."

"Enough to be ready for it," Jast admitted. "My wife has been after me to retire for some time now, so I thought I'd let First Speaker Voort have the honors of forcing me to do so. It seems to have put him into a very good mood."

"I should say so. What do you plan on doing now?"

"Now? Retiring, for the most part. I'm getting too old for these games of politics."

Indeed, Tark saw the grey in his hair and his lengthening beard, the fading energy in his eyes.

"So, you're dropping out of the plan that you started?"

"Publicly, yes. Privately, of course not. This is a plan to save

118

our people, but I'll need some more help at this point."

"Whatever I can do," Tark said.

"Then you must do whatever you *must* do. The Mission is entirely in your hands to change as you please. Simoth and the ISP Council will back whatever you decide, though I dare say you'll have some trouble with the Five Nations and the rest of the Ikaran people. Not that the Five Nations government will survive much longer anyway. Whatever you need, I'll do what I can to see that it happens."

"Then there are some changes I'd like to make," Tark said after a moment's thought. "For one, the Mission should be bigger. More personnel. Ever since the Accords were signed, I've known my destiny is to be a *real* Karth Kessai, to lead my people to the stars. For that, this needs to be more than a simple rescue and exploratory mission. A *lot* more, though I'm not sure if it's too late to alter the ship designs."

Jast cast a slow grin, one that had Tark giving him a curious look.

"You have been spending far too much time in these Catacombs, gazing in wonder at the *Slumberer*, my friend. Half of the cost overruns were my doing; the Mission Five ship is ready to hold up to two hundred people and their supplies, if it needs to."

"Two hun—why you wily old laravel. You had this planned from the beginning!"

"I suspected what you would want to do the minute Simoth and I agreed you would make the best commander for this mission. Tark, our world is dying thanks to the Tanians and soon everyone will know. Storms flood our lands and make it difficult for any craft of the air to fly, though I suspect that will also make it more difficult for the Tanians to detect our next launch as well. Even if they do, I know they have a fear of us. I am not sure what it is, but they have a weakness we have not detected. Possibly biological in nature, like our crew who died from exposure to microbes on Azur. On the surface, I see a strong race of space farers, but behind the façade

I honestly believe they are a weak people placated by luxuries and technology. They clearly underestimate us as natives. All the evidence shows we are stronger, we are smarter, we only lack the time they have had to develop. At any rate, before the *Slumberer* can perform its duty, we'll need an advance group, someone to scout things out for the bulk that will come later. Do you understand what I'm saying?"

Tark replied with but a nod, then gazed back out towards the *Slumberer* as he considered his next words.

"The expanded crew will include a broad selection of people from all five families, to act in the best interests of all."

"You shouldn't have any trouble getting that past anyone. People will see it as an affront to what they think my political plans are, while everyone else will see it as an opportunity to have their own included."

"It won't be like the First Mission. The candidates I choose will be for reasons of competency and quality."

"Agreed."

"Further, this will be a chance to bring us back to the old ways, back to the Grand Cycle. The Tanian influence has drawn Ikara into a downward spiral. We'll start off as a small isolated population. Two hundred so we have enough genetic diversity. The very best from science and the military that we can find. We'll include a couple of GenSeers and some Gate Keepers as well. We will be the first wave, and we will prepare a spot for the larger group that the Slumberer will bring."

"If you want to get your new crew used to the old ways of the Grand Cycle," Jast pointed out, "then you had best start now. I can arrange a location for a colony where the ones you pick can get used to life without emlash or Tanian gifts. We'll call it a training camp for the Mission; we just won't tell anyone outside the group just how extensive the mission is to be."

"A wise precaution," Tark admitted. "I will talk to Simoth, tell him ahead of time what I'll be proposing so he can make the alterations to my initial proposal that will get us what we need in the end."

"Then there's one other thing," Jast told him. "The only way this mission is going to be the kind of success that we need it to be… is if it's a failure. That means no communication with Ikara once you reach Azur."

For a long moment, Tark thought this over, realizing what it truly meant. No more contact, no more Ikara. They would be alone. It was a long moment before he finally replied with a slow nod of agreement.

"Keep an eye on your telescope in the new ISP observatory," Tark told him, "I'm sure you'll be able to spot the vessel once it lands. So that you know we made it intact and will be readying things for the final Mission, I will make one transmission, but it will be of a type that should alert you without revealing our presence. As far as anyone else will know, we did not make it."

"I will keep watch," Jast agreed. "In the meantime, good luck with getting everything ready for launch. At the rate both the Five Nations government and the weather's going, it may take a while."

"If it takes ten tallas or more, I will see it through," Tark promised. "You have my word on that."

Dantu Rathael

Dantu Rathael had recently graduated from the Academy. A bright and curious lad with much of his grandfather in him, he was immediately grabbed up by the ISP and offered a teaching position at the Academy. A talla his brother Micah's senior, he was as dark as the other was light, though a little shorter, stockier, and more muscular. Micah was quite precocious, and as such, Dantu used that extra talla as a badge of honor, doing everything he could to keep a step or two ahead of the adroit youngster. Dantu's tastes ran to riskier, more physically demanding sports, such as full-hold grappling and live-fire manhunts, both as hunter and hunted. The one trait he shared with his brother was the bright blue of his eyes.

Dantu's main curiosity, though, concerned the Tanians, especially after overhearing many a subdued conversation between his grandfather and father when he was growing up. So naturally, when he happened across certain pictures in his grandfather's possession, the lad's interest was more than aroused. The images that Halgor had supplied for Jast a long time ago were not yet enough to prove anything, merely to suggest. It was enough, though, to get Jast discussing it with Bellelorn while Dantu was in the next room listening. More than once, the name of the First Speaker of Volst came up as a very possible collaborator with the Tanian conspiracy, whatever the details of it might be.

This development got Dantu more than a little angry at the situation in general, and Volst in particular. Enough so to want to voice his frustrations someplace public. Quite naturally, it occurred in a bar after he'd had one drink too many. Micah was with him, but he kept away from the hard liquor. Therefore, they talked in tones that Micah wished were more hushed.

Micah was an intellectual recluse, his skin smooth and finely covered in near-invisible downy hair of the same shade as the locks that flowed from his head to his shoulders, his eyes the cerulean blue of Elmanith. They sat at a small round table, Micah hoping that the rowdy noise of the surrounding atmosphere would keep them safe from overactive ears. That, and the near-constant thunder of the weather outside.

"I'm telling you," Dantu said, his words a little slurred, "they're responsible. It's Volst's fault; they sold us out. They know what's going on up there and are trying their best to hide it. They and their Tanian friends should be marched one by one into the depths of the sea!"

"Dantu," Micah quietly whispered, "perhaps we should have this conversation somewhere less public?"

"Oh, come on, you know I'm right. We've talked about it. The Tanians are responsible for all this constant bad weather, and Volst is helping them. All because they want to think of themselves as chosen."

Dantu took another sip of his drink, while Micah responded in an even quieter tone.

"Let them think what they want, it doesn't change anything. I just think we shouldn't be talking about this here where-"

"Volst *are* chosen, and I'll fight any man who says otherwise."

Micah glanced up at the lumbering source of this declaration and gave a sigh as he completed his sentence:

"-about twenty Volst are also drinking," he sighed. "Dantu-"

"Don't worry, Micah, I can handle this."

Dantu downed the remainder of his drink in a single swig, slammed down his mug, and stood up to face the large man with the steel-grey eyes—a man who Micah knew his brother could handle. However, the five others standing behind him might prove to be a problem.

"Now," Dantu declared to his opponents, "there seems to be some misunderstanding as to what exactly I said."

"I thought there might be," the central man from Volst grinned wide, hands on his hips. "Did you want to rephrase what you said?"

"Yes, I do." Dantu took a step away from the table and closer to the group from Volst, while Micah shook his head and took his own drink to a more distant table. "I meant to say that Volst *are* the chosen…The chosen scum of Ikara. I'm sorry if I didn't make that clear enough before."

The other man responded with a growl, then a flailing fist. Dantu caught it handily, and stretched the man's arm out a little farther before slamming the elbow of his other arm up in a strike at the middle of the man's arm. A snap was heard, followed by a more painful cry, as Dantu shoved the man and his uselessly dangling arm into his companions. Then he swung at one of the others.

Two rushed to tackle Dantu, making bystanders leap out of the way. Meanwhile, Micah had seated himself at a table with a couple of Elmanith to watch the proceedings.

"Six against one," one Elmanith man remarked to Micah,

"certainly doesn't seem fair."

Dantu swung his right arm out to clothesline one man, while delivering a kick into the abdomen of the other. The first ended up sprawled on the floor, while the second found himself shoved into more of his friends.

"I know," Micah sighed, "but my brother's too impatient to wait for anyone else to join him."

The next man managed to get a solid punch in, the entire result of which was nothing more than a glare from Dantu.

"I'm too drunk to feel that lover's tap of yours and I doubt I would under the best of circumstances anyway."

It's not often you can surprise a Volst in a fight, but this one had a moment of disbelief as Dantu glared back at him, instead of doubling over the way he should have. Taking advantage of the pause, Dantu grabbed the man's collar with one hand, put his other hand to an arm, and ran him right across a table—spilling drinks into other Volst laps, not to mention a couple of Volst faces. He then spun around with a roundhouse kick to the one he knew had to be charging up behind him.

This one, however, was smart. He managed to grab Dantu's kicking foot and gave it a hard twist. Dantu launched himself out flat, his hands clutching at the edge of the table before he could hit the ground. He spun the rest of his body so that it faced the same direction as his twisted foot, which in turn brought his other leg around to smash across his attacker's face. The man fell back, letting go of Dantu's foot, and Dantu landed in a spring, pushing off the table up to his feet to face the original six.

Dantu surveyed his opponents. One had a broken arm, another held his hands to his belly, and the rest were still picking themselves up. Of course, he'd forgotten about the three who'd been seated at the table behind him, men with their drinks in their laps who now stood up to join the fight.

"Okay," Micah casually remarked to his new companions, "now the odds are a bit more even."

The first hit slammed into the back of Dantu's head, spilling him into the clutches of the ones before him, but he even turned that into a charge, which ended with his head pummeling into the chin of one of them. The man dropped while two others tried to grab hold of Dantu from either side.

Dantu was still recovering from the blow from behind, while the two held him before a third came to face him with a cocked fist and a grin. Dantu shook himself alert, just in time to use the pair holding him as a brace against which to bring *both* his feet straight up into the third man's chin. Another dropped to the ground.

When his feet came down, he used one to slam full-force into the knee of the man to his right. The Volst released his grip with a howl of pain, as his leg snapped beneath him. Dantu twisted in the grip of the remaining man, until his own hand gripped that of the Volst, whilst his free hand came crashing into his face.

Repeatedly.

"Did I mention," Micah calmly remarked while sipping his drink, "that I never got picked on as a kid because everyone knew that *he* was my brother?"

Dantu dropped the man to the ground, his face having now been rather thoroughly hamburgered, and he turned just in time to get tackled by the ones from the table (and the two that remained of the original group). Very quickly, there was a dogpile sitting atop Dantu, raining punches down upon him.

At least until one of them howled out in a near-soprano voice and fell over to the side.

"And my brother's not above groin punches either," Micah blandly explained.

Another fist smashed into Dantu's face, but this time, he brought both legs up and quickly wrapped them around the attacker's neck. He slammed his feet towards the ground, taking the man with him. The man's head never hit the ground, though, as there was another Volst in the way trying to grab onto Dantu's legs. One hard Volst head met with the other, and both dropped, dazed and near-unconsciousness.

"Of course," Micah continued with his running commentary for his Elmanith friends, "I could stop this by just telling them that our father in the First Speaker of Elmanith, but Dantu's been rather stressed of late and been needing the release."

"Your brother," one Elmanith finally ventured to say, "is quite the fighter."

"Dantu was the winner of the Inter-Nation Manhunt Games three tallas running," Micah lightly boasted.

"Dantu Rathael? You mean, he's *that* Dantu?"

Micah replied with a nod, and they watched with a new, more respectful interest.

Dantu was bloodied by the time he got to his feet, but at least he was down to two opponents, both of whom were regarding him far more cautiously as they spread apart to either side of the room and assumed wary crouches.

"You take back your words," the one on the left demanded.

"You'll have to remind me," Dantu replied, "what exactly it was I said. I'm a little drunk, you see."

The one on the left looked about to reply, then paused in brief confusion. He looked at his companion, only to receive a puzzled look in return. It seemed that between the alcohol and the fighting, they'd also forgotten.

"I... I dunno."

"Well then," Dantu shrugged, "I guess this means that the fight's over with. How's about I buy you two a drink?"

The others exchanged looks and shrugged to themselves, then relaxed their stances and approached Dantu with a welcoming smile.

"Here it comes," Micah quietly sighed.

The moment that they both got within hand-shaking distance, Dantu took his offered hand and used it (along with his other hand) to slam their heads together—hard. They dropped to the ground.

"Now the fight's over."

Dantu flashed a grin and looked down at the unconscious,

bleeding bodies arrayed around him. When he got to the last pair at his feet, he turned around to call out to the bartender:

"I *did* promise to buy those two a drink, so their next drink when they wake up is on me."

Dantu staggered over to the bar, pulled out some coins to slam onto the countertop, and made his way back to where his brother sat. Several tables were in shambles, and the bar itself was still filled with a good number of Volst drinkers. But even they started clapping and calling out their cheers. Dantu may have had a rude mouth, but he'd just beaten nine of their own and walked away with little more than a few scratches and bruises. Dantu replied with a smile, a drunken bow that nearly spilled him all the way to the ground, and a wave of one hand. Then he rejoined Micah, who was just finishing off his drink.

"Well, time to go," Micah said to the others at the table, "hope you enjoyed the floor-show."

Micah only spoke to Dantu when they finally stepped outside.

"Clear your head now?"

"Yes, I know of our grandfather, and the rumored suspicions he has regarding our benefactors. In fact, there are those of us who have been getting rather suspicious of things ourselves."

A few days later, Dantu was speaking in a lab with a thin Elmanith scientist with a pale complexion, green eyes, and shaggy blond hair, who wore a long white shirt, a loose-fitting pair of puffy blue and green pants bound at the ankles, and simple leather sandals. They were with a couple of others in white lab coats, one of whom was puzzling over what looked like some crudely taken photographs, which Dantu thought he recognized.

"In fact," the man continued, walking Dantu down the length of the lab, "recent evidence has come into our possession that is very suggestive of activity atop the Mountain. More activity than the Tanians have been telling us."

He stopped before the man and the pictures, only briefly

indicating them before continuing. It was enough, though, for Dantu to be certain. They were the same pictures that his grandfather had obtained from Halgor.

"Interesting pictures," Dantu said, hiding any sign that he was already familiar with them. "Where'd you get them?"

"Still don't know. An envelope was found on our doorstep one day. We're still examining them. If authentic, they suggest much though we are still without any conclusive evidence."

"The pictures aren't enough?"

"We are a consortium of scientists, Mister Rathael; we need solid evidence before we dare bring this up to anyone. The Families are too invested in the status quo to let anything past. We *have* been launching a few probes into the upper atmosphere and have very suggestive data concerning the weather. There are a few things to suggest links with the Tanians, but we need direct evidence; something that cannot be doubted. We need some better pictures of what's going on up there. The problem is we can't get anyone close enough. The Tanians are very watchful."

"Then don't use anyone to take the pictures," Dantu told him.

"What? I don't understand. How do you mean?"

"I mean," Dantu said as he pulled out a small roll of papers from his pocket, preparing to hand them over, "that Volst has been working on certain remotely controlled rover units. It's basically a flat platform on wheels with some control mechanisms. Fit something to take and transmit live pictures onto it, and the whole thing would be little more than a hand-span high and about two across."

He handed over the papers, which the scientist proceeded to examine. They were blueprints for just such a mechanism.

"If I may ask, how did you obtain these designs, Mister Rathael?"

"In a fight," he shrugged. "Well, not actually *in* the fight, more like afterwards. The day after, I went back with a request. They were significantly more polite this time, and this is what I walked away with. So, do you think this thing's feasible?"

"Very much so," the other said after a moment. "Yes, I think with this we can get the evidence that we need, then present it to the Five Nations Council. Very good, Mister Rathael."

"Just call me Dantu," he said holding out his hand. "And your name?"

The other took the hand most enthusiastically, giving it a shake as he replied.

"Ruel Elim, head of the consortium; Elmanith by training but Whycheral by birth. I'll let you know how we go, Dantu."

"Just make that report, then all the credit's yours," Dantu smiled back. "You can keep my name out of it."

Over the generations, the Voort family honor had taken a beating, yet the rise of the First Speaker of Volst had managed to prevent the drama and overthrows that were so prevalent in the political lives of Elmanith and Kartha. It was the rhythm of Nathor and Whycheral. The Volst kept their dirty laundry behind closed doors. As with any governing hierarchy, dynamics were shifted, loyalties were tested, traitors were exposed. However, they were all swept under the rug by the elders, and orchestrated by political engines that understood the concepts of subtlety and tact.

At least, that *was* the case until the *Observer* became the eyes of the world on the operations of the Tanians.

The Volst *Observer* had become the location for science teams assigned to keep an eye on the Tanian operations; these teams had been a source of pride for Volst. As the first broadcasts drew attention to an installation and level of operation that dwarfed the most ambitious project ever conceived, they also pointed out the importance of such investigative work, and did much to amplify the Volst standing. For the first talla or two, the Voort hegemony was able to keep a constant lid on their internal scandals and conflicts, and bartered a respectable level of trust from the Tanian Administrator Borosh. The level of esteem lavished on the Volst reporters was intoxicating to a people whose role in society had been diminished and belittled for a decade. It was a heady thing to be popular the world over.

Yet throughout all this was a balancing act performed by Thalamas Voort, that of promoting Volst pride with the *Observer*, while allowing only so much to really be observed in his deal with Borosh. Some were already beginning to wonder how the Tanians could put together such a large operation under the very nose of Volst, until Thalamas pointed out that they had merely built the *Observer*, and that it was usually Elmanith and Whycheral who supplied the personnel to man it.

To deflect such concerns, they'd constructed the Volst Oversight Platform, independent of Volst influence. Yet they'd built it (Thalamas hoped) a little farther away from the Tanian operations, so as to minimize any possible observations of anything their Tanian allies might not want to be seen. However, then came the tragedy that closed the Platform. Now few visited it, save the occasional field trip from some Academy students, who were there to see what they could learn for their various specialties. The Platform now mainly served as a lesson about the dangers of the Mountain, so it was meant to discourage any future ambitions.

Ruel Elim led one such field trip. He and a few students left, only packed with a few provisions. While the one Volst security guard was occupied with answering some questions for the students, Ruel and one of his students crept towards the edge of the Platform— and the one exterior access door that had been sealed off with red warning tape.

It wasn't much work for them to get the door open, nor to disable the alarm system. With furtive glances over their shoulders, they brought out the sole occupant of one of their provision bags: a wheeled platform barely two handspans across and only one high, on top of which sat a camera. They put it down outside, then Ruel took out a small handheld device and worked the simple controls. The wheels of the platform started moving on their own, and the device crawled a couple of cubits away before stopping under his command.

"It's working," Ruel whispered to the student, "now the relay."

From another provision bag, they took out a small box with an antenna atop it and carefully placed it just outside the metal door, adjusting the angle of the antenna before gently closing the access door. Ruel again played with his control device, and when one of the lights lit up, he grinned.

"All set up. The relay will transmit the pictures back to our camp midway down the mountain, and from there back to the Academy. All I have to do is adjust its course with this control box, based on what the pictures tell us."

"How far away can you be to control it?" the student asked.

"The relay will take care of that. We don't even have to start it up until we're back at our camp. Now let's get going before the others run out of things to occupy the guard with."

Later, once back at their camp and away from the eyes of security personnel on the Platform, Ruel and his students bent over their viewer, controlling the course of the little rover. What they saw left their jaws hanging open in shock.

———

As Jast had predicted, Mission Five was popular with the ISP, and Tark's changes in particular were readily approved. The Ikaran people, however, held it in lesser esteem, even with the looming suspicions of Tanian designs. Resources were slow to arrive, logistical errors caused cost overruns, and more people were concerned over increasingly virulent planetary weather conditions, quakes, and the reality of atmospheric losses—changes that couldn't be attributed to any known physical phenomenon. It seemed the Mission was in danger, as were any future missions.

Finally, Jast set it all out for everyone to see. He didn't do it himself, of course, but rather maneuvered a certain consortium of scientists into discovering it for themselves, ironically using (in part) the Volst Oversight Platform atop the Mountain. The Platform had been shuttered but not dismantled, and security around it wasn't quite top-flight.

Ruel Elim was giving the report before a combined meeting of the Five Nations government, the ISP council, and several dignitaries from all Five Families. Nothing was broadcast on the Wave, for fear of the Tanians overhearing, but it was well-enough attended that all significant parties were represented.

Ruel began with a series of charts, graphs, and more than a few photos, along with recorded measurements from a variety of instruments.

"The weather is a direct result of our increasing loss of atmosphere. As a portion of the atmosphere escapes the grip of our world, the outward rush of air creates these deadly storms. It appears our atmosphere is trying to reach some equilibrium. When it does that, or at least gets close to that, the process should slow down, but at that point, the planet will no longer support life. At least not the type of life we like. But what then is causing this atmospheric loss? Loss of mass from Ikara."

He clicked another picture into view on the screen overhead, and for a moment, no one was sure what they were looking at. It showed the top of the Mountain and the Tanian installation there, and the immense building of the Bridge, along with what appeared to be several machines digging and hauling. Far off to the right was a crater that the machines were coming and going to.

The problem was that there was no sense of scale. However, then a Tanian flitter craft came into view. All there had seen them during the kidnapping of the Speakers for their forced meeting, so they knew their size. This one appeared like a flyspeck against one of the earth-moving machines, but it was still at least a mile away. Several hushed voices began whispering in concerned tones as Ruel offered an explanation.

"This, and the following pictures you are about to see, were taken by a remote rover we launched from the Volst Oversight Plaform. It was only big enough to house the equipment to take these pictures, so as to remain as inconspicuous as possible. That vehicle you see in the center appears to be hauling away ore from a site on the other side of that crater, but further up you can see what appears to be the main point of interest."

He indicated a long, flexible metal tube leading from the edge of the crater to the Bridge building. As curious eyes sought to get a sense of the size of this mammoth tube, Ruel filled in the details.

"This tube appears to be pumping out material from deep within the crater for direct transmittal to one of the Tanian worlds via their Bridge. We have made some estimates, and this pumping tube appears to be over a thousand cubits wide. And photographic evidence suggests that it is not the only one in operation. The crater you see is over one and a half clicks wide, and was created entirely by the tunneling efforts of the Tanians. That, however, is far from the worst of it."

As voices rose, he clicked a button, and another picture came into view.

"This was taken at the edge of the crater."

The view was at the very lip, peering down into the center. They could see the pump-tube plunging into the depths of the crater, as well as a range of other immense pieces of machinery, which looked like they could dig out and haul away the entirety of the capital of Elmanith in about a day. That, however, wasn't what caused the collective gasp that followed. The bottom of that crater, including where the pump-tube led, simply wasn't visible. It was a straight, vertical shaft a mile wide, which went down as far as the picture could show, ending in a distant mist of molten rock.

"As near as we can make out, that hole dug by the Tanians goes all the way to the core of Ikara," Ruel finished up. "Gentlemen and ladies, the Tanians have been mining our world to death. Hollowing it out. They have deceived us from the very beginning. The Tanians have betrayed us and we were fools for not questioning them. They are not benefactors and givers, they are *Takers*."

The uproar caused by this revelation had nearly everyone on their feet, one person blaming another, and fingers pointing back and forth across the room. The mining was decreasing the mass of Ikara itself; this in turn made it unable to hold onto its full atmosphere, which had caused the extreme weather. The Tanians were knowingly killing their world, and they didn't care a thing about it.

It was Speaker Thalamas Voort of Volst, though, that desperately tried to offer a feather in support of his Tanian ally.

"All the more reason why we should take them up on their offer and leave Ikara for the stars. We've worn this planet out, it's time to leave."

He was drowned out by the far more numerous cries venting anger in the direction of the Tanians, many with cries of "Takers!" It was a representative from the Elmanith coalition who finally stood up to state it quite bluntly:

"Gentlemen, it is obvious now that the Tanian Accords were a complete sham, meant to stall us until they were finished with their scheme. These…these…Takers, had no more intention of following their end of the Accords than we should now have in keeping to our own. With this evidence before us, I motion that these Accords are hereby null and void."

The shouting didn't get any quieter with that call to action, though a lot of it now centered around what they could possibly do against the Tanians. Over and over, Volst motioned to take the Tanians up on their offer to vacate the planet. But Tark was present as a part of the ISP group, and therein saw his chance. He shot up to his feet and called out in a strong voice for all to hear.

"Everyone! It is obvious that we can't trust anything the Tanians say or offer. Our only chance lies in our own hands. Azur still awaits us, but we must have the chance to explore it for possible colonization. Mission Five will be the first step towards a foothold on Azur, but for that we need the funds to complete preparations. I ask of this esteemed body to pause in its internal squabbles long enough to set aside the money I've requested. The Tanians have betrayed us all, but we can still forge our own path through the Grand Cycle, and reach Azur!"

Only one dissenting voice came amidst the ensuing discussions, that of the Speaker from Volst, still trying to preach in favor of asking the Tanians to use their Bridge to walk to the stars. The vote carried, so Tark had the funds to complete preparations for the Mission.

Borosh

Administrator's Log, final day of Phase One Administration, Planet 3xStellarC-11344. Administrator Borosh. Final analysis and recommendation. Recording now.

"As Administrator, it is with great honor that I serve the Tanian Cause on the perimeter. I have endeavored to accomplish my goal, to serve my world, and fulfill my duty to the people of Tania in the field and on station. As we close our extraction efforts here and consider our alternatives, it pleases me to be honored with the opportunity to move to the Phase II extraction of Planet-3xStellarC-11344. I am very proud of the team that has undertaken this task and look forward to the next phase as well."

"Now, to the actual debrief. I will cover our particular mission parameters, as well as the collective objective results. Of course, the Matter Transporter and Molecular Sequencer process has operated magnificently, with only a few conditions that might be worthy of analysis."

"First off, in terms of mechanical operations, the M-travel leg of the mission was exemplary, and even set some corporate records. Sensory and analysis hardware operated well within parameters, and the vessel subroutines operated most efficiently on the way to orbit. Forty-seven point two-five hours of deceleration were well within mission parameters."

"Concerning the indigenous population, coordination was an easy process. In effect, we successfully turned the population against the world and against themselves. One fifth of the indigenous peoples have already committed to acting as our planetary liaison on another system, doubling our operational crew. While this is admirable, of course, the increase in the collective's population would defeat this mission's objective. So at this point, a Bridge crossing will not be possible. On the positive side, however, the shipment of biological matter from this planet back to Tania for use in the biomed system will be quite extensive. The sheer volume of genetic material scavenged will be in the millions of cubic cubits. This will be transmitted without the sequencer, so containers will be necessary. I did choose a few hundred specimens for the research lab. As with our previous arrangement, please hold them in containment for a thirty-day quarantine. It is a process we have used since the first MTS delivery more than a hundred thousand tallas ago and four hundred and fifty light-years away."

"As a matter of course, all arrangements between the Tanian outpost and the indigenous people are in my report body, so I will not go into the details. The entirety of the Tanian Accords, as they call it, are actually quite comical in terms of the very conservative approach with which we were able to bring to bear. Of course, we can make additional revisions over time."

"For the record, as of midnight last night, Ikara is dying. Mining operations have finally pushed it past the point of no return and at this point, there is no amount of technology that can stop its destruction. The good news is that we have achieved a profitability quotient of two hundred and ninety percent over initial energy expenditures required to initialize operations: a new record for a Class C world. Furthermore, we will be able to expand that profitability in the next few tallas as we establish the mining operation on the sister planet, as outlined in our original agenda."

"If it gives you any satisfaction, this is the first time in nearly seven hundred tallas that the mission has been such an unqualified success. Future operations will be more profitable too, as the system data may identify markers that make such successes even more likely."

"My replacement, Amishari, has been duly introduced to all the remaining tasks and she has the backing of Security Chief Lort. The time of my Bridge crossing is drawing near, so I trust that this report meets with your approval and I look forward to the planet-side debriefing that will ensue once I am home."

"In the name of the Tanian People, again, thank you for the opportunity. Ever in your service, Borosh."

Borosh wiped the sweat from his face as he stepped away from the viewer. For a moment, he worried that the recording might've captured his nervousness. He still had some packing to do, but his mind was focused on making his escape.

He jammed the last of his belongings into the final open crate with a sigh. He was feeling like a traitor, moving to withdraw himself before the truth became known. He felt the cowardice now, the abject detachment that being a planet-killer demanded. He'd been able to stomach it before, but now, as he readied all his worldly belongings for transmission, he knew what he truly was. For the first time, he felt guilt instead of pride.

Deep down, a small part of him wished he could make amends.

Then came the last message he would receive as Chief Administrator.

"Administrator, you have a visitor. Thalamas Voort demands to see you."

"I would imagine so," he thought tiredly back to the other. "Send him in."

It was pride that drove Thalamas Voort to go to the Tanians directly after he'd seen the pictures of their operations. The working relationship between Thalamas and Borosh had been civil, despite the harsh working conditions and a healthy disrespect of each other. But today, there had to be a visible show of reckoning.

Thalamas' actions might have seemed greedy to some, but he truly did believe that what he did was for the benefit of Volst, and by extension, all of Ikara. Now, seeing what he saw, realizing the extent to which Ikara was being threatened, and learning how Volst itself was being called into question, he was furious. He didn't even bother knocking. He just stormed into the office like a force of nature, to find Administrator Borosh seated behind his desk, a stack of small shipping crates stacked off to one side.

The smaller, gray Tanian, his large eyes wide and confused, tried to meet the turbulent Ikaran with the steady grace and diplomacy for which his species was celebrated, but to no avail. Thalamas was going to get an answer, and Borosh would provide it.

"Ah, Thal, my compatriot! It is truly an unexpected sur-"

Thalamas may have ceased his forward movement when he reached the desk. However, his force of will extended beyond, running over the words of the smaller bureaucrat and stomping on his politeness with an overbearing need for an explanation, which even a pacification protocol couldn't overcome.

"Borosh, you bastard! I could thrash you to the end of your life! How long were you going to take before you told me? The Accords call for equitable reciprocity!"

Borosh closed his mouth, clamping his lips tight like he was biting back a virulent response. He visibly swallowed, his eyes suddenly narrowing somewhat, the nictitating lenses blinking off the assault of words like a vessel weathering a strong tidal wave.

"I'm sorry, Thalamas, I'm not sure what you mean. I do believe..."

Although he truly wanted an answer from the Tanian, Thalamas clearly didn't want mere placations anymore, so he continued his press.

"There are *millions* of tons of ore being transmitted through your machines, and not just from the mountain but straight out from the *core* of Ikara! We had discussed the process and you had assured me there would be safety considerations made on our behalf, but from the images I just saw, you're doing little more than sucking our world completely dry. Tell me, Borosh: are you actually *trying* to kill Ikara, or am I missing something? I really want to believe you, but the video imagery I just saw seems very damning."

Thalamas' outburst gave Borosh time to figure out what the Ikaran was upset about. Some evidence of what they were really doing had leaked out. It was bound to happen sooner or later, but now he had to handle that eventuality. Borosh smiled like a Tanian again—the smile of a benevolent adult patronizing a younger kin.

"Thalamas, why do you let such trivialities upset you so? If some ruffians have violated the Accords, the agreement between your People and ours, we can certainly discuss withdrawal immediately from the process, and in the meantime, withdraw our support of the Five Nations."

Withdrawal would mean no more benefits for Volst, much less any means off a dying world. While he let Thalamas consider that point, Borosh pressed on.

"The Accords authorize us to extract the necessary alloys, as we have agreed, in trade for the advancements in technology you have already been enjoying, and the offer to join our confederacy as time passes and we find we can work together more equitably. I do believe the Voort family was one of the primary names on the proposed departure manifest. If that is out of order, then of course we can adjust it."

"Nuh... no. There are many considerations that can be looked at before we get to that point..."

Thalamas had been cut short by Borosh's abrupt, concise responses. It hadn't been the Volst's intent to suggest that the Accords were out of line, that the agreements reached by sovereign nations should be discarded, or that their chances to reach the stars should be cast aside. Thalamas swiftly breathed in and out, trying to clear his head. His passion had driven him to this point, but his personal issues had to take a back seat to what was best for his People. Therefore, he changed tactics. The problem had more than one means of solution.

"Administrator Borosh, forgive my intrusion. These times are trying and it was rash of me to storm your office like an impetuous child. But sir, there must be something you can provide me that would help us to protect not only our own sovereignty, but also your operation. These kinds of physical evidences do seem to reflect a cavalier attitude towards our safety. What can you offer that might mitigate the difficult position this leak has created for us both?"

Borosh pushed back his high-backed chair, stood up, and looked at Thalamas. The benevolence of his smile shifted, a nuance of some kind of mischief slipping between the cracks. Thalamas was passionate, yes, but his personal greed and compassion for his people were too much a part of his identity.

"Thalamas, we would not ever endanger the relationship unnecessarily. I will do what I can to get an explanation out to you, to help abrogate this situation and empower Volst. But remember, yours will be the first people to experience the Matter Transporter once we finalize our dealings here. We do look forward to your assistance in integrating all Ikara into the Tanian Confederacy. In the end, Ikara is a worn-out planet, but we would be only too glad to help you to worlds far more alive and full of potential."

"Well, I suppose…we *do* have the option of using the Bridge, after all. But I've been wondering…could you tell me a little about how this Bridge works?"

"Of course," Borosh beamed. "The Bridge consists of two components: the matter transporter and the molecular sequencer. Together they make up the MTS, or as it's more commonly called, the Bridge. The matter transmitter is essentially a device for creating and containing a singularity. All this component does is instantly transport raw molecular material to another Bridge to which it has been coupled. Now, that alone will only transport the raw matter, without any concern for form. That is where the molecular sequencer comes in. It reconstructs the matter back into its original form. This is how it allows a living creature to walk in one end and come out the other still alive and intact."

"It sounds a bit dangerous," Thalamas said doubtfully.

"Oh, I'll admit in the early days it was. Without the Sequencer online, you'll get nothing more than a puddle out the other end. But Visicia—that's the name of the multiplanet conglomerate from Tania that invented the MTS and coordinates mining operations—has had a few millennia to perfect it. Now, as you might imagine, it is a rather energy-intensive process, but well worth it when compared to any other means of traversing the stars. Of course, it still takes a ship many tallas to journey to the destination to initially set up the Bridge on the other end, but we use automated vessels for that. The Bridge is fairly commonplace now."

"Fascinating," Thalamas admitted.

Of course, what Borosh didn't say was that because it *was* very energy-intensive for the Company to make up for the vast expenditure in energy and resources needed to establish a Bridge (whether it be on a mining colony or a home world), it needed to actively seek out and extract as many worlds as it could. It had become a trap: create a Bridge to an uninhabited world, but to pay for it, the mining had to begin in earnest. To establish such a Bridge, the next world had to have that much more in the way of resources. Their shortcut to the stars had made them a culture of takers.

"But, how do you control them," Thalamas asked, "that is, how do you control to which other Bridge a given one goes? Communicating over the vastness of space would be impractical for wave or even anything light-based, as would be any manner of control system, at least until the point where the Bridge itself is operational."

"A very brilliant observation, Thalamas," Borosh admitted with a grin. "The secret is much like your GenSeers, if I have the analogy correct. You see, the likes of telepathy reach beyond normal limits of speed. There's an explanation that involves such concepts as entanglement, but you're not ready for that yet and it would be too great a tangent. The point is, in this way, communications can be sent nearly any distance, including control messages to our devices programed to set up the gate initially. This is what our Seers do, they send the communications across the stars, which our remote devices can then pick up. Of course, there can be a lot of psychic noise, especially near worlds with a native population, which is why every Seer must have an Oracle; the Oracle helps the Seer to tune out everything but what he must focus on, so that together they establish the initial connection from one Bridge to another. Once established, and thence tested, the link is locked and the Bridge connection stable. There are some more technical details behind all that, of course, and we have our own terminology that involves words other than Seer and Oracle, but these are the simplest terms I can put them in."

"No, it's… perfectly clear," Thalamas decided, only a little bit hesitant. "We have GenSeers to guide us, you have Seers and Oracles. They are your eyes."

"Exactly!"

As the two continued their conversation, the details played over Thalamas like molasses, burying his concerns in Tanian doubletalk. He left the office in a muddled state, convinced all would be okay, and that Borosh (and perhaps all the Tanian delegation on Ikara) had Volst's best interests at heart.

When the door closed behind Thalamas, Borosh let out a heavy sigh and clicked a button to send a message that would solve all his problems in one sentence. However, it was one more weight to prey heavily upon his soul.

"Security Chief Lort, please add Thalamas Voort to the non-sequencer list…Yes, that is correct. His will, indeed, be a one-way trip."

"Acknowledged, Administrator."

Tark

Tark tacitly refused Borosh's offers. He knew that Borosh saw him as a potential resource that the Tanians could use, and the offer did sound quite generous. It was a chance to journey the stars. But ever did he remind himself of the Tanians' true nature, and used such entreaties to keep Borosh's gaze away from the ISP, which still appeared to limit its research probes to the climate, as commanded by the Tanians. And the real work was done in secret. Along an Elmanith coastline, under cover of nearly constant storm fronts, Mission Five would come to completion with Tark as its leader.

He was leader of more than just the Mission now, because he

headed a new movement to reach for Azur (even under the watchful eye of the Tanians). He'd thought himself betrayed by his cousin Simoth when another had been selected for Mission Four, but now he knew the real reason. His destiny lay in carving a real foothold upon Azur ground, one to which other Ikarans would know to flock. It had always fallen to Kartha to supply the world's adventurers and leaders, and Tark was the Karthan chosen for this Cycle. The Tanians held out an offer to see the stars via their own well-worn and civilized pathways, while the Mission to Azur would be one fraught with dangers and unknowns. In the heart of a true Karthan, there could be only one decision to make.

Tark had the heart of a true Karthan.

As the launch date approached, Tark made more changes to the flight crew, changes that Jast's hidden hand made sure to see through. To some, it seemed that he was all but gutting the ISP of its greatest minds for just a single, extended mission. It was enough to make even his cousin frustrated.

With much on his mind, Simoth caught up with him the day before the launch. He literally had his hands full, carrying the departure protocols for the return flight in one hand, and the orbital mission plan that would guide the Mission to the Azurian landing site in the other. Both piles were a mixture of paper and lumen pads; so rapid had technology been developing that some engineers still wrote their calculations on paper, while others used lumen pads to enter their data and draw their diagrams. He climbed the gantry to the place where Tark was physically overseeing the installation of the last of the heat shields on the leading edge of the craft. It was menial work, and others could have achieved the same result. However, it was Tark's craft and, in the Commander's mind, his responsibility.

The stress was wearing on Simoth's face as Tark finally turned away from the work to behold his cousin. Simoth looked angry and on the brink of giving up. Amidst the cacophony of machinery, cargo transports, and screaming personnel, Simoth had to shout for Tark to even hear him over the din.

"Tark, you can't keep doing this! You took Ardeth and Barryl from the return mission complement, but they were also working on the orbitals for your arrival. At this rate, I may be able to get you to Azur, but unless I have more time or more of my personnel back, I can't guarantee we can get you home."

This information was the one part of Jast's plan that Simoth had not yet been privy to. Looking down at the papers held in Simoth's hands, Tark replied by slapping one stack of forms out of his cousin's hands, so the return-mission papers were now flying off the end of the vessel's nose. Simoth feebly tried to intercept the falling paper, only to make matters worse by splaying the notes and calculations out over a wider expanse. He stared after them with a look of futile desperation and a bit of anger at Tark. Like a mass of leaves liberated from a high branch, the papers drifted away, torn and shredded as they flew across the path of an active welder or spinning piece of machinery.

Simoth turned a rage-filled face to his cousin, ready to tear into him with angry words once he found his tongue, but Tark only looked on, calmly nodded, and turned back to his work. Only then did Tark say something, but with all the noise, Simoth wasn't sure if he heard right.

"We won't be coming back; Azur will be our home."

Simoth

"The rioting's getting worse," Simoth said by way of greeting as the other came out from the shadows. "Food shortages have become the norm of late."

Jast stepped up to him with a thoughtful nod as Simoth continued.

"It's all the changes in the weather. Between the tidal forces all over the place and the orbits of the two moons past any logical sort of prediction, it's playing havoc with the shipping trade. Add in the increase of complex salts and heavy metals being measured in the oceans and the mass die-offs it's causing in fish populations, and it's not looking pretty. Is there anything in your grand plan to account for all *that?*"

They were in the Catacombs, the one place where they could talk without fear of Tanian ears overhearing. Openly, bluntly.

"Yes," Jast replied, "getting as many people as we can off Ikara without the Takers finding out."

"And is that going to be starting with Mission Five?" To this question, Jast but raised an eyebrow, to which Simoth gave reply.

"I spoke with Tark. He sounds like he doesn't intend on coming back. Is that true? Am I to never see my cousin again?"

Jast paused for a moment, strolling about for a few steps before turning back around to face Simoth. Despite their differences, Simoth had become one of his greatest supporters. From the look on his face, all he wanted was a straight answer, and he deserved one.

"Every migration needs its first foothold," Jast told him. "Tark will be a true Karth Kessai, and for reasons we both know well, Mission Five will eventually be declared as lost. But, as far as not seeing him again…there is Mission Seven."

"Yes, the great Slumberer," Simoth nodded. "Are you implying then that I am to be on that ship when it leaves?"

"As much as Tark has a talent for leadership, your strength lies in logic and technology. Simoth, when the time comes, I want you to be the Mission Seven Science Officer. In your spare time, familiarize yourself with the *Slumberer's* navigation systems and sensors as much as you can, for when the time comes I suspect we'll all be in a bit of a rush."

"Agreed," Simoth nodded, "but who will then be the mission Commander? Tark was our best choice but he leaves with Mission Five in the morning."

"I've decided it will be one of my two grandsons: Dantu or Micah."

"Elmanith?" Simoth exclaimed. "With all due respect, it should be a Karthan who leads the way, as it has always been."

"They are still the best qualified. Don't worry, none of this need be announced until the time is upon us to awaken the *Slumberer*. I've not even told either of my grandsons; that will be your job when all is in readiness."

"Very well," Simoth sighed reluctance, "but there will be a lot of debate about the choice."

"Against which you will show a firm authoritative hand and a diplomatic face," Jast assured him. "If I did not have faith in your abilities then we would not be down here talking."

"I thank you for the vote of confidence," Simoth said, managing an insincere grin. "Now, if there's nothing more, I have a lot of work to get to."

With a final nod of the head and shake of the hands, Simoth turned away. As he started to walk down the tunnel, Jast heard him give one last remark.

"I'm going to miss Tark."

Launch

Ironically, the violent weather worked to the benefit of the Mission. Launched amidst a torrential storm of rusty-colored winds and never-ending lightning, the huge craft went completely unnoticed, even by the Tanians. (Perhaps it had something to do with their unknown Tanian sympathizer.) However, that same benefit also made it harder to track the progress of the Mission, or even be certain that it had landed.

"Contact lost," one technician reported.

"Last known trajectory," Simoth immediately snapped.

"From what little I can tell," the same technician replied, "they were headed straight for Azur, but...the angle looked a bit too steep. They were headed straight into the Azurian atmosphere. I couldn't tell you what happened after that, there's just too much interference on this end."

"See if you can bounce a signal off the Taker ship if you have to," Simoth snarled, "but just get me *some* sort of contact. That's my cousin out there."

"Yes, sir."

Simoth was just about to confer with another couple of technicians about ideas when Jast pulled him aside for a quiet discussion.

"Jast," Simoth started, "I think if we try to look for signs of their entry-trail then we might-"

"Simoth," Jast said in a quiet whisper, "the mission was lost."

"It may not have been," Simoth shook his head. "As I was saying, we might be able to pick them up if we-"

"No, you don't understand," Jast corrected him, "Mission Five is *lost,* broken upon contact with Azur's atmosphere."

"I don't think so," Simoth objected, "their angle of entry might have been just enough to…"

It took him a moment. However, comprehension dawned on Simoth's face as he realized what Jast was saying.

"I see…You know, there will be tears. And accusations."

"That is something I can handle," Jast told him. "It is best this way. For now, the loss of Mission Five was a horrible tragedy."

So Mission Five was recorded as a complete loss, but while some families mourned and others shot recriminations back and forth, Jast's main interest still lay skyward. He kept a telescope (secreted away on his own private property) aimed at Azur.

A few nights later, while Jast had his eyes peeled through the telescope, he saw it: a series of flares, barely bright enough to be picked out from this distance. To the uninitiated, it could have been anything from a forest fire to a volcano. Jast immediately brought Bellelorn over to his side to share the view. Neither said a single word. They just watched in silence through the eyepiece, smiles carefully spreading across their faces as the lights continued throughout the night.

One flare remained lit for a while, then dimmed back down, followed by another flare and another. After the third flare, a far longer pause was followed by another flare, and so on. So slow was the pace of the flares that it took a full hour before Ikara's rotation spun Azur out of view, but in that time, they'd seen enough.

It was a sequence of numbers. Both smiled, but neither said a word, as potential Tanian ears could overhear. The sequence began with three long pulses, followed by a pause, then one, then four, one, five, nine, two, and six.

Chapter Five:

Agora

"Tensions have never been higher," Amishari sighed. "Borosh really should have sent for a First Contact specialist the moment an indigenous population was discovered."

She sat at Borosh's desk—now *her* desk—going through the reports and other files left by her predecessor. Sitting opposite her was her new male assistant, taking notes on a lumen pad. They communicated in their usual silent, psychic way, though her tired sigh was audible.

"It looks like Borosh had a little project going," Amishari remarked as she went through the files. "Something to make the Ikarans more open to Tanian ways. Something about an Agora?"

"A reference to something out of their Grand Cycle," the assistant explained, "based on some interrogations with the ones stationed here."

"The Volst Oversight Team, yes I remember. Well, according to this, Borosh started a project designed to accelerate Ikaran mental skills along a pathway that would make them more amenable to our ways and give them a taste of true psychic sharing."

"The intent is to supply the first step to lead them into the Tanian way of thinking," the assistant filled in. "The Volst population is to be the test bed. If we can guide them into assisting us here, then we can perhaps use them as a workforce to exploit the larger blue planet in time."

"According to this he's already been giving them first access to anything we feed to the Ikarans, a policy that bolsters their sense of being chosen and has been contributing to keeping their various factions at one another's throats."

"Former Administrator Borosh thought that was the best way

to handle-"

"Yes, I was there," Amishari reminded the other with a sour look, then resumed her study of the files before her. "Apparently our engineers have found the inner workings of the Ikaran mind rather alien but they believe they have a good, first generation device ready to release."

"It is scheduled to be released to the Volst shortly," the other said after a quick glance at his lumen pad. "Do you wish me to confirm the release date?"

"Yes," Amishari said absently as she studied her screen. "Have our new toy released to-"

One file in particular suddenly caught her attention, an old file that predated the official first contact with the primitive vessel in orbit. It concerned a name she already knew was connected with the Ikaran attempt at a primitive space program, but this file suggested more behind this attempt than she realized. A lot more.

"-an Ikaran named Jast..." she mentally muttered to herself. She looked into his file some more, then called up a quick search of Ikaran activity that'd been observed over the past several tallas, specifically anything with the name Jast Rathael attached to it. As she quickly read, her head began moving in an almost imperceptible nod of approval.

"One change to policy," she finally said to her assistant. "Volst is no longer getting first pick. Send a message to the leader of the Whycheral faction. A First Speaker Jast Rathael, if these files are correct. Give him a few samples of this new 'Agorabox', as well as the plans on how to make them."

"Administrator? The plans as well? Even with the Volst-"

"Merely streamlining things. The Ikarans will get hooked on these devices, make their own versions to spread through the population more quickly, fulfilling Borosh's initial objective of bringing the local population into our fold – and all at their own expense. Now just see to it!"

"Yes, Administrator."

Of course, Amishari thought to herself, *if the undercurrent of these interrogation files is correct, there will be another effect no one will see coming. Then perhaps...*

"What's next on the agenda," Amishari said, snapping back to the present business. "How's the production schedule going?"

"Well ahead of schedule, Administrator. We have nearly thirteen hundred days left of primary operations. That is why Borosh felt he had the time to try and convert the local population and train them into being a passable workforce."

"Yes, I saw that mentioned in one of these files...here it is."

Amishari quickly glanced at the new file, but now saw something her previous brief examination had missed. The more she read, the colder her body grew.

"He...he changed the orders," she said in near silence. "Command already has it arranged. They aren't to be workers, they're to be-"

She stopped right there, afraid to say anything or to be seen (even by her assistant) with trembling hands. It took an act of will to contain herself and replace her features with those of an impassive Administrator.

"Administrator?"

"Nothing," she said, snapping back to her efficient guise. "Just see that the distribution of the Agorabox is performed as discussed, on schedule. And from now on, no more favoritism to the Volst; everyone gets things at the same time."

"That won't gain you any popularity with them, you realize."

"Not my concern at the moment," she stated. "That is all; you are dismissed."

The assistant gave a nod as he rose to his feet, then turned and left. Amishari didn't allow herself to react until he was out of the room, and the door had slid closed behind him. Her hands shook. Her breath was close to sobbing gasps, and she lowered her eyes, afraid to face the report on the screen again.

"Millions of Volst lives as so much biomass," she finally said, this time out loud in a near sob, "and I'm powerless to stop it. Maybe this Agorabox, but…this just can't go on. Not anymore."

As the tears ran down her face, she flashed back to a time long ago—a time when her own world had been in a similar situation. It was oh-so-many long centuries ago, though it still ran fresh in her memory, flashing through her mind's eye every time she rested.

She'd been a young science student when the Tanians arrived with their offers of knowledge, in exchange for what they could mine from the depths of their world's oceans. A world larger and more populous than Ikara. A world whose connection with her past had been long since forgotten, carefully erased over the tallas by her own actions.

A world called Nimbusi.

It had been a beautiful world, one with two moons, which the people were just beginning to explore with their nascent space program. The Tanian ship had looked massive to them as it arrived. They sent the ship radio messages, but it offered nothing more than automated replies. It was a probe, though a very large one. Amishari herself had been among those riveted to the public viewing screens, watching the live videos as the ship descended through their atmosphere like some majestic beast.

One of their defense crafts had performed flybys, hoping to tease out some sort of reaction. They even launched out a small missile to get the ship's attention. It worked. The entire world witnessed the ship suddenly transform into a speeding ball of flame. After that, the automated message changed.

"Please make no more approach to this vessel. You will be contacted by Tanian representatives after landing has been established."

It was the very first vessel from another world that anyone had seen, and they'd already started off on the wrong foot. The world's officials worried that if this probe was merely a sample of a larger fleet, they'd just angered something best left undisturbed. However, they couldn't just sit around while this megalith-looking cruiser came in unchallenged. So they watched it and tracked its course, and when it landed on a remote island, it was soon surrounded by half of the world's navies. The best of the world's scientists were quickly gathered to study these new visitors, but when this Contact Team failed to have more than a glimmer of an explanation about how the craft had crossed the stars, they expanded their query to anyone with a bright idea.

At the time, Amishari was just finishing her studies, her marks being the highest in her class and possibly in the university's history. Therefore, it was perhaps inevitable that she found herself onboard one of the ships with others of the Contact Team—watching, observing, looking for the least little sign of activity. She was there to see the craft's automated devices construct something that no one there had a clue about, and she remained curious and persistent. She worked her own instruments, which told her about every last magnetic flux the ship had produced prior to its activation. Then she came before her team leader and the Fleet Commander with an idea that had everyone else smirking or outright laughing.

"It's a wormhole generator."

"Amishari, I know you're a very bright young girl, but-"

"You watch," she'd insisted. "When that thing activates, there'll be people walking out through it."

There was much ridicule, but as soon as the Bridge was activated, the mocking stopped. The sensor readings of its energy were now completely off their charts, and a line of beings marched out through the resulting black globe. More respectful gazes now regarded her, and she quickly found herself first off the ornithopter when it landed on the beach to greet the newly arrived aliens. The rest of the team stood beside her.

In appearance, the aliens weren't unlike her own people, and upon seeing her at the front of the group, they assumed that she was the team leader—something her superiors decided not to contradict.

The offer had been simple: the Tanians would give the locals all the technological knowledge they could want, and in exchange, the

Tanians would be allowed to mine the depths of this world's oceans. Nothing the locals would miss, or were even be able to get to, as the mineral wealth was buried so deep beneath the water. If they had any questions, they could ask through one of their own people, which they'd elect as a representative. By virtue of her proven brilliance and their choice to let her walk out of the thopter first, Amishari had been chosen to fill that role.

As a result, she got to experience firsthand all the marvels of Tanian science. She was there as they built their mining devices more than a mile below the surface of the ocean, where no Nimbusian craft could ever hope to go. She watched them funnel all the ore they extracted straight through their Bridge, and she examined what she'd been shown until she was satisfied. Then she was whisked around on a tour of other Tanian wonders. The gifts the Tanians had given them seemed wondrous, and soon, everyone wanted more. Then she had the pleasure of announcing that the Tanians would recruit some of the population to accompany them through their Bridge to the stars, to help explore other worlds.

Amishari was the first to sign up.

The news spread quickly, and soon, everyone was demanding to be amongst those chosen. Fights broke out between factions struggling to be seen as the most worthy, and riots becoming increasingly commonplace. It became her job to assure the public that all would be given a fair chance. She turned out to be quite good in her role, so good in fact that she was the first one the Tanians made their offer to. When the mining operations were finished, she'd accompany the Tanian staff through the Bridge as one of their own.

She was overjoyed. A chance to walk the stars! Naturally, she agreed, and from there, she was given more access than she should have ever been allowed. She was even given her own Tanian flitter. The first time she was allowed to fly it by herself, she did what seemed natural: she went on a joyride. Just a short one. The craft could go to either of their moons and back in an afternoon, whereas anything her own people could create would take days.

That was how she discovered the Tanian's mining operations on the far sides of both moons. They were massive operations that looked like they could nearly hollow either moon out. Concerns were expressed, and reassurances given. However, she began to have greater suspicions. As Nimbusi began to experience a drastic increase in climate problems, she looked more carefully into the ocean mining, and that's when she discovered the horrible truth.

The Tanians weren't simply mining what could be found beneath the ocean's depths, but straight to the very core of their world! Therefore, Amishari discreetly alerted her world's authorities about what was going on, and from there, events exploded.

She was on the Tanian vessel when the attack came. Missiles launched from her world's military, and ships at sea began a constant barrage. Amishari thought that she might die along with the Tanians, and rightly so. Hadn't it been her own voice that'd prevented her people from more carefully looking into what these aliens had been doing? She was ready and willing to die if that'd mean an end to this Tanian threat.

It was not to be, however, for the same technology that can reign in the vast energies of the Bridge is more than capable of producing a protective force field, which is even able to easily keep out a barrage of nuclear weapons. After that, the Tanians launched a few of their own fighter crafts. Not many, but more than enough to handle the naval forces that had surrounded the island. After that, the script was clearly written.

After strike and counterstrike, the Tanians were forced to eliminate the world's military, but when that did nothing to quell the local populace, they proceeded to eradicate much of the world's population as well. She was there to watch it all, too afraid to do anything. She hoped to possibly use her position with the Tanians to stop them, but that was how the killing had started in the first place.

When the remains of the world's population let go of their fight and behaved like the cowed sheep they'd become, the Tanians finished their mining operations. However, the Administrator in charge of this operation voiced his displeasure:

"Does anyone *know* how much we've had to expend in personnel and materials for this little war? Every craft we've had to bring through the Bridge has cut deep into our profits, and then there's the effects of the war itself. All the radiation has polluted much of the rare earths and other minerals, making it *useless*. And it will all be too costly to clean up, leaving us unable to fully mine this world. Why, we'll be lucky if we even— Amishari, what's our profit projection look like?"

So closely did her kind resemble Tanians, and so much had she been around them by this point, that most of the Tanians had begun to think of her as one of their own. She'd been learning their ways, and her race was already psychic enough to communicate as the Tanians did. That was why they'd hoped to sway some of the population to the Tanian way of thinking; their psychic aptitudes would make them easy to employ.

"There is," Amishari said, wetting her lips then continuing telepathically, "a negative profit margin. According to projections, there's not enough to even pay for the energy expenditure of the Bridge."

"First the bloodbath and now *this*," the Administrator had fumed. "This is a disaster! Okay, we're cutting our losses and closing up now."

"Sir," Amishari hesitantly broke in, "the... local population will not survive another year between the radiation levels and the violent weather. In addition to the current conditions, it is projected that one of the moons will spiral into the planet as a result of over-mining."

"Not my concern! We're pulling everything out. Amishari, you have a choice: either stay and die with your people or join us out in the stars. You have the potential to be a good Administrator someday."

For a second, she considered staying, but that led only to certain death. She knew what these aliens had done, and no doubt would continue to do on other worlds. Going with them gave her a chance at life, a chance to await revenge.

"The…the Tanians are my people, Administraor," she said after a hesitant pause.

"Good girl," the Administrator briskly replied. "Someone get her a full medical work up. Now let's get off this rock. I've got to think of how to slant my report so none of us are to blame, myself in particular."

Many tallas later, another Tanian probe passed through that star system, sent to see if the radiation level had reduced enough to make mining operations possible once again. Amishari had seen the footage from that probe. The one moon had indeed crashed into the world of Nimbusi, blowing the cap off the old mile-wide drill hole left at the bottom of the ocean. Between the seawater rushing straight down towards the core and the impact on the moon itself, the devastation was inescapable.

Amishari was the last living being from Nimbusi.

Since leaving her world, Amishari's rise in the ranks had been gradual and methodical—with the intent of awaiting any opportunity to bring the Tanians down. She never forgot her Nimbusian birth world, but as the centuries stretched on, her hope for stopping the Tanians began to wane. Nevertheless, her hatred of them remained strong. She became quite skilled at blending in, and soon, only a very few (such as Administrator Borosh) were even aware that she wasn't Tanian. However, even he didn't know about her Nimbusian origins. No one did; she'd made certain of that.

In the seclusion of her own office, now a full Administrator with a project of her own, she was *finally* able to cry. By the time she actually left her office, though, any sign of tears and reddened eyes had long since been removed, and her features were once again those of the efficient Administrator, just as they had been when she was Borosh's assistant.

"Masters and Mistresses of the Elmanith Family Academy,

esteemed officials, and honored guests. Welcome, welcome I say! I am Baern Knobbre, honorary headmaster, and I welcome you to the Grand Cycle's annual Mustering of the Cadre! I am honored to be this talla's Speaker, in lieu of our National Speaker, Helm Rathael, who once again is kept from us by his duties. I invite you all to stand for the presentation of the Panoply!"

He looked small behind the Speaker's Stone. Baern, a pale and aging Ikaran, was dressed in a maroon robe with gold trim and a matching gold sash overtop, which indicated his importance in the Academy. He'd been a GenSeer in his youth and served as chief herald for the Elmanith family for decades. However, tragedy struck when a cavein on the shoulder of the Great Mountain crushed his skull and nearly killed him, depriving him of the Gift of Sight and leaving him half blind in one eye. This event had saved him from the call to suicide, which had struck many a GenSeer in times long since past. It was poetic that the person who'd initiated the search for those students most worthy was himself a blind man.

As the well-rehearsed orchestra, full of brass and percussion, began to play the Elmanith Anthem, the Five Banners were presented by reverent and resolute marchers, all held slightly lower than that of the host Family, Elmanith.

The first into the amphitheater-like Muster Field was the furthest away physically. The primary color of the banner of the Isle of Karth was the same hue as the blacks of their eyes, and the stylized Staff of Kartha, an emblem representing their constant search. Following it were the three students who'd applied for the Elmanith Muster.

Next came the steel-gray banner that matched the excavator family of Volst, which bore the unmistakable four prospects gazing in wonder from the shoulder of the Great Mountain at the verdant liveliness of the Elmanith capital city.

The banner of Whycheral was next. The green eyes of the ten delegated scholars who were hoping to be chosen reflected in the solid background of their emblem, the life-giving Tree of Albans (a legendary source of all edible foods).

Nathor's children were the last of the applicants by lottery. They carried with them their dark-umber banner, the brown of the soil reflecting in their soulful eyes. Upon their banner was the Phos: an emblem of the unquenched Koru, which blessed or cursed their efforts in the field.

Representing their magnanimity as host, the Elmanith contingency were the final to enter the ground, their banner held more upright. The deep, rich blue of their banner reflected in the dozens of cerulean eyes that looked upon it with such pride. The emblem borne upon it was the Chron: the shining silver symbol of the unending cycle of Ikaran culture.

When all the banners had reached their places along the outer ring of the Muster Field, their bearers brought their banners to a perpendicular position. The only movement on the field was that of the banners themselves, fluttering about in a slight breeze that whispered to the applicants. For a single moment, there was silence. Then they hoisted the banners to their full height, and in honor of the whole of the Ikaran People, the poles holding them moved forward with slow reverence towards the center—stopping once they'd reached a 45-degree angle.

Baern Knobbre, his voice clear and direct, continued his speech to the assembly:

"The Muster has long been a tradition in this Academy's history. Long ago, the GenSeers would determine a young child's potential aptitudes, but since then the Vorscht aptitude battery has become the standard to determine early in a child's life his genetic aptitude, historic placement, and career predilections. It is rare for a child to have but one choice. Far more likely they have eligibilities beyond their station. When possible, the student trains at home or with family counselors known as Advocates. However, in cases where the aptitude is particularly high, but the family is not of a privileged class or cannot afford to employ an Advocate, the student can create a profile and submit it for the particular Family's Academy Muster."

"With the Muster," he continued, *"any* Ikaran can pursue a

159

career, even beyond their personal aptitude. The Muster has long been the most equitable way to choose the best for each career in each of the Families. The Lottery was created after the discovery of emlash as a means to get the best of all possible minds together, in order to maximize the benefits of such technological advancements as quickly as possible. With this very program, the Five Families sought to each consolidate their own national identity, but it has since become a means of which those with a penchant for a particular career may cross international lines, moving from one Family's allegiance to another, and thereby promoting geopolitical cross-pollination without jeopardizing national sovereignty."

"And yet, one stigma was still attached to these under-represented families—those whom we call 'Unders' in short—and that was in the area of training and integration. Family Advocates are assigned to those whose background suits the Family, namely, their own descendants, while the Unders have to wait to be assimilated through their particular Field Advocates to choose to represent them. This is generally only done when an Under provides overwhelming evidence that doing so would improve their standing. No Field Advocate will endure a student who fails the transition, for such would destroy the validity of that Field Advocate forever. Thus they need to closely vet their prospects, which brings us to the drama and spectacle that is Muster Day."

He went on to speak of Family and National and Global Pride, but at least one of the attendees was paying more attention to one of the Nathorn Candidates. Micah was leaning against a banister in the stands above, dressed in pristine school-day brilliance: pale-blue trousers and amber tunic embellished with the Elmanith crest in spun silver on the lapels and right breast, and counterpointed with the deep-blue science sash and matching boots. He was cut from the family cloth and clearly looked the part, but right now, he was more interested in trying to get a better look at a brown-haired young woman. He grinned madly any time she happened to glance in his general direction—as if by doing so, he'd gain her attention from the midst of all around the stadium. He was only dimly aware of the speech finishing, and Baern asking the attendees, guests, and participants to stand and sing the Ikaran Anthem. Micah joined in, singing as proudly as any Ikaran, but he still had his gaze focused on the one below.

The Anthem resounded across the stadium, hundreds of faces unabashedly displaying the pride they felt with every word:

"From the dawn of the first morn.
Ikara! Ikara! Ikara!
Until the death of those last born.
Ikara! Ikara! Ikara!
We keep the pacts others have sworn.
Ikara! Ikara! Ikara!
And mend the wounds that time has torn.
Ikara, our voices praise! Ikara, our banners raise!
Though Koru will burn, the Cycle will turn, we will remain, and
we will learn."

When the last echoes of the refrain passed into silence, the Speaker returned to the lectern, looking down now at the circle of candidates and Advocates. The questioning of the Unders by the Field Advocates began, while the Elite and the representatives of the Five Families shuffled into the Academy building to get an early pick on their prospective seats, lockers, and beds. The Advocates walked from one Under to another—asking their questions and dismissing some based on their responses, while passing others by.

So focused was he, though, on the one girl that Micah was nearly knocked off his feet from the light bump against his shoulder when someone passed by. Upon turning, he discovered it to be his brother Dantu, wearing the Honors colors, his own tunic and jerkin of the same colors as his brother, but adorned with counterpointed blue and gold epaulets. And his sash had been replaced with the decorative gold chord of a Scholar.

"Dantu!" Micah gasped, greeting his brother with a firm clasp of hands. "Slumming around us undergrads?"

"You'll be wearing this braid too, in a few months," Dantu said, fingering the chord. "I see you're checking out the new candidates… or is it just one of them in particular that catches your eye?"

"The Nathorn in the beige and forest jumpsuit," Micah admitted with a nod of his head in the direction of the brown-haired young woman. "So far four different Advocates have questioned her and none have dismissed her."

That dark-haired little waif? Are you really sure she's your type? Looks a bit scrawny and ill-fed."

"Scrawny?" Micah protested. "Why, she's beautiful and brilliant. I don't see how you could call her-"

Then he saw the smirk on Dantu's face and relinquished with a light jab to his brother's shoulder.

"Her name's Aleka Nadiri and she's the top candidate from Nathor," Dantu said with a light chuckle. "The Downs quarters nearest the Stormwall. She transferred in via the Outland Lottery, the only student down there to do so this talla."

"You certainly seem to know a good deal about her, Dantu. She catch your eye as well?"

"I checked through all the incoming candidates," Dantu shrugged. "When I saw her profile, I made a bet with father that she'd catch your eye. Now he owes me a drink."

"Well, I'll admit, she's certainly caught *my* eye. Anybody here with her? Maybe I can start up a conversation with them and get them to introduce me."

"Her family's too poor to make the trip in," Dantu replied with a shake of his head. "She's got no-one to cheer her on."

"Well, she does now," Micah grinned, and with that called out to the assembly below. "Come on, Aleka, you can do it!"

Aleka was fidgeting and a little nervous, but still determined. Amidst a sea of Elmanith blue, she wore the only Nathorn earthen tones. She was fierce in her answers, and yet polite—as if her real purpose wasn't to be chosen, but to beat her inquisitors at their own game. Micah watched, entranced with her performance as one candidate after another was dropped, whittling the gathering down to half a dozen good candidates, of which Aleka was still one.

The number of eligible candidates was fewer than in past tallas, due to a combination of reasons, all of them political. In its reconfiguration to look into the possible causes of the recent global climatic shifts, the ISP recommended radical limitations on population growth and corporate advances, while the finger-pointing of one Nation at another had undermined the stability and trust between them all. The collective result of all of these complications was that fewer candidates could apply and make it through Muster.

"They're down to the final ones," Micah whispered excitedly to his brother. "One wrong answer means instant dismissal."

What had started with 24 Unders was now reduced to five, with four Advocates yet undecided. Any wrong answer would leave the field limited, and the pecking order among the Advocates would be determined by the first to flinch. The first to decide on an Under would in effect be the loser, for the best candidate would be the last one chosen. The observers in the stadium were quickly placing bets back and forth as to who would be the last to be chosen, and none of those bets were in favor of Aleka. Except one.

"Dantu, I'll bet you a drink that Aleka makes First Under."

"Hmm, between you and father that will make *two* drinks I'm owed," Dantu grinned. "You're on."

As they turned back to the action, two of the Field Advocates walked to the edge of the field, conferring. Such direct interaction was rare, and from the tense looks of the watching crowds, everyone was well aware of this fact. Finally, one of them relented and made a declaration.

The last Under to be disqualified had been identified. With that choice, just four remained, which fundamentally meant that all the remaining Unders would be joining the class. A shout of acclamation arose, most excitedly from Micah, as he saw that the dark-haired Nathorn girl was amongst the four. In fact, two of the Field Advocates were now facing her and snapping off questions in

163

rapid-fire succession.

"Out of all the planets in our system, which one turns against the Cycle?"

"Varisa," Aleka answered.

"From where did the burning men hail?"

"The unknown star."

"What else comes from the same point of origin?"

"The soul of all Ikarans."

"What powers the magnetic field of Ikara?"

"Ikarans themselves"

"Who brought the staff of Ikara to our planet and what was it called in its previous existence?"

"The Azurites, the Tree of Life."

The questions were amplified through the address system for the benefit of the onlookers, but the responses were not. This process took place so the applicants wouldn't embarrass themselves any more than they had by missing it. Yet Aleka spoke with a brilliance and discipline that seemed to amplify her answers anyway, and made the Field Advocates seem like the novices, instead of her.

A hand went up among the four remaining Judges. Fallon, Field Advocate of the Eastern Synod, had made his choice. Adapanth, the last of the Unders from Whycheral, was accepted. Now three remained, but for only a moment. The remainders fell in rapid succession: Granick of Kartha, Ballan from nearby Volst, and finally Aleka of Nathor. All were added to the scroll, and the Muster was complete.

Aleka had been chosen last, making her 'First of the Unders.' With that decision, she'd be the first among them to be honored with the Elmanith colors. She'd still be Nathorn until graduation, but once she left the Academy, her Family would forever be those of the Blue Eyes.

"Yes!" Micah cheered. "She made it! You owe me a drink, Dantu."

"A debt I will gladly pay," Dantu grinned. "Now all you have to do is convince *her* that you actually have something going for you."

"Watch me," Micah grinned. "While you're busy flitting around in space, I'll be introducing myself to the future mother of my children." They parted with a hug and mutual wishing of good luck. Then Micah swiftly walked down to meet the girl and tell her that, yes, he was that one crazy person up in the stands cheering her on.

Not long after, Micah transferred to Soils Analysis to see if an examination of storm-impacted soils might reveal where his theories had erred in his biomedical atmospherics courses. When he went on his field trips to collect samples of the iron-dusted fields from recent windstorms, it'd be Aleka who would attend as his field research assistant, asking him more questions than his professors would and relentlessly challenging his theories.

But then, that was one of the things liked most about Aleka.

Jast

The new Administrator was a complete unknown to Jast. He'd seen her beside Borosh on public appearances, but knew nothing else. Borosh hadn't exactly been an ally, but he hadn't been an outright enemy either (at least not all the time). It was more like the Tanian was walking a precarious balance, and on several occasions, Jast would make use of that balance for one small concession or another. Now, with the atmospheric concerns becoming too great for anyone to hide and the increasing ferocity of groundquakes, the Tanians seemed to be back-pedaling, looking for loopholes, and trying to reduce their footprint in Ikaran politics and economics.

To make matters worse, Borosh was now retiring, and this one before him was the new face of the Tanians. How would she react to what few concessions Jast had managed to get? How would she compare? Jast was ready for the fight ahead of him. With everything that was happening, there was little room for easy diplomacy or blatant sandbagging. To make any serious headway, he was going to have to be brutally honest, and perhaps even a bit rough on the new diplomat.

She'd chosen to meet with Jast at a small home he maintained in Volst, a place away from the prying eyes and ears of the general populace. He'd been in Volst anyway, looking over some things at the launch facility, so he thought it a mere convenience. However, considering the seclusion of this location, he wondered if the new Administrator desired more than his own personal convenience. As she entered his office, she stood in the doorway for a moment—not saying a thing, just staring at him. As if, by force of will alone, she'd communicate or draft him into silence. Jast didn't say a word, but used the opportunity to do his own sizing up.

She was slightly taller than her predecessor, while the pale Tanian's large and patient eyes were a severe shade of blue, rivaling those of Jast himself for the purest form of Elmanith's shade. Pale, thin, wiry hair (unlike that of the other Tanians) cascaded down over her shoulders, ending near the middle of her back. A pale blush powder tempered her pallid flesh, leaving her severe features slightly more palatable. To Jast, she looked fair enough, despite her height, which set her apart—her eyes easily looking over his head as she approached. She wore a dark jumpsuit that seemed to be the uniform of the Tanians, but around her throat wore a surprising Nathorn-style scarf, twisted and tied in the style of the Matrons and Sisters of Solace. She'd clearly done her homework and was familiar with the rise of House Rathael.

She carried a small satchel, which she now set down on the floor. Still not talking, she reached in and pulled out a small metal orb, which she then slapped to the side of the doorway through which she'd entered. It stuck to the stone and immediately emitted a high-pitched whine, which warbled like a bird. It wasn't loud, and Jast noticed that the running light on the camcorder he kept fixed to the ceiling suddenly winked off. She closed the door behind herself and slid the lock shut.

Something was amiss. She was more than simply a standard replacement for Borosh, but what was her goal? She picked up her satchel and made her way across the room, offering her free hand to Jast.

"I am Amishari Kael, new Administrator sent to conclude Tanian operations on your world. In particular, I wish to do my utmost to prevent such atrocities as have visited this world from occurring in the future. I was made to believe that you might also wish this. Was I misled?"

Jast had never shaved or trimmed his beard in his life, so by now, it'd grown to quite a prodigious length. It was something he was very proud of, though not of how much it'd greyed over the tallas. Likewise, the hair falling down from his head had become exceedingly long, ending in curled locks—another proud accomplishment that even his worst detractors couldn't fault him for.

"I'm so sorry, but I don't actually follow you."

"No," she corrected, "it's pronounced Ah, Me, Sah, Ree."

"What?" With a shake of his head Jast realized the point of confusion. "No, I wasn't trying to butcher your name, I was apologizing for not understanding your point, why you're here."

"Oh," and for a moment her cold expression flickered with a trace of amusement, "I see. Verbalizations are still sometimes a little difficult for me."

"Then let us start over," Jast smiled, putting out his hand. "I am Jast Rathael, First Speaker of Whycheral. I hope your ride here wasn't too bumpy."

"Administrator Amishari Kael." She perfunctorily took his hand in a quick shake, then stepped over to the waiting table and put down her satchel. This time, she took out a lumen pad and flicked it on as she took a seat. Jast stepped over and sat down in his own chair, bracing himself for whatever might come next.

"I understand that you have been in contact with us since before your official first contact via Commander Tark."

"I was quite a bit younger when I was kidnapped," Jast admitted.

"A decision made by former Administrator Borosh," she replied, as she called something up on her tablet, "for which you have made out rather well, I see here. Extended life in exchange for getting your people into more of a mind to cooperate with us. You've kept quiet, maneuvered your people into approving the Accords, and even falsified some of the official data regards the nature of your world's climate change problems."

"I'm a good little stooge, if nothing else," Jast said, flashing a sarcastic grin.

"You also," she continued, "are apparently responsible for pushing the agenda of your space program to explore the world you call Azur, even after Borosh gave orders that you were to limit yourselves to planetary science only. You have apparently even been funding the ISP through various channels of your own and more recently, there was a small probe that crawled its way across the top of the mountain for a better look into our operations. I believe you had a hand in suggesting that operation to others."

"A probe?" Jast said innocently. "I have no idea what you mean."

"I'm sure you don't," she said with the same level cold stare.

"Administrator, if I may be frank, what exactly is your purpose for this meeting, other than getting acquainted with the local native chieftain? And what exactly is that device you slapped onto the doorframe? Pardon me for being blunt, but my world is literally disintegrating as we talk."

With a last frigid look, the cold front finally broke. Amishari let out a sigh and relaxed back into the chair, looking at Jast with more emotion in her features than she had ever shown when around Borosh.

"Forgive the theatrics but in terms of trust, my Tanian masters are not the great examples they wish to portray. In fact, my Security Chief operates rather independently and often under his *own* authority. My pulse generator has deactivated all recording and observation devices within four hundred cubits of us; this space will be secure for a time, so we should endeavor to become more transparent. I am not your friend but I am here to help you. In fact, I already have…by covering a few tracks."

Jast raised an eyebrow at this statement, immediately understanding what she meant. Before him was the unknown benefactor, which had hidden traces of some of their launches from collective Tanian eyes. But why? She was still somewhat reserved, but it was apparent to Jast that she was now seeking an ally, just as he was hoping to gain one in her. A possible ally within the Tanian ranks? That was the one thing he'd been missing.

"Your masters? You aren't Tanian? I did notice some differences."

"No, I am not of the Tanian core world, but I have depended on the close similarities and a good deal of subterfuge, to convince them that I am loyal to their cause. My presence is a testament to the lengths to which I will go to achieve my own goals. In truth, I am more like you than you might believe, for my world too was destroyed by them. The most disastrous operation on Tanian record, in fact, but not even Borosh knows that is the particular world of my birth."

Jast thought about that notion for a moment. He had to be cautious. This situation could be a trap, luring him into revealing what he was really about. If so, he might betray any chance he had to save what remained of the Ikaran people and avenge his world. He looked at her again, now in a different context. If she was speaking the truth, then her ruse with the Tanians was genius, but to have achieved what she had, there had to be more to the story. Though she'd hinted that there were some timing restraints, he pressed her.

"They wouldn't just nominate you for this kind of position, unless there is a lot more to the story. This is not just a task they leave to a survivor of planetary genocide lightly. What did…"

Amishari looked away, blinking back the true horrors she'd perpetrated to be here, but she also knew where his questions were heading. She needed to get him back on track.

"You are correct, but we haven't the time to point out the atrocities to which I have been witness. One world after another sucked dry, their inhabitants treated like so much cattle. Long have I wished for an opportunity to shut down such tyranny. Ikara is lost to you, but perhaps she can be avenged, a chance to stop this from happening to other worlds. The Tanians are not your friends, you know this, but perhaps, Master of Whycheral, Father of the First Speaker of Elmanith, and former Chairman of the Ikaran Space Program, we can speak of vengeance and justice. Are you ready to be blunt?"

"What did you have in mind?"

She relaxed a bit more when he said this, then ran a finger across her pad to call up something new to refer to.

"There is a legend you have of something called the Agora."

"A collective joining," Jast explained. "A state that the Cycle tells us we had achieved once before, where all Ikara are as one mind, one soul."

"That's as much as the people from Volst told Borosh when he interviewed them, but I believe there's something more. You see, Borosh had our technicians looking into creating a sort of Agorabox that would allow Ikarans to join together mentally much in the same way as Tanians speak mind to mind. His hope was that this would put you into more of a mind to be like the Tanians, to make you willing to work with them."

"The Agora as a form of mind control? That's not the way it works," Jast said with a shake of his head. "According to the ancient legends, in the Agora everyone can see the other's soul, know their true intentions. No one controls anyone else by the Agora, but they are influenced by the deep truth of what they experience."

"That's what I wanted to clear up," Amishari said, now a trace of a grin forming across her face. "As far as my reports to the Tanians are concerned, this Agorabox will be a last attempt to tame the Ikarans. But for the Ikarans-"

"It will be a chance to finally spread the truth," Jast realized, "free of any and all political subterfuge."

"*And* any Tanian observations. The brains of Ikarans are

170

different enough that once these devices are properly attuned to Ikarans, no Tanian psychic device will be able to eavesdrop on them. You will have total collective privacy to do with as you please."

"That would be…perfect," Jast said with a slow nod. "With something like that I could-"

"Please, stop right there," she insisted. "I wish to know only the minimum; just in case worst should come to worst. Know only that I have selected you and Whycheral to receive these devices first, as well as the instructions on how to make them, so that your technicians may better attune them to the Ikaran mind. You may then replicate and distribute them at your own judgment. What you then do with them afterwards, I can honestly say that I do not know. It's safer that way."

"Agreed. Then when should I expect the first shipment?"

"It's all in my flitter right now, along with files for some other technologies you may find useful in the future. Just remember that once we're out in the open-"

"I shall speak only as an appreciative local for these marvelous new toys," Jast completed for her.

Amishari stood up with a wide grin, which momentarily let the true beauty of her features slip past her icy facade. She put out her hand for Jast to take.

"Jast Rathael, I have been looking for someone like you for a very long time."

Jast stood up, taking her hand and replying in kind. "And I you."

When Jast returned to his living quarters, there was a message from Bellelorn. It seemed that the most recent storms had devastated a Nathorn village near her home, and she'd decided to personally tend to some part of the rescue. He flagged the message for response in the morning.

He retired with his mind full of the possibilities that Amishari had brought to the fore. Before his journey to Volst to meet with this alien, he'd believed that he'd almost lost his cause before it began. Now there was a glimmer of hope on the horizon, at least for some kind of satisfaction.

As for Amishari, she'd finally found the ally that she needed for a war, which had started 400 lightyears away and 30 millennia ago. A regime such as the Takers wouldn't be brought down in a generation or even a single system, but it would end here on Ikara. From there, it'd spread like falling dominos. She herself would see to it now that she had found the one man who wouldn't back down, the one man who wouldn't be corrupted by Tanian guile.

———————

Jast awoke on the convey headed back from Volst, and wanted nothing more than to spend some time going over his plans. Amishari, his newest ally, had revealed a path for redemption, and the options it now opened up had eased his sleep.

The convey was making good time across the semiarid Whycheral badlands, headed for the northern palace just across the Nathor border. Bellelorn couldn't justify living beyond the Nathor boundaries; she'd always felt that it was a betrayal of her people, and he would never take her from them.

Now that the strategy to liberate Ikara was possible, his mind began to spin the way it had when he was much younger. He could see a way for all his misdeeds to be remembered without judgment, for his actions to be interpreted in a new, more palatable light. This plan pleased the aging patriarch, and it was a justifiable reason to celebrate his return from Volst.

As they rolled along, he wondered about Bellelorn's success in aiding her people through weathering these toughening times. He hadn't heard back from her, and she was usually quite punctual. The storms had been getting worse, but looking out of the viewport, there was no sign of the adverse weather so common these days.

They'd arrived in Whycheral, his adopted home, though he'd been there so long that it seemed like he'd been born there. It was the center of power for the GenSeers of old. For half a Cycle, every major decision the world's leaders ever made had been filtered through the GenSeers. It wasn't until he'd manipulated the system for his own purposes that he saw the dangers of genetic memory. How could it be controlled by those beyond its borders? Candlefall had clearly illuminated how easy it'd been to misuse the GenSeers' power, as people came to them for both insight *and* approval. The very thought of the enormity of the GenSeers' influence now nauseated him.

There was nothing left of the way the Ikaran people had once been. But with the arrival of the new Administrator, he had an inkling of a strategy, a hint of a plan to bring his people back from the brink. He simply wished he could only ensure that the world wouldn't die before he enacted that plan. He would have to act swiftly. Even with Amishari helping him, the Tanians could be delayed, but not denied. All he could do now was mitigate the losses, and perhaps give the Grand Cycle a chance to correct its own path.

He'd already completed the ISP formation while there was still a Five Nations government to sanction it. He'd also orchestrated the appointment of Simoth Karth because he admired the Karthan's adventurer spirit and the cleverness with which he'd manipulated the ISP. Now, with these new Agoraboxes, perhaps the people could regain their freedoms and reach for the stars. After returning from Mission Three, Tark wasn't just excited about space travel itself, but about moving the whole of the Ikaran population to Azur. If Jast could just keep everything on target for Mission Seven and the *Slumberer*, then at least a portion of that dream just might come to fruition. But he had to keep up with the planetary research as well.

Micah, Jast thought to himself, *it has to be him. Micah is about to graduate from the Academy soon, then I can see that he is appointed as Elmanith Undersecretary of Transportation and Planetary Safety. That will put him in a perfect position to keep abreast of what's really happening with both Ikara and the Slumberer, then with that experience ease into the role of Captain of Mission Seven.* Yes, the planetary research is important, but not for the reasons that people think.

"What we learn of Ikara," he muttered quietly to himself, "we can then apply to Azur."

_____

Micah

Micah walked alongside a brown-haired young woman with a slight build and a brilliant intellect that sparkled out through her eyes. They were in an arid lot just outside the Elmanith Academy, each with a little trowel and small jars ready for the soil samples they were there to collect. They'd bend down to pack away a small sample, then walk to the next site—all the time talking, but not as mere friends. They each had a certain sparkle in their eyes, reserved for the other alone.

"I've always loved the Tellar season," Micah was saying, "with its flowers and brilliant green leaves."

"Me too," Aleka sighed. "It's just a pity that there's so little of it growing this season."

"It's the winds," Micah explained as he bent down to scoop up another sample into a fresh jar. "You see, Aleka, the dust storms coming in from the badlands have been bringing with them an increasing amount of iron oxides and that's tough on plant life."

"The Iron Winds," Aleka nodded. "At least, that's what people have been calling them lately."

"We can measure the increased amount of iron in the soil, so it's just a matter of matching it up to the kind of particulates found in the winds. That's what I'm doing, gathering the evidence for the connection so I can present it in my paper. Most people think the fields like this have transformed from thickly-grown flowerbeds to near-barren fields because of failing soil, but I want to prove them wrong. I realize you're from Nathor and so, you're used to a lot of trees and such, but trust me; Elmanith isn't normally this barren."

"I was hoping to see more of the Elmanith wildflowers that I'd heard so much about," she sighed. "They're just so magical from the pictures I've seen."

Micah capped his jar as he looked up, the reddish haze from the sky above casting a flickering aura around her face as she looked up into the sky.

"From where I'm squatting," Micah quipped, "things are still looking pretty magical."

"What do you-" She looked down then saw the direction of his gaze and smiled, giving him a playful kick in the leg as he stood back up by her side.

"Seriously, though, these dust storms are becoming an increasing nuisance, worse talla after talla. Even the GenSeers can't find any trace of storms like this in past Cycles. Some say it's the Tanians, but I'm starting to suspect the Volst have over-mined more than they've admitted to."

"The dust from their iron mines," she realized. "But they say the Tanians have been doing some mining of their own as well."

"Exactly why I'm taking these samples, to find out one way or the other. The iron oxides of the Volst mines would have a different latent composition than that found atop the Great Mountain. I'm starting to suspect that Grandsire Jast knows what's going on but would rather I find out for myself."

"Or he wants to steer you clear of all that political rubbish he's always involved with."

"Hmm," Micah mused, pausing his step for a moment as he considered this, "that just might be a distinct possibility. Well, whichever the reason, we need to find out what's causing all this before we can do anything about it. If I'm right, these iron storms are already changing the entire planet."

"There might be more to it," Aleka told him. "For instance, even with all this dust in the air, athletes have been setting new records this talla, running a lot faster than ever."

"How does that connect up with anything?"

"I'm not sure yet," she admitted, "but these particulates of yours are also remaining airborne for longer periods of time, not to mention I've heard that the flight characteristics of aircraft are changing. It's almost as if...I don't know. You'll think me crazy."

"As if gravity's changing?" Micah suggested in more subdued

tones. "That might explain the laravel I saw being carried off in a windstorm last week. If that is what's going on, then the ISP's keeping a lid on it. Though, Dantu did say something about the launch speed for the next mission being calculated as being less than for Mission One. When he asked about that, they simply said that they've refined their techniques since then. Still, one mystery at a time. Everyone at the ISP is becoming more focused on the Missions and going 'into the Black', as they say, that not enough people have been paying attention to the weather. Most people assume it's just a passing phase of the Cycle, but...I don't know."

"You'll figure it out," she said with a smile as she wrapped an arm around his waist. "You're the smartest person I know."

"That comes from hanging around you," he grinned back, "though I supposed I've got to give some credit to my Grandsire."

"*Someone* has to," she quipped. "He's not exactly the most beloved person on the planet, after all."

They walked along a bit more, looking for the next patch of ground to sample—this time one with some growth around it, so as to check the difference in the soil's iron content. He was just content to be with Aleka.

"Before I entered the Academy, my father had a visit from Simoth Karth," he finally stated. "They were talking about Mission Five at the time when he saw me outside and came over to talk."

"Isn't he the head of the ISP? Your family certainly has its connections. What'd he have to say?"

"He asked what I thought of the Missions, of going out into space. I told him that Ikara is the only world I've known and that there's not much I could do to change it, so might as well discover what I could about *this* world. I saw my father in the distance listening in and I think my answer made him happy. He'd always worry that I'd get messed up in politics or something dangerous, so knowing that I planned on keeping my feet on the ground made him feel better."

"And *do* you plan on keeping your feet on the ground?"

"Well…Simoth ended that conversation by saying something like, 'Well, young man, let me know if you discover anything new or fascinating.' Had a bit of a sting to it, but I never forgot his words. It's kept me determined to do something to change Ikara for the better, purely so I can put it before him and gloat."

"Now there's a reason for excelling," Aleka grinned. "So you can tell somebody off."

"I'll admit my interests aren't always as grounded as my father might hope. I was forever asking questions about Azur, mainly to my Grandsire Jast or Simoth just so my father wouldn't worry."

"What sorts of questions?"

"Things like, how can Ikara and Azur be so similar. How can the two share the same star and both harbor similar life forms. And did these similarities have anything to do with the early creation story."

"Seriously?"

"Well, okay, so I got that last one from Arioch Entora, a classmate of mine. His parents bought into the myth that life originated in the stars and was dumped here by accident, that the burning men were in fact escaping certain death and that they were not just men, but a man and a woman. Yes, they were very weird people. At any rate, my questions finally got one in return when Simoth asked me how much I knew about the origin of life among the Stars, or how much I remembered about the twin planets. I answered his questions as best I could but then he began talking about this life being a preparation for the next dimension and some other stuff I didn't follow at all. I just kept nodding and acting like I knew what he was talking about. Something about what we perceive is not reality, but in the next dimension over, we'll be free of our current physical limits."

"I see. It all sounds…interesting," she replied cautiously.

"You were gonna say crazy."

"Guilty," she admitted with a self-conscious laugh.

"Well, he went on like that for over half an hour. And, yes, the man was crazy. I later learned he'd just returned from the Volst

Observer. I'm guessing he learned something about the Tanians, but he's never said what it was."

"Something that snapped his mind?" she ventured.

"I don't know what it was, but I've a hunch that Grandsire Jast has been steering me in that direction for quite some time now. For instance, before I met you he gave me a set of formulas that the Tanians had supplied. They led me to one theory but the formulas just seemed to be off somehow. Nothing that I could find in the way of errors in the formulas themselves, so I started to improvise instead of blindly accepting their given constants. There was a lot of work involved, and quite a bit of improvising on my part, but I eventually realized that I'd need more data. A different kind of data."

And that's why you took up planetary science?"

"It never would have happened if Grandsire Jast hadn't nudged me with formulas I suspect he *knew* to be wrong. You know, he's as sneaky as people say he is."

"I don't doubt it. He got *us* together didn't he?"

"Why, how do you figure that?"

"Simple," she shrugged, "he didn't actively move to break us apart."

"But, I haven't even told him about you yet."

"You think he doesn't already know? Jast Rathael, with eyes and ears everywhere?"

"Well…never mind about that. There was a point I was about to get to. I need to expand my fieldwork, get some samples from other places. I've arranged a deal with the Karthan government to do some work on an island in an archipelago they control."

"Far enough away to offer some good comparisons," she agreed. "So, you're trying to build up to asking me to come along as your assistant."

"Well…yes. And would you at least wait until I *ask* a question before giving your consent?"

"Sorry, but if I did we might be here until well *after* the world ends."

"You jest now, funny girl, but if I'm right...Well, let's not go there just yet. Anyway, it'll mean a couple of months out in the field."

"Just for studying soil?"

"Well...," he admitted. "Okay, so they also agreed to let me study the remains of Mission Two they've had stored up. It includes some bits of stone and sand the mission had collected, samples from Azur. From what I've heard from others who've had a look at these samples and except for the obvious difference in mass, Ikara and Azur are pretty similar."

"Then why do we have the storms and they do not?" she asked.

"Exactly! It might be just what I need to complete my studies."

"And then what?" she asked, eyeing him with a suggestion of something else. "Do you have anything else more...long term...in mind?"

He said nothing in reply, but slipped his arm around hers. Together, they walked arm-in-arm until the stars came out for the night.

Thalamas

This is upsetting *everything,"* Thalamas raged as he paced through his opulent office, several members of his staff quickly ducking out of his way. "A revelation of the Tanian excavations is *not* what we needed."

"Sir," one functionary began, "if all Five Nations were to approach the Tanians then perhaps they might fix things."

Thalamas whirled on him in an instant, an angry gaze fixing him in place.

"That is *not* what I'm angry about! The Tanians have promised to export all of us off Ikara to some other world, out to the stars, but if Whycheral goes public with these revelations and the general populace discovers what the Tanians have been doing, then the resultant rioting may just drive the Tanians completely away and *leave* us here. And now, on top of that, we get word from the new

179

Tanian Administrator that they will *not* honor our past agreements. They're already distributing everything *evenly.* Volst's newfound wealth will slip away in no time and that will leave Whycheral and Elmanith to carve up our holdings. *We* are the Chosen, *we* are the forger of the new path for Ikara, *we* are the leaders of this Cycle."

Thalamas fumed as his furious pace led him back across the room. He was angry at the Tanians, but couldn't presume to threaten them. Therefore, he'd vent his frustrations at the next available target.

"That scientist was born Whycheral and I'll bet they're the ones that put him up to that report. Whycheral has been a thorn in our side long enough." He spun around to face the others. "Maybe it's time we went to war with them, showed those mystic fools what Volst is *really* capable of."

"War?" one of those there spoke up, "But sir, not since the first cycle-"

"Then we're about overdue! We can't do anything about this new abrasive little Tanian Administrator, but we can certainly do something about those overachieving Whycherals."

It seemed as if Thalamas' mind was made up. They were a moment away from actual war, but Fate had good timing that day. For just before he would've given the final command to set things into motion, a messenger came in through the double doors of the grand office of the First Speaker, rushed over to Thalamas, and whispered a quick word in his ear. One which earned an interested grin across his face, and a wave of his hand towards the rest.

"Clear out this room then send in my new guest. He should be met with in privacy."

The room was quickly cleared, and none there, save that messenger, would discover who the unknown visitor was.

Jast sat back in the offered chair, smoothing out his beard while Thalamas sat opposite him. There were no others there in the grand office, no one to overhear what might be said.

"So, come to gloat?" Thalamas began. "The new Administrator's doing things a bit differently now."

"I have no control or influence over that," Jast explained, "I just came here to give you an advance warning of something and a chance at an exclusive contract."

"Exclusive?" Thalamas' steel-grey eyes narrowed, his interest mildly piqued. "I'm listening."

"Then to begin…For reasons I am not privy to, Administrator Amishari has selected Whycheral to receive exclusive rights to a certain type of device. We received a few samples as well as the plans for making it, and our scientists have since been working on making a few alterations to better adapt it to the Ikaran mind. It will soon be available to all Ikarans, but I am here to offer Volst a five-day exclusive access to this device."

"Five-day advance," Thalamas nodded, though still wary. "But what manner of device is this and why choose Volst?"

"My reason for choosing Volst is simple. I realize how upset the Administrator's new change in policy would have made you and I figure this is a small price to pay to keep the peace in Ikara. We no longer have a Five Nations government, after all, so maintaining the peace comes down to deals like this. Assuming you're amenable, that is."

"That all depends," Thalamas told him, "on what manner of device we're talking about."

Jast paused, taking a breath before launching into his explanation. As he spoke, Thalamas' eyes evolved from wary caution to wide-eyed wonder.

"The GenSeers of old had said that in previous cycles, Ikarans had come to know the peace of unity. Even in this cycle, no more pleasant a dream remains than to one day rejoin that common and placid state. Even in the most ancient of records, the promise of a union of the mind and heart called Agora beckons to us: Whycheral and Volst alike. Connecting to the Agora would be complete; one would be able to feel the comfort—and the discomfort—of complete integration. All its passion, fire, humor, happiness, and emptiness. The wholeness of it would elevate the operating level of every individual. According to the Grand Cycle, in that connection this Voice of the Agora is to be the beginning and end of Ikaran conscience. Everyone will belong to a whole, no longer to think solely of themselves, but in that state, everyone will find a purpose, a part to play."

"I am aware of the old legends," Thalamas snapped. "Get to the point."

"The point is," Jast continued, "The Tanians have given us a device designed to show us the benefits of their own form of sharing, but they did not truly know of our legend of the Agora. We have reworked what they called the Agorabox into something more truly like the Agora of fable. *That*, Speaker Thalamas, is what I am offering you a five-day exclusive for. Now, do you think that is worth a little peace between nations?"

Thalamas sat back, a grin quickly evolving across his face. Fingers steepling together, his gaze locked on an imagined future, with Volst once again playing a primary role.

"Volst will have the advantage, we will once again get what we deserve. The *Agora,* come to life."

Agora Life

When they first rolled the device out, it was considered something of a joke, a gag gift for the young. So few had access that it was only a novelty. Certainly, secrets that were hidden among friends—benevolent little things like youthful crushes and mental dalliances—revealed themselves, as Agorabox users truly were capable of reading the thoughts of others. So few had been granted access to the devices that it wasn't yet functionally connecting users (or manipulating the masses).

Yet in this toy, there came a spark, something to excite the young Ikaran. The device was a simple cube with a semi-rigid headband worn by the user, which functioned as a signal receptor.

It was placed on the forehead, then the device activated. The Agorabox drew input from the bearer, amplified the sensory input at a much-elevated level, and conveyed it to other wearers—further amplifying and harmonizing the experience. As the new toy caught on, the variety and styles rapidly expanded, and it quickly became a new kind of bauble that individuals could customize and use to outwardly express themselves.

With the device activated, one could get immediate feedback about what others thought, felt, or experienced, so those who sought public approval began to conform. From there, the appeal of the Agorabox quickly grew. It provided an interface and amplification of the will, so that one could equally embrace the process, regardless of position, power, or prestige. This centralized thought-pool became the new Ikaran identity, and if they thought about it (or on rare occasion, spoke about it), they called this new frame of reference the Agora.

For months, one young man in the streets had been trying to work up the nerve to ask a certain girl out for a date. He was too afraid that she might reject him, or worse yet, laugh at him. When he saw her wearing an Agorabox, he took a chance. He put his own device around his head and focused in her direction. A moment later, he was smiling; she'd been waiting for him to ask her all this time.

A thief was about to assault a merchant. Just a quick snatch-and-grab, then run away. He was wealthy, after all, so he wouldn't miss it, right? Based on the merchant's wealth and his own need, the thief felt entitled to the man's riches, so he ran up to the man, fully intending to snatch his wallet without pausing. But the merchant wore an Agorabox, and the thief had forgotten that he was wearing one as well. When he was less than two cubits away, the thief suddenly halted and stared at the merchant. In that moment, he knew.

The merchant had money, true, but for so many tallas, he'd worked and sacrificed to get where he was. Now he had a good home, but he also had family to support and many employees to pay. Therefore, as much money as he had, he had an equal amount of responsibilities. The thief felt all of this reality in an instant: the sacrifices, the setbacks, and the successes. In fact, he felt so much that he couldn't go through with his plan; he decided not to steal from one who worked so hard.

As the thief was about to turn away, however, something else happened. The merchant had seen the thief's thoughts as well, seen the poverty he lived in. And he could not help but feel the suffering as if it was his own. In a moment of generosity, he reached into his pocket and pulled out a pouch, filled with more money than the wallet contained that the thief had targeted. The merchant handed it to the thief without saying another word. By the time the thief walked away, both he and the merchant were close to tears.

The thief soon passed another man, whose mind was filled with joy. He'd just made it past the Academy Muster, and was happier than he'd ever been. He didn't say a word about it, but to those he passed, a wave of good feeling echoed from his mind. Smiles appeared like flowers blooming around him. Some gave him congratulatory nods, but others just reveled in the unexpected good feeling, which they in turn unconsciously passed onto others.

Word began to get around from the Agora users. In some cases, they were just watching them in the streets. One would pass another, then smile. Someone else would suddenly hug a complete stranger to console them in the grief that he'd had picked up on. Crime decreased, for no one with an Agorabox could harm another; it would be like harming oneself. One did not hurt the Agora, for the Agora is everyone, and within it, every life has meaning.

It was once said that the men who fell burning from the sky during the First Cycle had shared one soul, and from that soul came all Ikarans. It was as if the Agorabox brought the people back in touch with that one primordial soul. However, the Agorabox had one more positive influence on the Ikaran people: it helped them maintain a constant peace of mind. By being connected, they worried less about the future and were able to let go of any misgivings about the past. There was no reason to hoard or be unproductive. This presence cured the mind of the illnesses that came with technological advancements in the physical realm.

In Nathor, their desire to adopt and share anything regarding healing and well-being made the Agorabox a popular choice, nearly overnight. Of course, it helped that the Matron was married to the major supplier and proponent, and that she *gave away* several hundred units to the poor and needy.

The emotional and psychological impact was staggering, and it was more than anyone was willing to disengage from. The only disciplinary action that parents now needed was to threaten to disconnect their child from the Agora if they didn't behave. Even in the schoolyard, bullying fell away, for to give harsh words to another felt like berating yourself. As more people bought Agoraboxes, it became like an organism itself, with the individuals a part of the whole. Upon wearing an Agorabox, cruelty vanished almost instantly, as the collective desire for peace and happiness took root.

In this one device, a course correction had been given to the Ikaran people. The emlash and the pacification protocols of the Tanians had shifted the Ikarans' path from being a single, caring mind to having selfish divisiveness. This allowed the Tanians to apply their wedges into this this hostility and pry the Ikarans apart, pitting one against the other. But the Agorabox was changing all that by reestablishing the core of the one Ikaran soul. Tanians might've thought that the Agorabox would give a selfish people the means to devour themselves with greed, and make of them something closer to Tanian kin. Instead, it opened the door to cultural recovery.

One thing is certain: none of the Ikaran population would've survived the coming calamity, had it not been for the Agorabox. The Agora became the rebirth of Ikaran conscience.

It was ironic that it had been Borosh who put the Agora project into motion. For if he'd instead followed through with offering them access to the stars, then perhaps all Ikarans would have fallen. But as deeply as the desire for stellar travel was written into the Ikaran soul, the Agora appealed to the most basic instinct of them all.

That of harmony.

Jast

The newness of the Agora experience wore off within a few weeks, allowing the wearers to return to their regular activities. But by that time, the Agora had become a way of life; the open sharing of even the most mundane tasks provided instant pleasure and harmony. It became a positive feedback loop from which no one wanted to disconnect. This impact was concerning at first, as work output initially suffered, but the cultural shaming of someone who had selfish thoughts created its own regulatory effects. If someone acted in such a way, those who knew them would actively shun them, reducing the efficacy of the device and the resultant pleasure the shunned one would normally feel.

Anyone with violent thoughts couldn't conceal them, so very quickly, they had to suffer the intolerable punishment of psychic silence. As crime dropped away among wearers, it became a mandatory punishment within the courts to fit all criminals with Agoraboxes—in an effort to guide them back to a safer, more communal way of thinking.

Education rapidly changed as well. Since one could instantly understand difficult concepts through the communal sharing of subjects, learning became quite easy. Communicating without written or verbal language removed ambiguity and added compassion. In fact, if any *one* invention could be credited with undermining the control and manipulations of the Tanians, it was the Agorabox.

While deemed far too familiar a contact to be legally approved for business dealings, it did make competitors more sympathetic to one another's plights, which turned many of them into honest men. Governmental administrators found that they saved much time in committee meetings and brainstorming sessions; they could just link together around a table. During this time, many governments were on the verge of breaking down, and the fallout from the collapse of the Five Nations government was still being felt. There increasingly came a tendency towards decentralization in both business and government, as users could directly transmit their needs to one another.

Graft and corruption within the higher levels of government became increasingly harder to maintain, even with the coercive power of bureaucracy. The Agorabox forced upon them a new, frightful transparency, beneath the light of which no dark shadow can long survive.

There were, however, a great number of the elder Ikarans who resisted in the beginning, fearing such rapid changes. Those most vocal had been affected by the Tanian Pacification Protocols in their pre-contact desire to modify Ikara. Families were torn apart in the short term, policies of local governances became rapidly irrelevant, and services began to fail in small ways across the whole of Ikara.

Later known as the Silent War, every Nation of Ikara faced its conflicts as a result of the rise and return of Agora. And that was just as Jast would have it, not to mention Amishari.

It was during this time that Jast pushed for Mission Six. The Five Nations government had collapsed, but with the spreading popularity of the Agorabox, governments were becoming increasingly irrelevant as a concept. Jast never used an Agorabox himself, for that would open him up to collective examination, and he was not ready for that. If he was to save the Ikaran people from the coming calamity, his plans and thoughts had to remain his own.

That didn't mean, though, that he couldn't convince a few people of the necessity of Mission Six, and let the Agora take it from there. All he had to do was keep spreading Agoraboxes to everyone on Ikara and weather the waves of the Silent War. In fact, the first one he spoke to of a possible Mission Six was his own grandson, Dantu, who by now was a keen Agorabox user.

They were walking along a gardened path just outside the ruins of the old GenSeer fortress, before them a distant view of the Great Mountain. By degrees, Jast steered the conversation towards his thoughts on the Missions.

"We should never abandon thoughts of another ISP mission," Jast said. "We belong out there, but more importantly, there are a few things that need looking into."

"I want to see the Missions through more than anyone," Dantu sighed, "but Mission Five was a failure, all crew lost."

"Which is why we have to get back up and get another Mission going," Jast countered. "Dantu, our world is dying and it's about time everyone discovered why."

Dantu stopped, eyeing his grandfather suspiciously. But he couldn't tell if Jast knew something more specific.

"What do you know?" Dantu asked.

"Only something that has to be seen. The ISP is still solvent but we need the manpower, the will. If for no other reason than to prove the continued viability of the Missions, we need to achieve orbit. To orbit Ikara at least once and fly high above the Great Mountain, maybe even reach Azur to find evidence of what really happened to Mission Five. Dantu, we need this mission."

"Then why tell me? Why not get an Agorabox and tell everyone direct?"

"I have my reasons, and as for why I'm telling you…Dantu, I want you to fly this mission. Simoth will agree and convince the ISP council. That's a lot easier task now that there's no more oversight from the Five Nations government."

"I would be glad to fly the mission," Dantu said with eyes slightly narrowed, "but why do I have the feeling that there's something more to this? Are you playing another one of your games, grandfather?"

In response, Jast only smiled, wrapped an arm around his grandson, and directed their walk toward a clearer view of the Mountain.

Micah looked up at the statue of his grandfather, standing there in the middle of the Academy arboretum. It was a portrayal of him in his prime, tall and strong.

"Looks sorta like Dantu," Micah commented to himself.

"Where do you think your brother gets his athletics from?"

"Grandfather!"

Micah turned around to see his grandfather, his laravel faithfully padding along by his side, though far slower than in days past. The two greeted in a hug, the younger one clearly happy to see the older. Then they started walking through the flower-lined paths.

"I was afraid you would be too busy to make it, grandfather."

"And miss my favorite grandson so close to his graduation? Nonsense."

"Dantu's gotta be more in favor than me," Micah countered with a grin, "He's about to go into space on the new mission, after all."

"So will you some day; that I promise." Jast assured him. "So, how are things going for you? Have a girlfriend yet?"

"As a matter of fact," and here, Micah's face spread out into a broad smile, "her name is Aleka. Aleka Nadir. She can speak all *five* Ikaran dialects and is just *brilliant*. I've even taken her on as my field research assistant. I think she might be the one."

"Then why don't you use that Agorabox your father gave you to find out? I hear it's all quite the rage."

"Naw," Micah shrugged it off, "I prefer the old-fashioned verbal face-to-face method…Just like my favorite grandfather."

Jast gave a chuckle, slapped his grandson on the shoulder, glanced up at the statue of his younger self, and sighed.

"Ah, to look like that again. Unfortunately, too much Jaave juice and some other excesses have me looking like an old man, complete with paunch and balding cranium."

"Oh, grandfather, you've already lived longer than most any Ikaran. You have even out-lived Halgor."

"A simple combination of exceptional breeding and sheer luck, though I've a few opponents who have been spreading the rumor that I've either discovered immortality or made a deal with the Grand Cycle itself. Now I ask you, if I *had* done either, don't you think I'd put in a provision for spending eternity as a *young* man?"

Micah laughed in response as they strolled along. His father may have had issues with Jast, but Micah found a certain pride in being related to a man who was like living history itself.

"Friends ask me about you all the time," Micah finally said. "You're the Agora's biggest proponent and yet you do not use it. With your five export businesses in Elmanith and your ties to international commerce, you're more of a stabilizing influence than what's left of any of the national governments, and yet you keep so much out of the public eye."

"Sounds like you've been attending Professor Gadril's economics lectures again."

"Well," Micah admitted, "he *is* one of my professors. But he's right. You've seen emlash develop, built up the space program, done it all."

"None of which I would have been able to do had I *been* in the public eye," Jast countered. "Unlike a few contemporaries of mine, or have you been so isolated in this Academy of yours that you've not kept up with all the chaos out there? More than a few of the older statesmen and Family leaders have rather foolishly assumed that the Agora is a passing fad and that the people will soon come to their senses. And yet, even now, some of them are being rounded up, or engaging in their own counter revolutions to this so-called fad."

"I've heard," Micah replied. "A couple of them tried to use the Agorabox as a form of mind control, only to expose their own sins. Some of the others are being force-fed an Agorabox so as to get to the real truth of their actions. There's quite a lot of that sort of fighting everywhere. It seems as the people themselves are taking over their own governing and are enforcing the growing collective will."

"Their punishment seems to be one of two things," Jast told the young man, "either exile to the Badlands or removal from the gene pool altogether. Something to stay well away from, though I myself have underwritten four of the larger conveys that have hauled away the dissidents."

In his own mind, Jast was glad that he'd stayed away from the Agorabox. While it was the perfect solution for Ikara as a whole, it might have had him hauled away with the rest. Helm had kept good to his word of keeping a lid on his pre-Candlefall contact with the Tanians, and while Jast's intentions were always good, some might argue with his methods.

"You wouldn't have anything to worry about that, grandfather, you're one of the good guys," he smiled. "You've opened up more eyes about the planetary collapse and overly amounts of self-serving consumption than anyone else. Everyone looks up to you as their best hope for change."

"Ah, Micah, so much I wish I could tell you."

"Such as?"

"Such as…the trap of emlash, or rather its too-rapid development and deployment. There is wisdom in maintaining a measured pace. Emlash gave us our greatest advances and propelled the Five Families to the pinnacle of their power, and yet it opened us up for the destruction of our culture, a culture I mean to reestablish before all this is through. Then there are the Tanians: great gifts of technology and medicine, but at what price?"

You sound like a skeptic, grandfather."

"Skepticism I have well earned, my boy. It takes a very long time to become as skeptical as I am now. When I was your age I would have seen the Tanians as older kindred of the Grand Cycle, helping their younger kin. Well, maybe if it weren't for the prophetic abilities of a certain old GenSeer."

"The one that foretold of the Cataclysm. Yes, I remember the stories you told me as a kid."

"Good, because I had a very good reason for telling them to you. Now onto something else. How's your father?"

"About the same," Micah shrugged. "His problem is that, while he has become a very powerful political figure, he realizes it mainly arises from being your son. I've seen him in meetings where he wouldn't even argue or look into any of the finer points of something if it came with your name attached to it. I love him and all, but if he'd had to work harder for his success, I think he would have been a much stronger diplomat."

"Forever the Son of Jast," Jast sighed. "I regret it came to that, but let it be a lesson to you. No matter how much you may like and admire me—or anyone else for that matter—always retain a healthy bit of skepticism."

"I will, grandfather," Micah assured him. "Oh, but I should tell you. I overheard father talking to Simoth Karth about how to get the better of—and I'm quoting—the 'Old Man of Whycheral'. Nothing more specific."

"Helm tries to play his own games," Jast sighed. "But just you never mind about that. Stay out of politics and focus on your studies. Speaking of which, how do they go?"

"Well," Micah began, his tone taking a sudden eager upturn. "As you know, I'd previously completed my research to prove beyond a shadow of a doubt that it's been the Ikaran People, not the Visitors from Tania, who have been destroying the planet and driving the storm systems. Many agricultural families suffered on account of my reports, and not a few well-intentioned engineers lost their jobs for not foreseeing the same results that my formulas predicted. More recently, though, I've uncovered some errors in my analysis, so I transferred to Soil Science to get some different data points. I took Aleka along with me on some field research, but the answers I'm getting…I'm just not so sure."

"You'll get the answers," Jast assured him. "Soon…very soon."

"That's the point," Micah told him, "I think I *did* get the answers, I just don't like what I see."

As they came to the end of the path, Jast looked up in the direction of the Great Mountain, where he imagined the Mission Six vessel would be flying. Dantu should be coming into view pretty soon now.

"Oh," Micah said in sudden eagerness, "I almost forgot. Father was telling me how the Five Families had been boycotting Volst ports against any further shipments of Agoraboxes."

"I'd heard. It's been a great concern of mine."

"Well, just this morning I heard from my father. He sent in some people to break the embargo and get the Agoraboxes to market. The Families want him locked up, even some factions in Elmanith are after him, but they can't do a thing now. Father distributed the boxes immediately after to give *everyone* a chance to get into the Agora. I've even heard a few Agorabox users already calling him the Father of the Agora."

Jast looked at his grandson appreciatively, and for the first time in a very long while, replied with an honest smile that held no ulterior motives.

"I was hoping Helm would find a way to get out from under my shadow. I'm very happy for him, truly I am."

"I'm glad. I'll tell him next time I talk to him."

"No, please. Let him believe he won one against my wishes, that's the only way he'll get true satisfaction. I can afford to take a couple of hits, but Helm really earned this one. This could be Ikara's biggest move away from the Accords and my son is responsible. Let him enjoy it."

Simoth

Simoth was furious. As if it wasn't bad enough that so much had changed of late! The fall of the Five Nations government had once again left Helm as First Speaker of Elmanith, and the death of his father had left Simoth as First Speaker of Kartha, with little time for the ISP.

Now, though, there were these new toys of the Tanians: the Agoraboxes. They were of increasing popularity, and he was waiting on Kartha's first shipment. He'd met the transfer protocols to the letter, but had not yet taken possession of even one new device.

According to the intelligence reports from his spies in Volst, the devices gave their administrator complete access to mind control. It was a useful device, which would allow him to see into the thoughts of his enemies, pick them out from a crowd, and thereby solidify his control in such unstable times. His leadership had always been tenuous, maintained at the tip of a sword. However, now he'd finally be able to relax, knowing who his enemies really were.

"Jast Rathael is to blame," he muttered to himself as he sat there in his study, sipping at the dark burgundy concoction his physicians had prescribed for him. "That fast-talking bastard from Whycheral convinced me to squander the mysteries of the ancients and plunder the Catacombs. Okay, so be it, but now he's standing between me and my destiny as the greatest Karthan of all time. All because he can't get a reign on these people blockading the shipment. He's betrayed me, I just know it."

He took another sip of his drink. It had a sweet, robust taste, but it fell to ash in his mouth when he thought about Jast Rathael fingering the old scar on the right side of his face, which his mongrel laravel had given him.

"I've kept Kael's secret, provided secret support for the project. In fact, that's probably the real reason why Jast maneuvered me into control of the ISP in the first place. He knew I'd be First Speaker some day and he needed Kartha's cooperation to dig that old relic out. Lot of good it'll do anyway, with the governments falling like flies and everyone at each other's throats. And now the one device I need to pacify the population remains beyond reach because of a blockade."

Simoth's reverie was interrupted by the approach of a soldier. The man was in Karthan armor. The short greaves, boiled-leather chest plate, shield, and spear identified him as a Vocatis of the Ministry of Communication (what other nations might call a herald). Simoth was filled with tension as the man entered.

"Welcome, Vocatis. What news? Is the blockade broken yet?"

"I… assume so, sir."

"You *assume?*"

"Well, sir, they just appeared on the docks overnight."

"What appeared? Come on, speak up!"

"The shipment of Agoraboxes, sir. No explanation, just the shipment tags from Volst pasted on their tops."

"What?!" Simoth shot to his feet, surprise eliminating his previous sour mood. "But how? From where?"

"I don't know anything more, sir. Just crates of them. They want to know what to do with them."

"What to *do?* Why, start distributing them, of course. But be sure to get me one first!"

"Yes sir, First Speaker. Immediately, sir."

With a quick bow, the messenger left, leaving a grin across Simoth's face in his wake.

"Helm," Simoth grinned. "Gotta be Helm, his way of spitting in the face of the Old Man of Whycheral. Well, whatever broke through the blockade, we finally have the Agoraboxes, and I have some lovely ideas for the first thing I'm going to do with *mine*. Yes, sir…"

Within a few weeks, the shipments of Agoraboxes had been scattered throughout Kartha, mostly in the hands of the criminal element, who'd mistakenly thought to use it as a mind-control device. However, such uses had their own corrective element, so there would soon be very little of the criminal element left in Kartha.

Bellelorn

Bellelorn, Matron of Nathor, sat in the recording studio, while the technicians made ready. She had her speech written out before her, while Jast Rathael sat off to one side, out of view of the camera.

"You're okay with this?" she asked of him. "You could still go into the Agora with me."

"I cannot and you know why," he said back in quiet, gentle tones. "Some secrets must remain secret if I am to complete my plan for our survival."

"I long for you to remain by my side," she sighed. "I am afraid of what might be the result of what I do today and wish your hand within my own. Many users of the Agorabox are already beginning to suspect that the technological wonders supplied by the Tanians may be responsible for our ills, and maybe even the Tanians themselves. Rumors circulate as to my stand in matters and concern for what I am to announce, while I am concerned for how they may react."

"You will do fine," Jast said, his hand reaching gently out for hers for a light squeeze. "There is not a person in all Ikara who does not love you…myself most of all."

"I love you as well," she replied with a smile, "which is why I fear for what I must do, that it might forever separate us."

"I will be with you always," Jast assured her, "with or without the Agora."

She looked at him with a sigh, then glanced around at the technicians readying up the equipment. With his hand, one of them signaled how much time was left. Keeping in mind the few minutes remaining, she gave a few last words to her true love.

"Long before I was born, my grandfather had been an advocate for Nathorn independence. It was before Candlefall when it seemed as if Elmanith would absorb the other Families into its own promise of unity. He was for a unified Ikara, but one under the Grand Cycle, not a tyrannical single leader. It was a dark day when an assassin had done what the others could not, and ceased the overreaching dictates of Elmora Elmanith. No-one was ever punished for that act."

"That was what initially promoted my family into Elmanith politics," Jast replied with a nod. "After that came Argos then Tollwyn in a progressively decreasing quality of Elmanith leadership. My name got a little mixed up in things after that, as you know, and some thought that it was a plot of my father's to get the Rathael name into significant prominence…and maybe it was."

"But then you gave Helm the right of Speaker and all but severed relations with him in the name of diplomacy. Jast, you have sacrificed so much to do what you needed to do, I do not wish that you lose anything more. I do not wish that you lose…me."

"Bellelorn," he gently replied, "we were both born to serve

a greater need than our own. Your grandfather had the right idea. Enough blood was shed in the Great War of the First Cycle. No planetary government can be built upon blood and the meanest of aspirations if it is to last. It must be built of a true unity of mind and soul. That is the chance that the agorabox gives us."

"I know," she sighed, "I just…"

She paused for a moment, before doing the one thing that she couldn't express in words. She reached over and kissed him. Short though it was, the moment seemed an eternity. So much so that she nearly missed the signal from one of the technicians. With a last regret in her eyes, she sat back down in her seat, arrayed her hair, faced the camera, and gave a slight nod. When the lights came up to present her to the people across the waves and around the world, Bellelorn was at peace. She knew that it was truly the only way in which Ikarans could finally regain their place as the masters of Ikara and direct their *own* destiny.

"There is a tide moving," she began her speech, "against which we can only choose to falter or to stand. I step before you now, raising the standard high that you may have the courage necessary to do what is seemingly impossible.

"Oh children, my family," she continued, "my love. Long have I struggled to find the words to say, the song to sing, that would take your hurt away, but there has ever been only one way, and that is to surrender my place at your head as Matron of Nathor and instead stand by your side.

"We are intended as a people to live a life of nature, in tune with our planet's father who made us. In every Cycle, the mother's lash finds us; she lifts us up from the millennia of tribal life and challenges our minds with advancement. In every Cycle we heed the call and accept the challenge, only to find the technology we create brings out the worst in us first of all. But if we can survive that short period then we can eventually go back to our understanding of unity with all things. For in the end, we are not our technology; they are simple tools and it is up to us to recognize them as such.

197

"Our attachments therefore must remain to the one, the only, of which we are all children. From there, in the midst of our travails as we are now, we can search the stars for our brothers. We know from the Grand Cycle that they are out there, amid the stars, and it may soon be our time to discover them once again. If we succeed in this, if we climb among the stars, the end of our lives will mean a life eternal among those who are called God. Our true selves are a native people, our task to make it past our current challenge. If in this life we can harness the power to destroy all life and choose not to do so, then we have again succeeded. It must be, though, that every single one of us choose this path; only then can we advance to the next step in the Cycle of the universe. One alone cannot do it; we must *all* do it and we must all do it *willingly.*

"Thus, I am hereby asking for all governments of the Five Nations to surrender their authority to the Five Families from which we all descend, and to do so swiftly and gently. Though there be conflict inherent in the system, we must not fall prey to vanity or vengeance, for such would be admitting that we have become our captors and that the Tanian Way has become the Ikaran Way. I believe you will rise above the error and rediscover the peace of our past."

She paused for a brief moment, casting a last glance out of the side of her eyes at Jast—a last longing desire—then reached down and pulled up that which also lay on her desk: a wide headband with an Agorabox fixed to it.

"I will meet with you now, my Family."

Without another word, and in full view of every Wave screen around the world, the now-former Matron of the Nation of Nathor surrendered herself to the peace rediscovered in a little metal box. Bellelorn embraced the Agora, and Jast couldn't have been happier on her behalf.

Dantu

Dantu had a certain amount of celebrity status, which was only amplified by the growing pockets of Agora use. Therefore, interest in a sixth mission grew to supply what was needed, even without any formal governmental entities to supply them. As a result, Mission Six made it off the launch pad and into orbit with Dantu in command.

The parameters of the mission were expanded to include a flyby of Azur, so that they could seek evidence of the survival of the Mission Five crew and its vessel. The pictures they took of Azur from orbit were of even greater detail than before. From its vast herds of prairie animals to its wondrous range of terrains, it was enough to make Dantu and his crew as giddy as schoolgirls at their first dance. Alas, though, they could never find any sign of Mission Five.

However, on its way back, Mission Six did discover something of far more monumental importance. To decelerate prior to landing at home, they had to make a couple of orbits around Ikara. His suspicions about his grandfather still fresh in his mind, Dantu had cameras ready just in case. He suspected there would be something, but he never would've even considered what he finally saw as he snapped one picture after another.

"I just know there's something that grandsire wanted me to- what's that?"

The Great Mountain was a well-known landmark situated on the far side of Volst near the edge of the vast Ikaran Sea. Yet as they came into view of the far side of the Great Mountain—the point farthest away from any nation of Ikara, which was hidden from view by the bulk of the Mountain itself—there was something new. Perhaps too recent to have yet been discovered, or perhaps in too remote an area of the world. Nonetheless, it grabbed at Dantu's attention like iron filings to a magnet.

"By the Cycle! Get the cameras on this or no-one's going to believe us, even *with* an Agorabox."

For Dantu and his crew, it was unfathomable, and the pictures they took were staggering. They could easily see the great hole in the center of the Mountain. But even more plainly visible was what lay along the developing plate ridge, still forming under the eastern edge of the Great Mountain and extending almost to the Ikaran Sea. A magma rift had formed, creating a seemingly bottomless chasm running for a hundred leagues.

"The Tanians," Dantu gasped, "what have they done to our world?!"

Once Dantu returned from his mission, Dantu's first step was to show the pictures to anyone he could, but certain factions within the ISP and Family hierarchies were still obsessed with their own personal agendas and grabbed the image files away.

"For a scientific analysis, before an unnecessary panic is started," one man had told him. "You understand."

But Dantu and his crew knew what they saw…and all of them wore Agoraboxes.

Amishari

"Administrator Amishari, first report as Administrator."

She leaned back in her chair, making a psychical dictation to be transmitted as plain psy-text, devoid of any emotional inflection.

"The substantial mass of the world the locals call Ikara is enough to easily achieve profitability. Furthermore, the one great mountain, rising as it does to the edge of space, provided a prime site for the extraction process out of sight of the locals. The optimal extraction from this world represents a loss of thirty percent of its mass, resulting in an eventual loss of ninety-five percent of its atmosphere due to decreased gravity. The core pumps have been working constantly in the decades that this operation has been underway, liquefying and extracting the core then sending it straight through the Bridge. The equipment and energy necessary for this entire process, including maintaining the interdimensional Bridge, is on the order of a small star by the time it will all be finished, but with the content of minerals and resources being pulled out, we have long since passed the break-even point.

"We even managed to obtain some help from the locals. Under the administration of Borosh, the Volst segment of the local population assisted us with extractions closer to the surface by constructing advanced digging machines and even supplying some workers, all at their own expense, in exchange for a few technological trinkets. Their efforts have left large underground trenches that the rest of the Ikaran population remains ignorant about, and they have supplied us with more of the planet's heavy and ferrous metals.

"Nearly eighty percent of desirable ores have been mined and I have begun the partial winding down of operations. The original vessel that shipped the Matter Transporters is being dismantled and moved through the Bridge in between bursts of the still-flowing core material, of course. Critical drive components are being walked through the Bridge and those of the operational staff no longer needed for operations are also being withdrawn for reassignment. This will amount to some eight thousand of the ten thousand current staff.

"There will be some catastrophic results for the local people, however. The loss of such a mass means loss of gravity, not to mention the loss of magnetic shielding from a spinning core that is by now seriously compromised. We have already recorded significant atmospheric losses, increased incidence of violent storms, and the overall planetary stability has been irreversibly damaged. The planet's orbital rotation has changed from a two percent variation in tilt to around ten percent tilt which is causing ocean sediments to move back and forth according to seasons and make trenches and mines collapse. More recently, the collapse of such mines and digging sites has caused leftover iron particulates to be picked up by the winds, creating storms of iron particles that are responsible for dumping hundreds of tons of material onto the planet's surface. In short, Ikara is dying and there is nothing the locals, or even ourselves, can do to stop it."

She paused for a moment, just long enough to wipe away a tear before gathering her thoughts enough to resume.

"The introduction of the Agorabox seems to be having the

intended effect of pacifying the Ikarans. Already, pockets of them seem happier and more sedate. As such, I have commissioned the construction of a worldwide network centered in a single Agora tower. We are already working with the locals on its construction, being sure to let the Ikarans provide the bulk of the materials and labor. If successful, I am sure we can subjugate the people completely and turn them into useful and productive workers.

"This will mean," she continued, "that there will be no need to harvest them as biomass and feedstock. On that matter, I have noted that former Administrator Borosh has the majority of the Volst segment of the population scheduled for transmission across the Bridge but without the Molecular Sequencer initiated. This will mean that…millions of people will arrive as unliving masses of biological material. Even though he is no longer Administrator, Borosh seems to have kept oversight control of this last operation of his, I assume so that he can qualify for the credits that such a deposit of mass would bring him. However, I urge the committee to reconsider as these are fully intelligent creatures and not mere animals. Also, consider the tactical aspect that our mission will be here for several more tallas, so many missing people will create questions that will be difficult to answer."

She paused once again, trying her best to keep her emotions under check, so that she could finish her report. She almost failed, but with a last surge of willpower, she found enough control to finish it off.

"In summary, all operations will continue as scheduled, unless I receive orders to the contrary. Report ends."

She clicked off the recorder and leaned back with a sigh, which quickly turned into a sob.

"Not again," she said to herself. "Please by the Powers not again. I just hope I'm right about this Agora phenomena."

When she finally left her quarters, all signs of her weeping swept away. Someone grabbed Amishari's attention: a slightly taller, older man with short-cropped bluish-white hair, and a stride as precise as the uniform he wore and as stern as his position demanded. Amishari had been dreading this encounter, for now that she was Administrator, he would be keeping an even closer eye on her.

"Lort," she said as he approached. "What news does my Security Chief bring me now?"

"Just a few irregularities I wish to discuss with you," he said. He brought up a lumen-pad he'd been holding in one hand. "First, there was a trip you made to the locals, but no record as to the purpose."

"Merely getting acquainted with native leaders," she flatly stated. "They'll be easier to deal with if they trust me."

"I see," he said, glancing back down to the list. "Then I see the shipments of parts for these pacification boxes you talked them into wearing."

"The locals call them Agoraboxes, but yes," she admitted. "A program begun by former Administrator Borosh that I feel still holds some merit. Now, was there anything else? I have quite a busy schedule."

"No, not right now." He performed a short bow of his head, a sharp click of heels together. "I will let you know when there is."

With that, he left, but Amishari showed nothing more than her usual featureless expression. Beneath it, however, she felt a swiftly growing dislike for this particular Tanian. Borosh may have been the result of the system in which he was birthed, but Lort represented the system itself. He was the coldest Tanian she'd ever met, and he wouldn't hesitate to turn on anyone, even Borosh, if he had cause to.

The timing was *almost* perfect. After months of the rising popularity of the Agoraboxes, Amishari (in cooperation with a collective of voluntary Ikaran workers and engineers) began construction on the planetary Agora: a single large tower with the capability to connect everyone up to it, no matter where on the planet they were. It was to be an Agorabox network, allowing users to share their thoughts and feelings with anyone, anywhere. It would be the perfect solution for Dantu to finally get word out to the planetary populace about what he'd seen on Mission Six.

Unfortunately, the imperfection of the timing was due to Thalamas Voort and the people of Volst. They had just enough exposure to the Agorabox to take what they deemed was the next logical step.

"Volst will lead the way to the stars," Thalamas proclaimed in his final speech. "The Agora has shown us the way and now it will be the people of Volst who will share in our communion with our friends from the stars. We have but the beginnings of Agora here on Ikara but the Tanians have had their own version for many Cycles. We invite the rest of Ikara to follow us, for when you do, you will find that Volst has built for you a new home, and we will have plenty of new experiences to share with you via the Agorabox. I myself will be the *first* to cross the Bridge."

The brief ceremony was being held in the confines of the mammoth construction that housed the Bridge, crowded now with innumerable people from Volst, and more being brought in via Tanian flitter every minute. Thalamas spoke from atop a high-raised platform, behind him the Tanian representatives in attendance. Administrator Amishari and Borosh both gave smiles that neither truly felt. Behind them, a cavernous room rose a hundred stories, which no Ikaran had been allowed to see until now. The Bridge.

A spherical hole in space, it was nearly a mile across—a deep black void, which was still yet dwarfed by the roomful of support mechanisms that surrounded it. Into one side fed one of the pipes, which recent evidence suggested burrowed deep into the Ikaran core; however, it was conveniently out of sight, blocked by the very presence of the Bridge itself. Ramps led up to it from the side, enough to take in hundreds of thousands of people every minute. The room itself was filled with the faint throb of power, a static tingle that made arm hairs leap to occasional life. The sheer size of the Bridge dwarfed anything conceived before on Ikara, and yet it was nothing compared to the distance it would allow them to cross.

Security Chief Lort remained off to one side, ever at the ready, eyes taking in every last detail. Meanwhile, his security team stood scattered about, with weapons ready just in case. If the marching millions before them showed even a trace of subversive intent, they had no qualms about shoveling *dead* bodies through the Bridge.

Over a million people crowded into the Bridge room. More lined up outside in a trail stretching as far as the old Volst *Observer*, where flitters deposited the new arrivals. From his brief speech, Thalamas earned a cheer that echoed strangely in the vast confines. It was to this glad roar that a grinning Thalamas turned for a last bow to his people, then one to his Tanian benefactors.

Then finally, Thalamas gave a last word to Borosh himself.

"I will see you on the other side, my friend."

"I will come through after the very last of your people have departed," Borosh replied with a smile and warm handshake. "Have a good trip."

Thalamas took his hand in a quick grip, then turned to face the black, large eye of the Bridge. With a brief intake of breath, he strode boldly and unafraid, ever the one to lead his people by example. Once he reached the horizon of the Bridge, there was no flash of light or anything dramatic. He simply vanished into the darkness. There was a great cheer, then Tanian workers let the ropes fall, holding them back to usher the Volst forward.

They needn't have bothered, though, for the people of Volst charged forward, all of them eager to be about their journey to the stars. The Tanians were hard-pressed to keep them from tripping over one another.

Borosh maintained a smile for the recordings and the Ikarans, but beside him, Amishari was as grim-faced as ever. When he spoke, it was in their silent Tanian way, so the true emotions behind Borosh's smile could be felt.

"This was the only way it could be handled. Those Volst were ready to revolt if we didn't give them what they wanted. And I was really tired of listening to that Thalamas."

J. R. Austin

"Twenty million people," Amishari replied. "Twenty million sentient beings."

"I would quibble over the term 'sentient' in this case, but look at it another way. That's over one and a half million cubic cubits of biomass credited to Ikaran export."

"Of which you get your percentage."

"It's got to be done anyway," he mentally shrugged, "so why not make some money off it. Makes for a nice little retirement fund."

"Twenty million," Amishari repeated, this time slower. "That's men, women, and children."

"Not anymore. Listen Amishari, I've had some hard decisions to make on this project and there's no-one that will fault me for any of them. This world can no longer support the population it once could have and the Company has decided that this would be far too many mouths to feed. Besides, it would cost too much to properly pacify and train them. Simpler this way. They're all going to die anyway, so why not get something out of them."

"Twenty million-"

"Okay, now stop that," he cut her off with a harsh thought. "Besides, you still have to handle the rest of them. You'll just end up doing the same as me and your cut will be a far larger amount, so just shut up. We're going to be here a few hours before this is up, and I'd rather not spend it listening to your complaints. I don't like it much myself, but that's the system. Now try to manage a smile for the walking bags of meat."

"Twenty million…You know, there's a few children in there that look almost like Tanian kids."

Borosh flashed her a glare, which she returned with a cold scowl. She managed to not say (or think) another word, though every now and then, she'd indicate something by giving a nod of her head (or the psychic equivalent of one) to one or another in the crowds below that had caught her attention. It was just enough for Borosh's gaze to reflexively follow. A young child holding onto a doll as she eagerly leaps through the void, a pair of newlyweds obviously looking forward to their new life, a pregnant woman every now and then. She went on like that as the masses surged past, and with each directed glance, Borosh's smile hid a greater degree of displeasure.

Amishari had still yet to say or think another word more. She just sort of looked around. For the first hour, they stood there watching smiling Ikarans from Volst pass on by, all cheerful for their new lives, yet ignorant of the doom that awaited them as vat-filler. And for nearly every minute of that first hour, Amishari managed to subliminally direct Borosh's attention to the individuals amongst the masses, each with a story told in their eyes.

"Okay now, that's enough," Borosh finally snapped at her. "We've killed *billions* over the millennia. What's a few million more? They're all just cattle anyway!"

Only then did the fierce glare in her eyes lighten, and the grim line of her mouth ease into the most slender of grins, for her nearly subliminal attack had earned its result. Borosh had not *thought* those words to her, but in an uncontained mental frenzy, he had screamed them out *verbally*.

It was then he noticed that—while she hadn't said a single word—she *had* been engaging in some nearly inaudible humming. It was much like what the Tanians themselves would use to pacify the Volst before conversing. Only this particular hum was designed for quite the opposite effect. She'd learned her lessons well.

Borosh's heart froze cold. In that same instant, the nearest of the marching millions stopped, the last syllables of his words still clearly ringing through their ranks.

"They…they're going to kill us! It's a trap!"

"It's a trap!"

That one word echoed like a battle cry, and the march to supposed freedom became a sudden charge to battle. The ones nearest the Bridge tried to break away, only to be tossed through by one of the Tanian guards. Very quickly, it evolved into a Volst stampede away from the Bridge, many feet running over their own fallen. The larger men amongst the Volst grappled with the Tanians.

Some of them pointed towards the platform where Borosh stood, and shouted demands for his death.

"Don't just stand there," Borosh glared at Amishari, "you're Administrator now. *Do* something!"

"I would remind the former Administrator that this is still his operation," she calmly replied. "Or did you wish to forgo your jurisdiction of both an unauthorized early retirement and the resulting commission?"

He spared a final look of displeasure at Amishari, then took command and called out his orders:

"Close the outer doors! Tell the ones lined up outside that we're having some technical issues. Lort! Every security team down here *now*. Full weapons! We'll *shovel* them through if we have to!"

From the overlooking catwalks that ringed the staging area of the Bridge, Lort and his guards ran with weapons ready. At the far end of the facility, the massive access doors thundered closed. Those at the far end didn't yet know what was going on, but they'd soon find out. Shots rang out as beams of light flashed out from the Tanian rifles, cutting down everyone they touched. In mere moments, Borosh had transformed from the hero of millions into a butcher.

Amishari backed away. The guns above could take down dozens of people at a time, but in the staging area, only a hundred security personnel were facing nearly a hundred thousand Volst.

As the bodies piled up, some amongst the Volst risked the climb. Much to the amazement of the Tanians, they proved quite adept at scurrying up pipes and other objects that'd seemed unclimbable moments before. They'd forgotten that life near the Great Mountain had made the people of Volst prodigious climbers.

Soon, Lort and his security team were in the unenviable position of engaging in hand-to-hand combat with a people who averaged some eight to nine inches taller and fifty pounds heavier than themselves. Borosh saw a security guard being unceremoniously flung through the air, then tossed over the edge of the Bridge.

"Kill them all," Lort shouted out. "They're just a bunch of

unarmed diggers and engineers!"

A full-blown riot had developed, and Borosh found himself in the middle of it. Three of the nearest security personnel had gathered around him, as the rioters started up the platform. Some Volst wanted to throw Borosh through the Bridge one limb at a time, and the trio of guards wouldn't be able to fight them off for long.

Borosh looked quickly around for Amishari, only to see that she was with the technician by the controls, and the security shield was glimmering around them.

"Amishari, *do* something."

"I am," she replied, her voice as inflectionless as ever. "I am securing access to the Bridge controls until Security Chief Lort has dealt with this problem. As per protocol."

Amishari's face reflected no emotion one way or another, but what she felt inside was quite different. As in situations before, she'd used the strictest adherence to protocol as an excuse, a means of setting something up. Then she stepped aside to watch and hope. All Borosh could do was fume and panic.

Twelve Ikarans climbed the pipes adjacent to one of the catwalks and charged the heavily armed men, who were firing down on the unarmed Volst, killing them by the dozen. At first, the guards seemed fearless. Then suddenly, a helpless look came over their faces, as one of the twelve grabbed two of the guards and jumped over the side with them, killing all three instantly. This action set a new perspective on what the Volst were willing to do—not for themselves, but for one another. The heavily armed men suddenly didn't feel so brave. They began firing down the catwalk, killing each other as the newly formed Volst team began to disarm the guards; the rioters took their weapons and used them against their former owners.

Bjarn, a young man of twelve tallas but twice the size of any Tanian, yelled from the catwalk:

"We have their guns! We have their guns!"

He tossed several to the people below. The Tanians had never anticipated a firefight with the people of one soul, and they began to fall during the battle that ensued.

"Get me out of here! I don't want to die on my last day!"

The only reason he was still alive was because Bjarn and his band of brothers were afraid to shoot their own people, who were standing near him. Borosh backed away from the mayhem.

Meanwhile, Lort was nowhere to be found. He was hiding from the firefight and strategizing his next move.

Amishari was standing behind the glass, and thus, from Bjarn's standpoint, she was wide open for a clean shot to the head. He raised his weapon, placing his sites between her eyes and gently started to squeeze the trigger. However, before his weapon discharged, Amishari locked eyes with the young Volst. She knew the security shield around her didn't have a protective frequency against Tanian weapons, but she had something else that would protect her more surely than any shield: knowledge.

Amishari lifted her right hand, her thumb and adjacent two fingers pointing towards the heavens; her ring finger and smallest finger remained closed, pointing downward. Like many well-studied Volst, Bjarn knew what the sacred hand signal meant, and he respected it. No one else had seen Amishari make the gesture.

Instead, Bjarn opened fire on a group of guards, who were throwing his Volst brethren through the Bridge. The Tanians guards were almost completely eliminated, save the small contingent with Borosh. Then the molecular sequencer came online, and new guards began to appear through the Bridge. Lort was busy prepping his final solution and buying time with this act.

Over a thousand guards arrived. There was barely enough room to accommodate them, as they arrived literally on top of the Volst, standing on the edge of the transfer area. Three Volst managed to jump through the Bridge before the sequencer was deactivated.

"Kill them all!" The battle cry came from a large ginger-haired Volst, ringing out across the death chamber as the Volst (armed and unarmed alike) descended upon the guards.

"Come over here!" he yelled to Bjarn.

Bjarn bolted across the room to create a diamond formation with three other Volst. It was a tactic they'd learned while playing ball in school; it was difficult to attack any of their teammates if they had eyes covering all ends.

As the security guards were being overrun, it was Lort who took the reins of the situation and showed them why he'd been selected as Security Chief of this operation:

"Gas them! Masks on. I want this place dead in two minutes!"

Borosh heard this order and blanched. He had no mask on, having planned on leaving after what was supposed to be a rather tedious ceremony. However, when the guard next to him pulled his own mask out from his belt, Borosh snatched it from him and kicked the guard into the angry mass below.

Seconds later, grenades launched through the air into the crowds, each one impacting with an explosion of yellow gas. Dozens of grenades at a time exploded until the entire staging area was filled with a jaundiced cloud. The children and very elderly dropped first, but even as some of the larger men began to falter, there were still many who continued to fight. They threw their last breaths into their efforts, determined to take the enemy down with them.

"For Ikara," the large ginger shouted out, "for Volst! We die that the rest may…may…"

As he collapsed, Gantar, another tall Volst, with muscles hardened from long tallas working the mines, had beaten back Borosh's one remaining security guard and approached the old Administrator with anger clearly written across his face.

"You will die by my hands today, you foolish little man. Your yellow gas will not save you."

It was Borosh's turn to experience justice, but now he wasn't so brave. Through the black mask, Gantar could see Borosh's enlarged eyes and fearful red face screaming and gasping for air. Gantar picked him up with a single hand.

"No! I am your friend! This is a misunderstanding!" Borosh

cried through the thick filter on his gas mask. To Gantar, he sounded like a small rat in a bag.

For that feeble attempt at reconciliation, Gantar let out a sinister laugh and after a contemptuous glance he began howling with glee as he leaned back, holding Borosh's arm. Dragging the small Tanian around as a child would a doll, he grabbed Borosh's throat, ready to rip it out in front of the alien onlookers. Borosh looked upwards at Amishari and Lort, a pleading look upon his face.

A breath away from his own death, Borosh felt the huge man falter from the toxic gas, dropping him a moment before collapsing to the ground. Gantar's fall left Borosh gasping and wondering if he was truly alive. Bjarn and his team of heroes had already perished, and their bodies lay on the floor near the edge of the Bridge.

When all was said and done, Amishari maintained her impassive features, even while looking at the spread of a hundred thousand bodies piled around the staging area. The last of them fell from one of the upper catwalks as he finally succumbed to death. Then not a single body moved. In the eerie silence developed, she finally remembered to signal the technician beside her.

"The compressors," she ordered. "Clear the air."

As a hum came to life from somewhere above, she had time to assess the situation. Nearly two-thirds of the security personnel had been killed by the rioters; perhaps it was proof enough for her to urge less violent measures in dealing with the Ikarans. There was also enough evidence to lay the blame of this on Borosh, and he knew it. In turn, Borosh had nothing overt with which to accuse Amishari, save a little friendly bickering. It wasn't her fault that he'd lost his temper and unwittingly yelled out his dark intentions.

After the gas cleared, Borosh was first to rip off his mask, while Amishari lowered the security shield from around the Bridge controls.

"I think," she began, "that under the circumstances we should-"

"Get these bodies all shoveled through the Bridge immediately," Borosh roared, both verbally and telepathically, "this is still my operation, and it's running too far behind."

"But, Borosh, I would think that considering-"

"As I said, this is still under *my* jurisdiction and I'm getting that commission! As you say, all strictly according to protocol."

He didn't see the slight sigh of defeat that escaped her lips. He just saw her—hand on her pendant—nod up to Lort. The messy work of pitching bodies through the gate began.

Those outside didn't know how long they waited, nor the reason why. They were simply told that there had been some manner of a technical glitch, but that it'd now been fixed. They saw the great doors once again slide open, and they cheered as the march was resumed. Borosh and Amishari were once again standing side-by-side on the observation platform. However, this time, there were a couple of extra security guards nearby.

To the remainder of the ignorant millions now marching past, Borosh was once again a hero, but to Amishari, he was something far lower. He wouldn't fall for her subliminal distractions again, though neither would he report to anyone about them. He had too little evidence to oppose her long history of service to the Tanian people. She wondered if he felt any guilt about his actions, or whether he was as much a part of the system as anything else.

When finally the last Volst marched into oblivion, there was an odd silence. Not one Tanian worker spoke; for long seconds, the only sound was the hum of the equipment. Borosh finally broke it, a slight nervous accent to his movements as he finally faced Amishari.

"Well, time to go now. Ikara is all your problem. Try to remember that they're all just a bunch of primitive animals. It helps. Have the Sequencers put back online, if you will, Amishari. Wouldn't want to end up as pudding like the rest."

She said not a word, just turned and walked back to the Bridge control panel, making sure that the Security Chief's gaze only saw her back. She pressed some buttons and got a response. Then while Borosh was looking at the Bridge with a combination of eager anticipation and nervous concern, she pressed another control and

213

cast a cold grin to herself, before turning around and presenting Borosh with the same icy glare as before.

"Molecular Sequencers online," she told him in a level tone. "Enjoy your retirement."

"I'll try," he replied.

She watched as Borosh marched off, up to the black horizon, then gone an instant later. She spared a brief moment for a stony smile to herself, before snapping into a more commanding manner.

"You," she pointed to the nearest Tanian technician, "it's your job to keep an eye on the Sequencers, is it not?"

"Well, yes, but you said earlier that you could-"

"Never mind that, your duty to the *Company* comes above all else, now check the Sequencer and see if former Administrator Borosh made it through safely."

"Yes, Administrator," the other replied, confusion in his thoughts.

He hurried over to the same panel where Amishari had been, while her cold calculating gaze followed his every movement. He'd been at the panel for but a moment when he called out with a gasp, both psychically and audibly.

"The Molecular Sequencers are still offline! They were supposed to be...I don't understand it," he said, spinning quickly around, "this means that Borosh is...dead."

"And it was your responsibility to double-check the settings," she reminded him sternly while pointing her index finger at his eyes. "The fault lies on your shoulders."

"Y-yes, Administrator."

"As such, the punishment will be yours. You are hereby docked half your reserve pay to be forwarded to the family of former Administrator Borosh."

"Yes, Administrator."

"As far as the percentage he would have earned from the recent shipment of biomass since he didn't quite make it to the other side to claim it, it forfeits to the current Administrator, which just happens to be myself. Now get this place cleaned up and back to normal operations. We still have a lot of resources to transmit."

"Yes, Administrator; immediately, Administrator."

She kept a cold eye leveled in his direction, but it was a shield from her real thoughts: the same shield she'd had to maintain during her long employ with the Company. Ikara was fully in her hands now, and no one left might think to return to check up on her activities. The Company had its money, and now, by some accident, would have one less retirement account to pay.

Jast

Jast walked across the tarmac to the waiting convey, a small crowd of observers seeing his passage and eagerly pointing it out to others. Many of them were users of the Agorabox, snapping a quick memory to be shared with their friends. It was a public convey, though more of a first-class passage. He entered, found a couple of empty plush seats, and sat down in one. There was a small scattering of other passengers, several of them Agora users.

A moment later, another sat down next to him: a familiar woman with pallid alien features, who greeted him with a brief flicker of a smile.

"They'll let just about anyone travel by convey these days," she said verbally.

"You used a contraction," Jast said, noting how like a native Amishari was now talking..

"I've been practicing," she replied. The convey engines rumbled to life, the craft starting to taxi down the length of the tarmac before lifting into the sky. Amishari lowered her voice. "So, Ikara seems to be in a bit of a turmoil since your wife made that broadcast."

"Pro-Agora contingents are calling for the complete dissolution of all governments," Jast replied. "Any sort of centralized authority, for that matter. Including the ISP, schools, and research groups. A bit extreme, if you ask me, especially with the space program."

"It's just birth pains," she told him. "Once you get more

scientists and technicians into using the Agora, people will be better able to understand their need."

"You mean, once they discover Ikara is doomed and that we need the ISP to get off the planet."

"That too."

"Speaking of which, how goes the Agora tower?"

"Construction should be finished quite soon," she replied with a nod. "Then users of the Agora from anywhere in your world will be able to interact, to…spread news of what they hear and see."

For a moment, Jast eyed her; she had something to say, something that for some reason she didn't want to discuss someplace more private. Very well, he would play it her way. In the short time he'd been working with her, he had come to trust her motives.

"So," she said. "Has anyone decided what to do with the Volst lands?"

"A lot of abandoned buildings," Jast agreed. "The ones that survive the increasing quakes should make great homes for those who need them, though the lack of good Volst engineers will be missed. A few of them stayed behind, mainly those connected to the ISP, but the vast bulk of them are enjoying life…wherever your people sent them."

"Yes," she sighed, "about that."

Emotion flickered across her face, one eye twitching as her control started to slip. She shifted her gaze to the window of the conveyer; she wouldn't be able to look Jast in the eye as she told him what she needed to articulate.

Jast, you know what I've had to do to earn the trust of the Tanians and of Borosh so that I could confirm my role here and give us the fighting chance we need. And even then, I tried—oh by the powers I tried to stop it—but it was the last piece of business that Administrator Borosh maintained jurisdiction over before stepping down. There was nothing I could do. I *did* try; I am *so* sorry."

"Amishari," Jast said, his eyes searching for any clue, one hand close to trembling for fear of what she might have to tell him, "what are you trying to say? What's happened?"

A single sob escaped her lips, unheard by any Tanian. She quickly regained control enough to continue, though Jast might have wished she hadn't.

"The people of Volst walked through the Bridge, just as Borosh promised, but...Jast, the Sequencer was inactive. Not accidentally either, but by Borosh's direct order and confirmation from Company headquarters. Millions of people—men, women, and children—walked into the Bridge, smiling and cheering for their new lives amongst the stars, but...they came out the other end as buckets of organic sludge; more profit for Borosh and the Company. They're dead, Jast, every single one of them. The entire nation of Volst was converted to raw organics to feed Company profits. I...I don't know what to say. I had to stand there next to that monster Borosh and *watch* every single one of them walk to their deaths. I tried to engineer a riot and at first, it seemed to work, but the Security Chief gassed all the rioters with none of the rest of the people waiting outside the wiser. Every single last one of them just..."

Tears were now streaming down her face, the cold discipline of her features breaking. It was as if she could feel the loss of every single one of those millions. And with her alien empathic and psychic abilities, perhaps she had.

"Except for a few saved as...specimens, they're all gone. Jast..."

She let her voice drift off and finally turned to look Jast in the eyes. Jast's own face was flecked with emotion, though he shed no tears. The sheer shock of it had put him far past crying. He said nothing, just reached an arm out and pulled her close, letting her cry on his shoulder. A few sobs later, muffled by her contact with Jast, she said a few broken words.

"Seen it too many times...It's got to stop, *must* stop. So many dead, so many..."

To see one of the Takers break so completely was telling enough, and Jast himself didn't know *how* to react. Millions so callously killed, and all for simple greed. It was beyond words, beyond comprehension. However, in that thought, he knew why she'd insisted their meeting be someplace public. Looking around, he saw that they had the attention of everyone on the convey.

Half of them were Agorabox users. Jast himself didn't use one, but Amishari was psychic enough for the little boxes to pick up on what she felt and why. It was a very stunned group indeed who'd be transmitting their experience to other users.

Word of the horrible tragedy spread through wearers of the Agorabox.

Protests against the Tanians started up in earnest, some groups call for further violent actions.

Micah completed his research and graduated. More importantly, his revised formulas proved that the Tanians were in fact responsible for the bad weather and the iron winds, as well as the coming doom of Ikara. The world was soon to die, and there was nothing anyone could do could stop it.

Aleka broadcast the findings over the Agora to anyone that would listen, and very quickly, Micah found himself being hailed as a hero for uncovering the final proof of Taker treachery: that the Tanians had sabotaged their world, and all for selfish greed.

Soon after, Micah found himself appointed the Elmanith Undersecretary of Transportation and Public Safety, while Aleka was drafted by the ISP to be part of the next generation team: a group of scientifically and philosophically elite individuals who'd facilitate the move to Azur.

Nothing remained of the old formalized governments. In the end, the only centralized force that persevered was the Ikaran Space Program. It was now consolidated under the one Family with enough wherewithal to continue its operations within their own economy: Elmanith. In the same move, the ISP expanded its operations to all manner of sciences, even those not directly space-related.

Finally, for no reason that he would care to give, the renowned

Jast Rathael resigned from his position as First Speaker of Whycheral, leaving in his place the newest crop of GenSeers to run things. He retired from public life, many saying it was because of his age, though some who were on that convey had other theories. No record of his activities appeared thereafter. There wasn't even any indication about how much longer he might yet live, but while change rocked its way through the Ikaran soul, a collective Agoran tear was shed for the news that filtered out from that one convey trip.

Glossary

Azur: Earth

Azurian: Star-traveling races that have made Azur their home. They include, but are not limited to, Caucasians and Native Americans from different places in the Universe. Most of them have some blood and DNA of the first men: The Azurites.

Azurite: The original people of Azur. A onetime very advanced space-faring civilization. Azurites are very dark-skinned people, mostly from the area of modern-day Egypt and Ethiopia.

Burning Men: The almost mythological beings, of whom all Ikarans are descendants. They were actually a couple (male and female) from another galaxy, who shared one soul. They brought the first humanoid life to Ikara during the First Cycle.

Candlefall: The fiery event of meteors landing on Ikara, combined with a mysterious craft hovering over the Great Mountain (Mons Olympus). It appeared as a candle to those viewing its arrival from the Great Black. Many events are dated in relation to this event, such as B.C. (before Candlefall) and A.C. (after Candlefall).

Emlash: Electricity. It is a construction of the English words "mothers's lash."

Gatekeepers: Offspring of the early SoulSeers who work as guards and judges across the land. They have mastered the connection of humanity to the one soul. They carry with them a set of keys to pathways. By rubbing each key and finding the matching one for the subject being examined, they can often determine intent.

Genetic Memory: A phsycial record contained in the DNA of huminids, which records every event of every person in their ancestory. Genetic memory allows those who can read it to determine the future, based on past events.

GenSeers: The coven of mystics who read gentic memory and can transcribe the happenings of previous Cycles. They can deduce, and sometimes predict, the potential outcome of future events based on these readings. Most, but not all, GenSeers hail from Whycheral, where the best Academies for the trade exist.

Grand Cycle: The system of Ikaran belief that time is in fact not linear, but cyclical, in nature. Time is a place in the Universe. And history repeats itself, but in different ways. It is the spiritual center of all Ikaran life.

Ikaran: Those who are from Ikara. To the uninitiated, they are called Martians. The word also means "of one soul," so to be Ikaran is to be part of the physical manifestation of that one soul.

ISP: An acryonym for Ikaran Space Program, similar to today's program NASA. The ISP has many objectives, both public and hidden.

Karth Kessai: An Ikaran who has traveled into space. Tark Karth is recognized as the first Karth Kessai of this cycle.

Koru: The Ikaran word for the sun.

Talla: One Ikaran year, which would be 687 days on Azur.